HEART OF DRACULA

IMMORTAL SOUL: PART ONE

KATHRYN ANN KINGSLEY

Copyright © 2020 by Kathryn Ann Kingsley

First Print Edition: July 2020

ISBN-13: 979-8-65327-416-9

ASIN: B084NFB7PM

KATHRYN ANN KINGSLEY

All rights reserved.

No part of this book may be reproduced in any form or by any electronic or mechanical means, including information storage and retrieval systems, without written permission from the author, except for the use of brief quotations in a book review.

This is a work of fiction. Names, characters, places, and incidents either are the product of the author's imagination or are used fictitiously, and any resemblance to locales, events, business establishments, or actual persons —living or dead—is entirely coincidental.

A FOREWORD

Usually, I take this time to thank everyone who supports me while I go on this crazy-train journey toward of being a writer. And to all the usual folks—Lori, Evan, Kristin, Michelle, Sylvia, you readers—thank you. But I thought I might take a second to do something a little different.

I know many of you who read this are aspiring authors yourselves. I know you haven't finished that manuscript, or you aren't brave enough to hit "submit," or you don't think you can handle the aftermath.

Do it.

Write that thing. Publish that thing. Yes, you'll get bad reviews. Yes, you'll have to deal with your friends and family reading something you wrote and the embarrassment that comes with that.

My father has read "the desk scene" in *Steel Rose*. Process that for a moment.

But it'll also be something you get to hold up to the world and say, "I did this."

I mention this in the beginning of my Dracula duet for a

reason. I began writing, like few people would likely want to admit, with fanfiction.

I know, I know.

The horror.

Stay with me.

I started writing Dracula fanfiction when I was young. I did it because nobody was writing the fiction I wanted to read. I wanted to read stories where the villain got the girl for a change. Where they got to win for once. They are always the better and more interesting character.

I also wrote stories because I daydreamed them in my head and needed to get it all out on paper to make it stop. It only freed up space for my head to move on to the next one.

It was many, many years before I was brave enough to post my silly stories online. I made a few fans—*Sylvia, I'm looking at you*—and I slowly realized I was spending so much time building my own world within someone else's that it was time to break free and do my own thing.

I took the leap and put my stuff out there. And it's been a wild ride. It's had ups and downs. And it's a slow climb. But it is absolutely worth it.

Now, here's a simple fact for you.

I'm not special.

You can do it too.

My writing story began with Dracula, and here we are coming back around to him. I've made friends, garnered a few fans, and have had a blast. And I hope to continue for many years to come.

So to you, the one sitting on the manuscript you're afraid to put out into the world, I say push the button. Send the email. Hit submit. Be brave. Be silly. Tell the stories you want to tell. Get the things out of your head and share them with the world.

This story is for you.

1

Maxine Parker's life ended with the sound of a knock on her front door.

Squeak. Clack, clack, clack.

A brass ring in bad need of oiling let out its preemptive squeak before the figure on the other side rapped it against its plate. Not urgently, not impolitely, and with nothing except simple social propriety.

It did not help the sense of dread she felt as she sat on the stairs of her home, gathering the skirts of her long navy dress around herself as she stared at the back of her front door, wondering if she should simply ignore the call of those on the other side. She did not know who was standing there, summoning her to answer, but she could *sense* one thing from them—death.

Maxine was very good at sensing death. Especially as of late, considering what had befallen Boston. Murder came to the city on the inky wings of the night, summoned by a crimson moon that never wavered and, by some means, defied the motion of the Earth to remain full.

Most of the residents of the city ignored the screams and

howls in the darkness, the sounds that belied what hunted its prey was not human. The papers attributed the disappearances and remaining gore to a pack of wolves or coyotes that had taken up residence in the Boston Common and the Public Gardens.

But wolves could not leave a man's head impaled on the wrought-iron railing of the Granary Burying Ground. But the papers kindly skipped over the details of that particular night. *No need to incite a panic. People might run for their lives.*

Many had already done exactly that, but many either believed they had no reason to fear or they had nowhere to go. As for her? She fit in neither category. Her excuse for remaining within her walls was far less valid. Or far less sane, at any rate.

It was the whispers she heard in the night's calls that inspired her to remain. There was an intelligence behind the death, and it was calling to her. She could not understand why, or for what purpose it bade her stay, but she felt compelled.

Spirits whispered often to Maxine, and she always listened. They had successfully guided her through her life up until this point, and she would never refuse their council. She had some part to play in what had befallen her city. She believed in fate without question. Perhaps not that all choices were immutable, but that some were inevitable, like death.

Death came for all, no matter the choices that were made. No matter the circuitous path a mortal might take to escape, all roads must someday cease. And whoever knocked upon her door felt like such things. The end of one journey, and the beginning of another.

Her life, as she knew it, was now over.

Squeak. Clack, clack, clack.

Heart of Dracula

The soul that stood on the other side of her door was still patient and wonderfully polite. That was the first indication that it was not a ravager from the gates of Hell come to rend her asunder. More importantly, it was barely before noon and the sun was out, and therefore that meant those who waited for her—and they were plural, she now realized as she felt three distinct emotions on the other side of her door—were not a pack of the demons that now stalked the night.

But that did not mean they did not her bring danger all the same.

Rubbing her hand over the back of her neck, she shut her eyes and let herself reach out through her mind's eye instead to focus on those standing on her stoop. Two men and a woman. The older of the two men caught her attention first. He was stern, resolute, dignified, and felt every inch a soldier. The younger man was easily distracted, his emotions flitting from one to another with little hesitation. He was bored and nervous in the same breath. The woman was eager, excited, and anticipated greatly the answering of the door.

Standing from the stairs, she brushed her hands down the folds of her dress and reached for the black silk gloves she always kept tucked into her bodice, even while inside her own home. She slipped them on before heading to the front door to answer it. The gloves were necessary. Immensely so.

Unfortunate as they may be, they were for the benefit of everyone.

Taking a breath, she let it out, steeling herself for what might come. She sensed a magnitude about this moment. This was why the spirits had called her to stay.

My life is about to change.

She was not a psychic in the truest form of the word. She could not see the future. She could only see the present and past—often in rather excruciating detail—and it was easy enough to see the strings of where she stood and predict the next thread that was to fall in the loom.

And a black stitch fell into place in front of her.

Fate was fate. It could not be avoided.

Maxine opened the door.

Upon seeing her, the older man who had been the source of the knocking pulled his hat off, and a young, beautiful blonde woman elbowed the other man beside him. The young man jumped and nearly ripped a wide-brimmed leather hat, a style rarely seen on the east side of the Mississippi, off his head. The over-eager action knocked a hand-rolled cigarette from behind his ear. He scrambled after it, and the woman rolled her eyes.

If death has come to me, it comes in a strange guise.

"Excuse me." The older man interrupted her thoughts. "Are you Miss Maxine Parker?"

"I am."

Her opinion of him carrying the air of a soldier was matched by his appearance. He had short, dark hair graying at the temples. Kept in a style that was all function and no form, he was every ounce the utilitarian creature she expected. His eyes were creased at the edges, and she knew it was from worry and not from laughter. He had seen grief. He had seen loss. He knew death, and he knew it well. The children behind him—they looked not much younger than Maxine herself, but they felt more youthful all the same—were marked with their own tragedies, but not nearly to his extent.

She could picture flashes of their memories in her mind's eye. Bits and pieces of what they carried around with

Heart of Dracula

them in their souls. She had to push them away to keep from being overwhelmed. But she saw a trail of blood had led them here to her. They may not mean her harm, but they brought harm all the same.

The older man reached a hand to her. She hesitated for a moment before meeting him, taking a moment to ensure that she still wore her gloves. It was a reflexive action.

"My name is Alfonzo. Alfonzo Van Helsing. And I am hoping we might speak with you."

―――

Walter rose from his bow. He kept his gaze downturned. The sunlight hurt his eyes. It did not trouble his Master, who stood in front of a window, gazing out at the city beyond, pale hands clasped behind his back, his forefinger and thumb rubbing slow circles against each other as he thought.

The elder vampire cast an imposing and stark shadow over the floorboards and across his own shadow, mingling them together into one. Walter may not wish to stare into the sunlight, but he did not worry about it burning him overmuch. It would take significant and direct exposure to harm him, although its presence was hardly enjoyable.

He did not speak. He would wait until his elder addressed him. He knew better than to interrupt his thoughts.

Walter did.

His compatriot did not.

"Why can we not hunt in the streets at night? Your monsters can. It is a travesty and gloriously unfair," Zadok whined from where he sat, draped on a chaise lounge by the wall, far out of the reach of the sun's late-morning rays. His feet were up on the back of the wood frame, his head hanging off the portion where his feet were intended to go.

Walter shut his eyes to keep from rolling them.

His Master kept his voice even and devoid of the annoyance Walter was certain was there. "They are allowed a few a night. They are not free to kill with abandon, and I will not command them to starve. You have taken three pets since we have arrived in this city. You are not bereft."

"One died last night." Zadok squinted over at the window then covered his eyes with his arm. "I'm down to two."

"That is your fault. It is no concern of mine."

"I didn't kill him. He killed himself."

"I fail to see how that changes my statement. Make do with your two remaining toys, Zadok, and be happy I allow you that much." The elder vampire paused. "Walter."

"Yes, Master?"

"The ghouls are becoming too bold. They killed a man and left his head on a rail the other night. They must take their prey and eat below grounds in the tunnels. Ensure those responsible for the misstep are dismembered and fed to the rest."

"As you wish, my Lord."

"Tell Mordecai he is to see that the rest are kept hungry for a week. I will not have them ruining my plans over their insatiable bloodlust." The elder vampire's voice was a low rumble and did not need to be loud to be heard. It carried easily in the room, especially to their preternatural ears. "And tell Mordecai to keep his lust leashed as well."

"I will do my best." Walter felt his eye twitch. He was not fond of Mordecai. It was nothing personal. They were simply very different men. Attempting to convince the captain of his Master's demon horde to keep his desires curtailed was quite like attempting to hold back the tide with a teacup.

Mordecai was an incubus, after all. Some things couldn't be helped.

"Soon, this city will be ours, and those within it will be the same. We will stretch our grasp, and we will etch our new kingdom into this fledgling country. You will all be fed as much as you can desire. But now is the time for patience. We must play the game. One must not spook the flock if one wishes to catch more than one sheep."

"Yes, Master," Zadok said through a heavy sigh. The Frenchman did not care to be lectured, yet often found himself in precisely that position of his own accord.

The elder vampire tilted his head to the side slightly, long black hair falling along his shoulders in dark tendrils. "Both of you must stay on your toes. We have unwelcome company in our city. I smell them on the air. Hunters have come."

Walter felt his eye twitch. "How many?" While he was not overly concerned, any hunters always meant more, and more meant trouble.

The elder vampire paused. "Three."

"Only three?" Zadok snickered. "Send me after them tonight. I will deliver their heads to you by dawn. I will—"

"One of them is a Helsing."

Zadok fell silent. Briefly. For as long as Walter suspected the Frenchman was ever capable of staying in such a state. It lasted a whole fifteen seconds, which was a remarkable feat on his part, before it shattered. *"Merde."*

The older vampire chuckled and turned to face them, crimson eyes shining even in the dim light of the room. "Walter. One last thing for you, once you are done with the ghouls and Mordecai. This is a delicate matter. I trust you to treat it accordingly."

He would complain about being sent on so many errands while Zadok had neglected to receive one, but he knew better than to speak his thoughts for two reasons. It would result in little more than having his arm torn from its socket and fed to the creatures who lingered below. And Zadok could not be trusted to fetch the mail, let alone be given a task of any importance.

So, he simply nodded and said nothing. "What is it, my Lord?"

His sire smiled. It was an unkind one. It was the expression of the pleasure of a predator moments before the kill. "The hunters have gone out of their way to meet with a young woman. I will need to find out why. Find me everything you can learn about one Miss Maxine Parker."

Bowing low again, he folded one arm at his back and the other at his waist. "It shall be done."

May the gods help you, Miss Parker. For I have seen that look on him before, and it spells your doom.

Maxine made tea.

What else was one supposed to do with guests? Manners demanded she serve them tea and cookies. She might have spent the better part of her life living in a Roma caravan, but it didn't mean she hadn't first been raised in "civilized" society and taught all the ways she was meant to act.

Even if she was rather terrible at such things.

Even if she did hate it.

She guessed she hated it precisely because she was terrible

Heart of Dracula

at it. People rarely hated things they were good at. *Focus, simpleton.* She poured her three guests their tea and sat at her spot at the table, filtering her own through the strainer and into her teacup. She took it with a single cube of sugar and nothing else.

The younger man in the leather duster and hat apparently took his with four cubes. She couldn't imagine it tasted anything like actual Earl Grey by the time he was done. She couldn't help but smile at him, finding his sweet tooth disgusting and charming at the same time. The young man smiled back. "And you are?" she asked.

"My name is Eddie Jenkin." His accent was thick and labeled him clearly as somewhere west of Boston. Although being east of Boston and still being American was rather a trick, so she supposed it wasn't hard.

"And I am Bella Corallo," chimed the blonde woman. She had a beautiful smile, one full of happiness and life. One that perfectly covered the tragedy Maxine could sense dwelled in her past. She wore it better than the other two. It might even be invisible to the naked eye.

But Maxine's empathic gifts extended to more than just her ability to read emotions. Flashes of memories came with it. Images of Bella as a young girl, cowering under a bed, weeping. Clutching a ratty stuffed animal to her chest as blood pooled on the ground nearby.

As for Eddie, there was more grief than there was fear. A loss—something taken from him. A small body in his arms. But both flashes of sensation carried one thing in common. Tears.

"What is it?" Alfonzo broke her out of her thoughts. "Are you all right, Miss Parker?"

"Hm? Yes. Sorry." She shook her head and forced a smile back on her face. "Forgive me. It isn't often that I am around people with such stories. It is hard not to get lost in the hallways looking at the paintings on the walls."

"I...don't think I understood anything you just said," Eddie muttered. He glanced at Alfonzo as if to ask if she was crazy. She didn't take it personally. Most people assumed she was. Or they were too afraid to accept what it might mean if she wasn't.

She shut her eyes. Correction—she tried not to take it personally. It still stung. She opened her eyes again after a moment and knew her smile was now marred with the sadness that always seemed to plague her. "What is it that brings you all here?"

Alfonzo was the one to answer, and she wasn't surprised. He was clearly their leader. "You were recommended to me by a colleague. He said you are quite talented in your ability to identify artifacts and answer certain...enigmatic questions regarding personal histories and motivations." He scratched at his stubble with his fingertips. It was obvious he wasn't a diplomat. He was dancing around the subject with all the grace of a drunken boar.

Maxine laughed at the piss-poor attempt.

"What?"

"I am an empath, Mr. Van Helsing. Is that what you're implying?"

"I. Uh. Yes." He blinked, clearly surprised she had come out and said it. She knew he was shocked. One, because she could see it clearly on his face. Two, she could feel it from where she was sitting a few feet away. Emotions traveled in the air around her like the scent of flowers.

"And you wish to request my assistance?"

Alfonzo cleared his throat and nodded. "We can pay you, if that is what you require."

"It depends on the nature of the work and how long it

Heart of Dracula

will take me to complete." She paused thoughtfully. "And the risks involved."

The three of them traded glances.

Maxine sighed. "There are risks, then."

All three of them nodded.

"Well, then," she leaned back in her chair, "allow me to give you a piece of advice when dealing with someone with my talent. Do not lie to me. I can sense it as easily as I can see the sun. Do not hide things from me, as I will find out in due time. Tell me the full of what it is you wish me to do, and I will tell you if I can help you and whether or not there is a price involved."

She often took unpaid work to help those who needed someone with her particular gifts. But that was not to say she was a fool, nor was she a pauper. She had learned how to turn her trade into an asset. It had bought her the brownstone she lived in, after all.

"How do we know you're for real?" Eddie sniffed. "No offense."

"None taken." She watched him for a moment and let herself examine the "painting on the wall" a little closer. She let her vision go unfocused as she dug deeper into what she could sense from him. "I can prove it to you, Mr. Jenkin, but I fear it might become personal."

After a long pause, and likely exchanged looks from the others, the young man reluctantly replied. "That's...that's fine."

"I see you holding a body in your lap. A young girl. Blood stains her dress, her hands...and her mouth. You killed her. But you loved her. It was an act of kindness that made you do what you did."

She heard a chair screech loudly on the floor as he jumped to his feet. That wasn't an uncommon reaction to her gift the first time it was witnessed. She let herself come back to the moment and pushed away the rest of the memory. She looked up at Eddie and saw him staring at her wide-eyed in shock.

"You're—you're a psychic?"

"Yes, but I cannot read minds. Not like you may think."

"Then how did you—how—"

"I read souls, Mr. Jenkin. And you carry that moment around with you like it is emblazoned on your sleeve, I'm afraid. It has come to define you."

Eddie walked away, rubbing his hand over his face and went to stand by the window and gaze through the glass down at the street below.

She felt her heart break for him. The memory she had dredged up was the worst day of his life, and he was now reliving it thanks to her words.

Maxine knew she was an overly sympathetic creature.

Alfonzo reached into a leather satchel he carried with him and pulled out an object wrapped in red cloth. He laid it down in the center of the table, crimson velvet over white lace. He parted the fabric and revealed a small brooch lying in the center of it. She guessed that it had belonged to a man by its design. In the center was a ruby, thick and dark, the color of blood.

Instantly, it made her skin crawl. She felt goosebumps spread out over her arms underneath the sleeves of her dress, even in the warm summer air. When Eddie, Bella, and Alfonzo came to her door, she had known they had carried death with them. She had assumed it had been their own doing. It was not.

It was the doing of whoever had once owned that jewel.

Cold swept over her, and she felt as though something

had breathed icy wind down her spine. She shivered and leaned farther back.

"You can sense it already," Bella said, watching her with a bright-eyed look of awe and curiosity. "It's true what was said about you. You read from more than just people."

Maxine greatly disliked that she had a reputation. Reputations meant trouble. But they also meant business. And therefore, they were a necessary evil. "Why have you come to me?"

Alfonzo spoke up. "We need your help to find the creature who owned this."

Creature. Not "man." Mark those words. She watched them warily. "And tell me...who was it who once owned this?"

"The one we've come here to kill. The one responsible for turning the moon to blood and controlling that which runs the streets."

No one commands the moon. "I told you not to lie to me. I told you not to withhold information. Already, you haven't learned." She shook her head. "Give me an answer, Alfonzo Van Helsing, or our time is over. To whom did this pin belong? Who have you come to Boston to destroy?"

Alfonzo paused before he finally said the words she knew he dreaded to utter. "The King of Vampires. Vlad Tepes Dracula."

2

Maxine set the bottle of rum down on the table with a heavy *thunk*. She uncorked it without any explanation—she assumed none was needed—and poured some into her tea before sliding the open glass bottle across the table to her three visitors.

Eddie snickered and reached for the bottle. "Thank you, ma'am."

"I'm not old enough to be a ma'am. Call me Maxine, please." She sipped the tea, glad for the sting of the alcohol. Something told her she would need it.

"You're older than me, and I wasn't raised wrong."

"I'm only twenty-three," she laughed. "Should you even be drinking? Is it wise at your young age?"

Eddie shrugged a shoulder. "Twenty. Plenty old. It isn't my first, if it makes you feel any better."

"Where're you from? Somewhere west, I assume."

"Yes, ma'am—er, Miss Maxine. Colorado."

That would do it. She watched her three guests with curiosity. She felt such an array of emotions from them. Determination, hope, sadness, grief, and an immense

Heart of Dracula

resolve. "So. Let us start at the very beginning." She sipped her tea. "Vampires are real."

"Very real, I'm afraid." Alfonzo was the obvious leader of the pack.

"And they can command the moon itself?"

"This one can. Vampires have plagued our kind since the beginning of mankind's history. They are at least as old as civilization. And we are part of a secretive few who strive to keep the beasts at bay. We hunt them. Now we hunt the one who rules them."

Beasts. She looked out the window at the gardens below. Her kitchen overlooked a small courtyard that was protected from the street by a high brick wall. She spent much of her spare time caring for the plants she kept both indoors and out. The azaleas and roses were in bloom, and she could see bees drifting from one to the other, eager to gather pollen. They cared nothing for the troubles of humans.

That was why she enjoyed them so much. Flowers were untouched by grief or sadness. "The murders." Maxine sighed.

"Yes." Alfonzo reached for the bottle of rum and added some to his own tea. "The papers attribute it to wolves. I promise you that what hunts the night is far worse."

"I know." She shut her eyes and felt her awareness expand as she did. It took a great deal of focus to keep from prying into the souls of those who sat across from her. She may have been young, but she was practiced. If she had left her gift unchecked, it would have driven her mad long ago. Survival required skill, and so she learned. A bee was not impressive because it gathered pollen. It learned what was required. "I can feel the creatures that hunt when the moon turns red. Hungry and twisted things. But there is a design to them. Something more than ravenous need drives them. Something intelligent commands them."

Alfonzo grunted. "Good. We can skip ahead, then."

She opened her eyes to look back to the older hunter. "Pardon me?"

He shrugged. "Usually, the first hour of this kind of conversation is me trying to convince people I'm not a lunatic."

"The problem is that you explain it quite poorly," Bella chimed with a teasing smile at her older companion. "And you are a lunatic, so there's no helping that." The young blonde turned to her, a kind and sympathetic look in her blue eyes. "The King of the Vampires commands the creatures you have felt. He has begun a siege on this city. He works to cut the transportation lines in and out. Soon, he'll do more than curse the moon and take a few lives to feed his hordes every night. He will unleash terror on this city. Thousands will die if we do not stop him from raising a new empire of the dead."

"Well, doesn't he sound charming." She smirked into her teacup.

Bella chuckled. "He is. That is another issue. He commands other vampires as well. He is an ancient, powerful thing. We are here to stop him."

"If he is ancient, why do you think you can stop him where all others have failed?"

"What makes you think others have failed?" Alfonzo had an oddly pleased and knowing smile on his face.

"The way you speak tells me that he has done this before —that he has taken over cities before, or tried to. Since he still walks the Earth, it tells me that no one has been successful." She paused and scrutinized Alfonzo. He was still looking at her with the expression of a man who knew he had a straight flush and was betting as if he had a pair. "Or is that not true?"

"He cannot die. He cannot be destroyed, and believe me, hunters have tried. He has been beheaded, burned, hanged, dismembered, and buried in a silver coffin flooded with holy water. Yet he always returns."

"You fight the inevitable, then." She spun the teacup idly between her fingers, watching the little hand-painted flowers on the porcelain as they rotated in and out of her view. "You battle against a creature you cannot truly defeat. You ask for my assistance in a game that cannot be won."

"We can't kill him, but we can stop him. And that is what we seek to do. To spare this city and to spare the lives he would see ended."

She squeezed the muscles at the back of her neck, trying to ease the tension that was working to give her a headache. She was prone to them. Maxine joked that if she sneezed too hard, she'd have a migraine for days. She blamed it partially on her gift and partially on bad luck.

When some of the knot eased, she put her gloved hand back on the table. Her gaze drifted to the ruby brooch that sat in its center. It burned in her perception like the ember of a flame. It reeked of tragedy and destruction. She had no desire to hold the burning coal and learn precisely how it might harm her. But, sadly, she assumed that was what they wished her to do. "And how am I to help you destroy this 'Dracula'?"

"He is biding his time, and we need to find a way to draw him to the surface," Bella interjected. She struck Maxine as an intelligent woman. And perhaps a little dangerous in her own right. Her dress was a pale green, and it offset her blue eyes, although Maxine suspected that was likely by accident. There was little of the woman that belied any sense of "culture" or "fashion." Maxine could tell by her posture that Bella didn't wear a corset. She could see pockets and slits hidden in the folds of the skirt, and she wondered what Bella carried that she might need to produce in short enough order that she needed to conceal them in her skirts. She could tell Alfonzo and Eddie were both armed. The former with a knife in his belt, the latter with two guns in leather holsters. It did not trouble her, but it made her wonder what the woman carried that made her similarly formidable.

As someone who also did not conform to the ideas of what a woman was meant to be in the eye of society in 1897, Maxine instantly felt a fondness toward Bella. It was a camaraderie that came with two souls fighting the same battle, if clearly in very different ways. "You wish for me to help you find him. And how can my gifts do such a thing? I am not a true psychic, I warn you. I cannot peer into a bowl of water and see all that is, or any of what may be. I am not certain if our mutual connection explained to you or was aware of the particular limits of my gift."

"Father Uncquist was quite forthcoming with details." Bella chuckled. "We know quite a bit."

Maxine laughed and shook her head. "Never trust a monk. Let alone one who drinks as much as he does. Nice man, but a bold-faced liar. And he cheats at cards." The way the three hunters laughed revealed they did indeed know Father Uncquist and were aware of his predilections.

"Let me explain to you, then, precisely what I can do. Then you can tell me exactly how someone like me can help you defeat a vampire king." She couldn't believe those words had left her mouth. She had no clue vampires had existed until this moment, although she knew the myths and legends as well as anyone. Her world was often bent

Heart of Dracula

toward morbid endeavors by nature of her gift, and often she had been told of creatures that stalked the night that were no longer human. Or who had never been. While she had never seen proof of one for herself, she had no issues taking things on a little faith. The hunters were not lying. "I deal in souls, as I said. In the simplest fashion, it can be reduced to that. I hear them, I sense them, and I can touch them."

"What do you mean...you can touch souls?" Bella furrowed her brow.

"I mean precisely that." She put her hand on the table, palm up. "I wear these gloves to protect us both. I am an empath, yes. But that is the same as claiming a sparrow is a bird only because it has two wings. I experience the emotions of those around me as if they were my own, but it is because I can hear their souls whispering to me. If I were to touch you, skin to skin, I would be reaching far deeper than that. It allows me to see into a person's very being. It is unsettling at best for both parties, as you can imagine. And dangerous."

"I...see. Father Uncquist told us you aided him in finding the other half of a broken artifact."

"I did. Humans are not the only things that carry souls, or something akin to it. Objects carry a history to them, as do buildings and locations. People know this instinctually. You can tell if you hold a blade in your hand that has taken lives or one that is used to slice butter. Everyone has the gift that I have. You feel connections to people around you, to the places you visit, and to the things you touch as I do. I simply can hear it much louder."

The three of them sat there quietly for a moment, watching her with various degrees of interest and curiosity. Bella seemed to be nearly overflowing with the need to ask her questions but kept glancing at Alfonzo to see if their leader would speak first.

"If you were to hold that brooch, what would happen?" Alfonzo asked after a long and thoughtful pause.

"I suspect I would see a memory. Objects carry the past with them. They contain threads of everything that has happened around them, imprinted by the emotions of what they have witnessed. Some memories are far more impactful than others. Think of them like rocks thrown into a river. If I were to hold a steak knife in my hand, for example, I could not see every meal it has shared in. They are small pebbles. Barely enough to disturb the surface. If I were to throw a boulder, I could change the course of the stream. If the steak knife took a life, that is more unique. More notable." She looked down at the brooch and felt only dread at the idea of holding it. "From that, I think I will find a continent dropped into an ocean."

"You are correct in being wary to touch it." Bella folded her hands in her lap. "That belonged to him."

"I guessed." With a reluctant sigh, Maxine picked up the item in question. She could feel it pulse even through the layer of black silk protecting her. It did not contain just one memory—it contained many. It was a tangled web of all it had witnessed. "I am not sure how it will help you find him. I can only see what this has witnessed, not where he is or where he will be."

"Let me ask you this." Alfonzo leaned his arms on the table as he talked. "Can you identify one soul from another?"

"Of course."

"Then if you were to see the memories of whomever owned that jewel and found yourself in a room with him, could you identify who it was?"

She blinked. She laughed and leaned back, watching Alfonzo with renewed respect. He was better at cards than she had given him credit for. "Clever. Very clever. Yes, I could." She turned the brooch over. Nothing was etched on the back. "You want me to play bloodhound and sniff out the King of the Vampires."

Alfonzo smiled. "Exactly. We will keep you far away from danger. You will never see a battle. We only need you to lead us to him."

"I expect this will be exceedingly dangerous, even with your assurances." She ran her thumb over the ruby of the brooch. "I have not seen the things that howl in the darkness...but anything that has the magic to turn the moon to blood would make mincemeat of me in less than a heartbeat's span of time."

"We can protect you," Eddie insisted. "We promise."

She smiled sadly. "I believe you mean your words. I do not doubt your intentions. But I have seen enough tragedy and witnessed enough horror through the minds of others to know that intentions do not beget reality."

"I won't mislead you, Miss Parker," Alfonzo added grimly. "You are correct. We have come here to save this city, not to spare our own lives. We are prepared to pay the ultimate price to save the lives of the innocents who call this place home. You must be willing to do the same."

"Well." She placed the brooch back on the table and took off the glove of her right hand. "Let me see this King of Terrors for myself, and perhaps that may convince me."

Picking up the brooch in her gloved hand, she paused. Taking a deep breath, she readied herself. She did not know what waited for her in the ruby's dark depths, but she knew it was not going to be pleasant. She dropped it into her bare palm.

It was a throne room.

That was an assumption, to be fair, but she could think of little else for which a room such as this could possibly be used. The ceiling soared overhead easily a hundred feet, disappearing into the darkness of the dimly lit space, giving it the illusion that it could go on forever. Gothic archways with their austere finials rose from the corbels of columns and stabbed like jagged claws at the shadows.

From the heads of large, carved gargoyles dangled burning cauldrons on thick iron chains. The monsters were grotesque, resembling the art of Hieronymus Bosch, and were equally disgusting in the way the chains were mounted —impaled through the lower jaw, upper, or both, or wrapped around the maw, or through the eye sockets of their skulls. They screamed in silent torture.

And there, at the end of the corridor, was a throne. It sat up on a row of long stairs that were carpeted in deep crimson fabric that matched swaths of fabric that hung in the wings.

The throne was equally as horrifying as the gargoyles. It was a twisted monument of monsters and their prey, creatures with claws and wings and horns writhing around bodies of humans caught in terror and death.

Whoever had designed a place like this had one singular goal. They had one simple message.

Fear me.

And Maxine could not deny that it worked. This place carried a sense of death and danger. She knew the carpet was stained red from more than dye. This was a place of suffering.

But it was only a dream.

It was a memory, caught in the jeweled broach she held. It could not hurt her. This was merely imprinted on the stone. But the one thing she knew—simply *knew* without question—was that this room belonged to the man who had owned the gem. Even without the hunters having told her it had belonged to a king, the nature of the two were one and the same.

Red satin and black velvet. Fang and claw. Death and blood mingled with the scent of roses. She walked up the carpet toward the throne, gaping at its magnitude. The flickering shadows of the firelight made the figures seem to dance and come to life. There was a strange, artful beauty to it. They had been carved with remarkable craftsmanship by a master, even if their subject matter left much to be desired.

Death had never frightened Maxine. She had always accepted that it would come for her. She had seen more suffering through the eyes of others and in the memories of the objects she touched than one person should ever know. It gave her an interesting perspective on the matter.

But this was not the acceptance of death—this was revelry within it.

Death may not concern her...but dying like the ways that were depicted very much did. Simply because she did not fear the journey did not mean she was not troubled by the idea of being eaten alive. And being eaten alive might be the least disturbing of the ways the throne depicted.

When she finally reached it, she let her fingers trace over the armrests. More flashes of the creature to whom it belonged rushed over her. There was a deep disdain for all around him. Hatred. Violence. *Wrath.* All the world was small to him. But beneath it all...she found loneliness like that of a mountain peak looking at the valley below. All the rest of what she felt was a bridge of cards stacked over a chasm of emptiness and sorrow. Grief and loss ran through it like a raging river.

Enormity. That was what she felt. He was a bridge, a river, a mountain—the metaphors ran rampant in her mind. He was not a man. He was an element of nature.

Perhaps there was more to this story the hunters told.

She let her fingers trail over the armrest again. "Who are you?"

A hand fisted in her hair and yanked her head back. A voice, little more than an angry hiss near her ear, accompanied it. "I could ask you the very same."

She screamed and dropped the brooch.

Maxine came back to reality lying on the floor of her kitchen, locked in a cold sweat. She was panting. Someone was crouched next to her, their hands on her arms, gently trying to help her up. She shoved away from them violently. "Don't touch me!"

They lifted their hands from her obediently and moved back, showing her their palms in a display of harmlessness. "Sorry."

It was Alfonzo. She must have fallen from her chair. She saw the brooch lying on the ground near her. She was shivering and she shook her head dumbly, trying to form words. Trying to think of an explanation for what had happened.

Impossible. That was impossible. But it happened, so therefore it clearly was not. "I'm sorry." She sat up and tried to pull herself back together. "It is not your fault." She slipped on her other glove and reached out to pick up the brooch now that she was protected from it. "You cannot touch me, for your sake and mine. I react poorly when I am startled, that is all."

"What happened? What did you see that scared you?" Bella asked eagerly. She was fetching a glass of water from the sink.

Standing on shaky legs, Maxine returned to her chair

and placed the brooch on the lace tablecloth. "It was not what I saw that was the problem. I saw a throne room fit for the devil himself, but that was not why I screamed." She was still trying to process it and to piece together the bits into a cohesive explanation. When Bella handed her the glass, she thanked her and gratefully sipped the water. "It should not have been possible..."

"What happened?"

"When I touch something, I see a memory. A reflection of a time long past. It isn't changeable. It is like experiencing a moving painting or a zoetrope that might animate around you. I'm an outside observer."

"Paintings on the wall," Eddie muttered as he put it together. "That's what you meant."

She nodded.

"And?" Bella sat back down as well, her bright blue eyes shining with curiosity.

"This painting reached out and touched me." After finishing the water, she poured a shot of rum into the empty glass. The water was nice, but the rum was necessary. She looked over to Alfonzo. "Tell me all you can of this Dracula."

3

"Master? Are you well?" Walter pressed his hand to the elder vampire's shoulder. Dracula had collapsed against the wall as though he had suddenly grown weak.

Dracula chuckled. "Fascinating..." He straightened, tugging on the bottom of his vest to smooth the lines. "I am fine, Walter. Indeed, I am more than fine." He looked down into his pale palm and flexed fingers accentuated with sharp, deadly nails, as though he were remembering holding something. He tightened his hand into a fist and walked down the hall toward the dining room that also served as the war room. "Come."

Walter followed silently, curious as to what had overcome his Lord. Curious and concerned. But he knew to stay silent and keep his worries unvoiced. He would be told all soon enough. He took his position standing by the table as Dracula sat in his chair, the movement smooth and graceful despite his height and stature. Such things were to be expected from a creature such as he.

It left him feeling like the whelpling that he was, despite his own centuries of age. Walter was nothing to scoff at,

Heart of Dracula

since he served as the right hand to the King of Vampires. But next to the one who had sired him, he often felt like little more than a mortal toddler. A brash, clumsy, noisy thing.

Dracula steepled his hands in front of his face and gazed thoughtfully at the table. Walter suspected he was both seeing the notes and maps left upon its lacquered surface and yet taking in none of it all at once. His voice, a low rumble, carried easily. "What have you discovered about Miss Parker?"

"She purports to be a spiritualist—an empath. She claims to be able to divine great secrets from objects and to see all the hidden truths within a human soul. If the hunters have gone to her seeking assistance, I think we shall have little trouble in dispatching them. She is a charlatan, nothing more, and if they can be gulled into—"

"She is no fraud." Vlad chuckled darkly, a sadistic and amused smile spreading across his features. "No, my dear friend. She is far more interesting than that."

Walter furrowed his brow. What had happened in the hallway was connected to Miss Parker; he was now sure of it. But how, he hadn't the foggiest idea. "What would you have me do?"

"I would meet her in person." He paused, shutting his eyes. "Find some aristocrat in this city who fancies becoming as we are. Send Zadok to seduce him and convince him to host a gala. We shall ensure our dear hunters have reason to attend by creating the suspicion that we may also be present. If we are lucky...they shall invite her to join. We may be able to destroy them and collect her in one night."

"Collect her?" Walter carefully kept the dread out of his tone. Whenever his Master found himself in the mood to play with mortals, it never ended well. For anyone. He wanted this business with Boston to be concluded and finished as quickly and cleanly as possible, especially after the debacle they had just suffered in London. Walter had hoped he might be spared his Master's fascination with baubles and toys a few more years than he clearly was to be allotted. *Not again. Please, not again.*

It would be enough that the whole of the American army would be on their doorstep in a few months' time. They did not need to feed danger within their walls.

Let this be a passing fancy. Think wisely, Master. For once, I beg you, do not be entranced by the promise of—

"I have reason to suspect she may be...unique, Walter. Truly unique. And I wish to see for myself what it is that I have found. Opportunities such as these come along so rarely, after all."

Walter felt his hopes crumble, and he let out a low breath. "As you wish."

"You do not approve."

"No, my Lord. We will have a war on our hands, and we cannot have you distracted by a mortal...bauble."

"That is a fair criticism." Vlad leaned back in his chair and smiled thinly. "But wars are so very common in the end. This shall not be my first, nor shall it be my last." He waved his hand dismissively. "Your concerns are likely of no import. What I witnessed shall prove to be a fluke, she shall be utterly uninteresting, and you shall have my full attention dedicated upon the battlefront as you so wish."

"I do not wish for a war, Master, I have made that quite clear." Walter shook his head. "But I serve you. Ergo, I follow you where you lead. I am honored enough that you let me speak my mind."

"True loyalty is more valuable than gold, my dear friend.

Heart of Dracula

For even that immortal metal will tarnish before a heart like yours might wander." He sighed, crimson eyes slipping shut. "I am more grateful than you can fathom. Never hesitate to speak your opinions. They are wise. That is why I turned you—and that is why I keep you at my side."

Walter smiled faintly and bowed his head. He might be a servant, but he took great pride in the friendship that accompanied that service. "Then allow me to say I think this entire endeavor will end in disaster."

Dracula chuckled again, his amusement seemingly genuine. "Noted. Now, please, go. Find us a suitable home to stage our masquerade ball. Take Zadok. He needs a chance to stretch his...predilections. Allow me my dalliance and curiosity. I have not felt such excitement in many, many years."

And so, their fate was sealed. As was the fate of Miss Parker. "Yes, my Lord." Walter folded an arm across his waist as he bowed low. This was a mistake. This whole ordeal would end in nothing but tragedy and setbacks to their cause. But he was grateful that anything at all amused his Master. It had been rare in the past few hundred years.

The alternative to this coming mayhem was far worse. His Master might slip into the coldness of apathy, never to return. That was a far worse fate indeed. He only hoped the hunters were fools enough to die quickly.

It would be a nice change of pace.

Walter knew he was never that lucky.

MAXINE and the hunters had moved into the parlor to talk. The conversation had already stretched on for an hour, and they had only just begun. It was hard to focus on the words they were saying, yet she knew it was all crucial information, and she tried to retain it all. Yet she couldn't stop her mind from dwelling on what had happened when she had grasped the brooch.

That creature is to blame for what occurred. It is not because of anything I did. If he is strong enough to reach through the connection of a bauble such as this... Who is this monster that has come to lay siege to Boston?

Sadly, it seemed they knew surprisingly little about their quarry. Vlad Tepes Dracula had been a mortal warlord and was now an ancient vampire. He hailed, unsurprisingly, from Europe originally, although no one seemed to know quite where. He had masqueraded as several mortal men through the course of a few hundred years.

And from time to time, he would raze a city and declare it his own domain, such as he was apparently attempting to do now with her home.

Maxine was sitting by the window, looking down at the city below and the figures that walked past from time to time. "What is his goal here?"

"To build a kingdom for his immortal monsters." Alfonzo shrugged.

"Yes, but why?" She placed the remainder of her food on her plate and put it aside for the moment. She had made them sandwiches and apologized for having nothing else to serve them. She had not been expecting guests and employed no servants to help her.

"What do you mean?" Alfonzo asked.

"I assume they spend the rest of their time scattered amongst the populace, yes? They gather around him for strength in numbers or because he somehow commands them. But how is this preferable? Why is he staking his

Heart of Dracula

claim here, knowing he will attract not only the likes of you, but soon the full public force?"

"Because he wishes to bring death and mayhem to this world."

"That is the response of a zealot, not a man who knows the answer." She smirked over at Alfonzo. "It's quite fine to say you don't know. I would rather you not fill in the blanks with suppositions. It will only make my job harder."

Eddie snickered. Bella smacked his arm with the back of her hand.

Alfonzo's jaw ticked. It was clear he wasn't accustomed to being scolded like a schoolboy. "The vampire means this city harm. Simple as that."

"Of that, I have no doubt. But I do not yet understand his motive. It may help me to understand him."

Bella looked at her quizzically. "And why would you wish to understand him? He is a monster, nothing more. We are here to stop him."

Maxine paused as she looked out the window again thoughtfully. "It is in my nature to try to seek out the 'why' behind a person's actions. It is my gift to divine the threads that make up a soul and see their whole. In my experience, cruel actions are rarely done without context. And understanding such things, to read the fabric of a man, might help us prevent this from ever coming to pass again."

"He is not a man," Alfonzo argued.

Bella ignored Alfonzo. "How so? Do you seek to reason with him? To negotiate? It cannot be done. Many have tried in the past."

"Perhaps. But there is little else I can do. I carry no guns. I wield no weapons. I can play your bloodhound and hunt the wolf that stalks the streets at night. There is no other benefit I can serve, save that I might learn more about who he is and why."

"Knowledge is always valuable," Alfonzo admitted. "And we will record anything you learn of the vampire—of his past, of his motives, of his powers. If it does not aid us, it may aid those to come."

She smiled over at the older soldier. "Then I will seek to learn as much as I can." She looked down at the brooch. She had continued to turn it over in her hand, feeling the strange sensation still pouring from it. It had ceased to give her the chills. Like stepping into a cold bath, she was adjusting to its presence. "You call him 'the' vampire. As if he is the only one."

"He is the only one that matters. Others can be killed, where he cannot. Maxine…I hate to ask this of you. But if what you can glean from him might lead us to a way to stop him permanently, I cannot pass up on this opportunity."

"I never said such a thing was possible, but I do not know that it isn't." She ran her gloved thumb over the face of the ruby. "Something tells me he will subvert many of my expectations."

"Will you agree to help us, then? It will put you in great danger."

"I suspect the deed is already done. My life ended when you knocked upon my door, Alfonzo Van Helsing. You wish to bring hope with your fight, but you leave death in your wake. He was in my vision. It is too late."

Alfonzo looked off, the lines of his face creasing deeper. "I did not mean to bring him to your door. I did not know what would happen. But you are right. If he was there—if he sensed you—he knows you are a player on the board. You could flee the city, and I would not blame you for doing so. Yet I ask you, will you help us?"

Heart of Dracula

Maxine shut her eyes and let herself feel the room around her.

Alfonzo. Tired, but determined. The weary warrior who must lift the sword and defend against the invading army. The wish for family, for peace, and love. Yet he was no fool; he knew it would be denied. He saw in her a chance for a new page, a kindling of hope that his dreams may yet come true.

Bella. Curious and eager. Everything was something new to learn, something interesting to master. A scholar at heart. She felt like a daisy in the rays of the sunlight in the first days of spring. She was the embodiment of resilience, though she might look fragile on the surface.

Eddie. There was some deep personal mission that ran through him like a vein of silver in a rock. It defined him and it didn't, all at once. She resisted the temptation to pry. It was not her right. He was wary, nervous about this whole situation and, of the three, seemed the least ready to charge onto the battlefield.

He was also in love.

Oh. The young man's focus was clear. Bella. It brought a smile to Maxine's face, and she looked back out the window, letting her awareness of her guests fade. Eddie did not wish to rush to his death because, unlike the other two, he had more to live for than his cause. It was bittersweet. Love rarely ever followed logic or reason when it came to where it chose to place its focus.

As if she would know. She had never been in love herself. Although she felt it enough through the eyes of others around her, she suspected that wasn't at all the same as living it.

How much love would the vampire murder when he took the city? Saving Boston would be a noble cause to pursue, as short-lived as it would be in her case. Literally and figuratively. She looked down at the gem in her hand. She could feel it calling to her. Whispering *come and see*. It was the lure of secrets untold, of knowledge to discover.

Of danger.

Of a creature who would join her there in her visions.

It should scare her more than it did. As it was...she was intrigued. There was more to this mysterious creature than the death and the murder it seemed he spread around him like a plague.

It would mean her death, she knew. If she fled the city this very moment, she might escape with her life. He may not send his minions to follow her. She might live to see another day. But they were all assumptions based on nothing. In fact, all she knew of him—although it was very little—pointed to the opposite.

He had been able to reach through a thread of a connection so slight that it was imperceptible to all others and touch her mind. She could not imagine what he might think of such an imposition. Was it an insult? A curiosity? An annoyance, or uninteresting altogether? She could not say.

But in all her life, short as it might be in comparison to his, she had never experienced anything quite like it. It was terrifying...but she wanted to try again. She wanted to touch the flame. God help her, doom her to the pits, she was going to walk proudly to her own demise.

Shutting her eyes again, she let out a small breath. This was going to end very poorly. "Yes. I will help you. I will sniff him out, and I will learn all I can from him. Right until the moment I suspect he will rip my still-beating heart out of my chest."

Alfonzo chuckled. "We'll do everything we can to keep that from happening."

Heart of Dracula

"I appreciate that." She looked back over at the older soldier and shared a smile with him. They were both aware the odds were good that none of them survived. "If I am to die, I suppose it is better that I go with meaning. We rarely get to pick how we exit this world. At least this will be interesting."

"That is quite true."

"Then I will begin. Return tomorrow morning, and I will tell you what I have found. Or you will find my corpse, one of the two." She stood from beside the window and placed the brooch on her mantel. "I suspect he is not a creature who likes to be encroached upon."

"No. I suspect he is not." Alfonzo stood from his chair and motioned for the other two to do the same. "We have work to do as well, after the sun sets. We will be back tomorrow before noon."

"Perfect." She tried not to laugh as Eddie shoved the remainder of his sandwich in his mouth.

Alfonzo walked up to her and extended his hand. "It's been a pleasure, Miss Parker. Thank you for agreeing to help us. I know the magnitude of what we ask."

She ensured she was wearing her glove before placing her hand in his. Alfonzo did not hesitate when he shook her hand to say goodbye. Bella and Eddie could not say the same, as they both glanced down warily before touching her.

Maxine was accustomed to the sting of being a pariah because of her gift. But it never stopped it from hurting. It merely became easier to bear after all the years.

"Tomorrow, then."

And, with that, she showed them out. Eddie mumbled a goodbye through his food and waved back at her as they left. What an adorable, silly young man. With a shake of her head, she shut the door behind them and threw the locks.

Vlad Tepes Dracula had surprised her once. He would not do so again. She would not bother trying to protect her home from him. What wards she might be able to place on her home would be useless in the end. One, Roma magic was unpredictable and stubborn, and two, she was terrible at it.

While she was a decent empath, she was an abhorrent excuse for a witch. The Roma sorceress she had traveled with had given up trying to teach her the traditions quickly. *"Your gift is elsewhere. Now, get back to work."*

She chuckled at the memory of the old woman shooing her away to have her go pretend to be a psychic. It was amazing how much money she could make from those who believed she could see the future only because she could see the past and present. It had not been honest work. But it had meant shelter over her head and food in her stomach.

She nevertheless went about locking the doors and windows and changed into her house dress, not wanting the uncomfortable steel boning of her corset to dig into her side if she woke up on the floor a second time. After slipping on a necklace that bore a few simple symbols and charms, including her favorite, which was a painted glass evil eye, she was ready. She returned to her parlor and, plucking the brooch from the mantel, she sat in the center of the floor, cross-legged.

If I am going to find myself on the carpet anyway, I might as well start off that way. Lessens the chance of a head injury.

Taking off the glove on her right hand, she held the brooch in her left again. "Well, Mr. Dracula. Let's try this again, shall we?"

She dropped the stone into her bare palm.

4

Maxine found herself standing once more in that nightmarish throne room. She turned around slowly, taking in the space, and waited. Waited for *him*. But the room was silent. Nothing but the whisper of a breeze that sent the tapestries lazily drifting. It gave the room the appearance of breathing.

"I know you're here." Her voice echoed in the large chamber. It felt like an empty expanse. It felt as lonely as a tomb. "There's no point in hiding."

A laugh echoed through the space, low and dark, dangerous and promising both violence and a great joy taken in bringing such things to pass. "And why would I hide from you?" His voice was a deep baritone rumble. It sent a chill up her spine, and she shivered.

When she turned, there was no one there. "If you are not hiding, then what, precisely, are you doing?"

"Observing."

"False. You are attempting to scare me. You can observe me well enough standing face to face with me, and not lurking in the shadows like—" She paused, deciding it may not be a grand idea to insult him.

"Like what, my dear?"

The voice came from behind her, and much closer than before. She whirled and gasped, taking a step away from the figure who had appeared there. She felt the color drain from her face. *Yes, I suppose I shouldn't be surprised. This is precisely how a King of Vampires should probably look.*

He was tall, towering over her, and broad shouldered. He was a monolith of a man, and he surpassed her by easily a foot or more, and she was of average height. Long black hair reached past his shoulders in dark tendrils. They were a sharp contrast to his skin, which was so pale it was almost gray. Full lips were barely a shade darker. His ears were slightly pointed at the tips, accentuating his incredibly inhuman appearance. For while all the rest might be in the right places—he did not have a third eye, nor horns or scales—there was no mistaking what he was.

But it was his eyes that arrested her to the spot. They were crimson and flashed as they reflected the firelight around him like a wolf in the darkness. He was dressed in blacks and deep cardinals, perfect and regal finery, over which he wore a long peacoat that nearly reached the ground.

Not that she looked for too very long. While his gaze was intimidating, it was also dangerous. It felt like turning her back on a hungry tiger. He was watching her with a strange expression that all at once seemed predatory, amused, and curious. He arched a dark eyebrow. "Well?"

"Well...what?"

"You did not finish your sentence." His canines were a bit too long and a bit too sharp.

I am an idiot. Did I expect a vampire not to have fangs? She

Heart of Dracula

forced herself to focus on what he was saying, although it was not hard. He commanded attention.

"You were about claim I was lurking in the shadows 'like' something, were you not?" He took a step toward her.

She immediately retreated one in turn. "I fear I have forgotten what I was going to say."

"Now you are the one lying." His lips turned up at one side in an unfriendly and patronizing expression. "You are merely rethinking your decision to berate me. A wise choice." He took another slow step toward her, his hands clasped behind his back.

She took another step away. "Well, then, Mr…" She paused. "What precisely am I to call you?"

"I have had many names. To others, I am most recently Count Vlad Tepes Dracula." He swept one arm in front of his waist and bowed deep. She did not miss that his fingernails were long, sharpened points, like claws. He straightened slowly, red eyes catching the firelight and flashing dangerously. "But to you, Miss Parker, I would be only Vlad."

She swallowed. She wasn't quite sure why his words made her as nervous as they did. "That is an assumption of a level of personal intimacy I was not aware we shared."

"You have invaded my mind. Twice in one day, no less. You pry into my thoughts. I would call that rather personal. As for intimate…" He tilted his head slightly, his gaze pointedly traveling down her body once and back up. "No need to rush the inevitable."

She laughed. That seemed to catch him by surprise, and he furrowed his brow in confusion. She did her best to smile. "Forgive me. I thought you were making a joke."

"No. You once more lie to me. You know my comment was not made in jest. You wish to dismiss it. Why?"

"You are a vampire tyrant bent on destroying my city. Flirtatious commentary is hardly appropriate. Therefore, it must be an attempt at humor."

"Mmh. And a third lie."

"Neither statement was false."

"Perhaps not, but the latter is hardly the real reason you seek to ignore my *flirtatious commentary,* is it, Miss Parker?"

"It seems foolish to call me Miss Parker when you would have me call you Vlad. As it is clear you already know my full name, you may call me Maxine." She hurried into her next thought. He was right. Usually, it was she who could sniff out the lie in the room, not the other way around. It was unnerving, and there was enough about him that was troubling already.

That he was a terrifying King of Vampires was top on that list. Second was that he knew her name and likely knew who she was and, therefore, where she lived.

"A pleasure to make your acquaintance, Maxine." The glint in his eyes betrayed that he had caught her attempt to steer the conversation away from his comment. "I look forward to meeting you in person and not in...whatever this is." He glanced around them with a thoughtful look. "Is this a dream, or a vision?"

"I am not sure what this is, to be blunt."

"Oh, grand. You do not know the results of your gift." He sighed. "How disappointing. I thought you were more formidable."

"No, you misunderstand. I know what this *should* be. But what it should be and what it very clearly is are quite different."

"Explain."

It was an order, and she bristled at the idea of being given a command by him, just as much as she did at his easy

Heart of Dracula

dismissal of her. One was understandable, and the other was an odd reflex to being insulted. As she wavered on the edge of doing anything the vampire said, his crimson gaze turned back to her.

"I have demanded countless things from countless souls, Maxine. I suspect I will demand far worse of you in the days to come. If what I require of you is painless...I recommend you do not fight me for the sake of it alone. You will have plenty cause to find yourself quite rationally obstinate in due time."

"What an odd speech. You ask me to take your small intrusions with grace because there are larger and crueler mandates to come." She laughed again. "You are a tyrant indeed."

"I will not argue the title."

"Why not? Do you agree with it?"

"I am merely tired of fighting against such childish insults." The lines of his face grew weary. "I am very old, my dear."

"How old?"

"A conversation for another time. When we are in person, and I am not trapped in this dreamworld of yours." His expression shifted back, and she realized now that she could see it anew that it bore a strange kind of playfulness. "Perhaps over a bottle of wine."

She skipped over both his mischievous tone and his comment. She would not be lured down that road once more. "This is not a dream. It should be a memory."

"Interesting. Go on."

"When I touch something, I see the imprint that time has made upon it. They play out for me as a living painting. They are nothing more than pages from a book long penned and immutable in their events. I am a silent and passive witness. What *this* is"—she gestured between them with the wave of a hand—"I do not know."

"I am not one to ever be passive or silent." He smiled. "In any matters." His gaze drifted over her body once more. This time, she could not keep the warmth from creeping up on her cheeks. His smile grew as it clearly did not escape his notice. "Tell me, my dear Maxine, why is it you have come to intrude upon my memories?"

"I would like to propose an accord with you first, King of Vampires. Before we go any farther, I wish to have one thing settled."

"Oh?" He was amused. Deeply amused. If her gift of empathy had not told her that, the devilish grin on his features would have done the deed. "Do tell. Please, do not make it boring. I have such high hopes for you."

Every word that came from him was like a small piece of a puzzle slipping into place. This conversation was painting a portrait of a man, although she could not say she liked what it was showing her. "And what would constitute boring?"

"Demanding that I spare this city, or your life, or some such trite and trivial nonsense." He waved a hand dismissively.

She laughed. She couldn't help it. "Human lives are trite and trivial nonsense?"

"Yes."

It was said with such finality and cold determination that it brought a shiver over her. She glanced away, unable to hold his gaze. It was too much to withstand. There was so much ice and stone behind it that she felt as though she were looking up at a mountain and asking it for pity. She might stand a better chance with the rock. "Then I shall strive to not be boring."

Heart of Dracula

"You are doing wonderfully so far."

"I have done nothing but stand here and make an utter fool of myself. You have low expectations, Vampire King."

It was his turn to laugh. "Perhaps." He took a step toward her. "Perhaps not."

She took a step back.

He grinned.

Summoning the best glare that she could under the circumstances, she tried to hold her ground. "Stop stalking me."

"No."

She stammered. That was not what she had been expecting. She grasped the fabric of her skirt in her gloved hands, needing something to do with them. "The accord, Count, is simply this—"

"Vlad." He interrupted. "To you, I am only Vlad."

"Very well." She shook her head, not understanding why he, who clearly thought of himself as a grandiose and powerful figure, would wish her to refer to him by his first name alone. The throne room in which they stood told of a man who wanted people to fear and worship him. But that was not who stood in front of her. Overwhelming as he may be, he did not seem intent on terrorizing her any more than was clearly unavoidable. "Vlad. I propose that we agree not to lie to each other in the time that is to follow, however brief it may be, before you tear out my throat."

His eyes flickered with something akin to eager excitement. "Oh?" he purred. "And why is that?"

"My abilities allow me to hear a lie as it is said. And yours allows you to see through mine, it seems—"

"No, you're merely terrible at it."

"I—I am not!" Now she was flustered, trying to defend

her aptitude at an undesirable talent. "I—" She broke off in a frustrated growl.

He laughed. It seemed to fill the hall, resonating within the stones. It was a real laugh, pleasant and amused. When it faded, he was smiling. "Tell me, why should I agree to an accord with my enemy? And you are my enemy, no doubt. You consort with hunters who have come to end me."

"From what they have told me, such things are not possible."

"I can be killed. I merely do not stay that way." He shrugged. "Tell me, my darling Maxine, what danger do you bring me? Why have the hunters sought you out?"

"I am no threat to you. I am an empath." She did not fight the smile that brokered for freedom. "Unless you wish to be bored to death as I explain your current mood to you in excruciating detail."

He grinned at her joke. "But they have come to you all the same. Why?"

She watched him for a moment. But she had offered to make this deal with him, and she wished him to trust her enough to speak the truth. "I give you this as a show of good faith. They want me to lead them to you and to sniff you out like a bloodhound using the brooch they gave me. It is through contact with that stone that I have brought us both here to this vision."

"I see. And you would do what they ask of you?"

"You seek to kill thousands of innocent lives. Yes."

"Hm. Very well." Then...he vanished. Simply vanished from her view. His shadow remained, and it rushed under her as though it were now a sentient creature.

Before she could react, hands settled on her shoulders over her dress. She tried to yank away from him, but they held her firm.

Heart of Dracula

"I agree to your terms, darling Maxine. And I find them very interesting indeed." His voice was a whisper by her cheek, his breath cold against her skin.

Goosebumps raced over her, and as she felt him lean in closer to her, meaning perhaps to kiss her, she doubled her efforts to pull away. "No! You can't!" She pushed hard, and he let her go. Turning to face him, she eagerly put several steps between them. "You can't touch me."

"Can't?" He tilted his head slightly. "Interesting choice of words, my dear. I have heard 'don't' a hundred thousand times. But can't? What do you mean?" As if to challenge the concept, he took a step toward her and reached a hand toward her cheek, sharp nails and gray skin stark in contrast to the black fabric of his sleeve. "What magic protects you?"

She drew back. "None."

"Then define 'can't.'" He stepped closer, meaning to press his palm to her cheek.

"Stop!" She backed away again, twice the distance he had closed. "I meant as I said. You can't touch me. No one can."

"Fascinating..." He lowered his hand. "Your gift. You read more than from objects, don't you? If I were to touch you, you would be trapped in my memories?"

"It is far worse than that."

"Explain."

She paused. "And so begins our accord in full, vampire. I shall answer your questions, and you shall answer mine. Both of us have agreed to speak the truth."

He smiled, a predatory thing. "Yes. We are agreed."

"To touch me is...is to die. A slow and painful death of attrition." When he did not speak, she continued. "I am an empath, yes, but by a different way around that most others might be. I hear the whispers of those around me on a far deeper level. When I touch someone—when they touch me—it is not their flesh that I endanger. It is their very soul."

That eager excitement glimmered in his eyes again as he took a careful step toward her. "And you have killed in this fashion? How?"

"I...have torn a man's soul from his body. He starved to death as a result." She swallowed thickly at the memories that seemed to lift bile into her throat. For more than one reason. She shook her head. "Spare me from recounting the details. A conversation for another time, please."

"As you wish. But I will ask for the tale soon. What you say you have done is impossible." He took another slow step toward her. Not wishing to frighten her, it seemed. "You can hear not only my emotions but my soul, then?"

"Yes."

"And what does it tell you? What can you feel from me, my darling empath?"

She hesitated, her eyes slipping out of focus as her attention drifted elsewhere. "Your soul does not whisper. It is the roar of ocean waves on the rocks of some distant shore. Some might be the babble of a stream or the rush of a river...I think you are far more than that."

"Good. What else?" He took another slow, careful step as he approached her.

"I feel...hunger."

"An easy guess. I am a vampire."

"No. Not like a wolf. Although, yes, that is there, I hear something else. Something deeper. A hunger for—" She paused and blinked out of her awareness of him. She looked up at him, uncertain if she should finish.

"Go on. Please."

"A hunger for life."

He straightened his shoulders, taken aback by her

words. He said nothing, his crimson eyes flickering between hers, as if trying to understand. After a moment, he finally broke the silence, his voice a low whisper. "I am dead and have been for a very long time."

"You do not seek to be alive, though, do you? You hunger for that which such a state of being might bring." She reached out carefully, unsure of what she was doing. She needed a clearer photograph. The portrait of the man that she was building was becoming more than simply a tyrant. She needed to understand him, although she was not quite sure why. She placed her gloved hand against his chest, over where his heart might be.

She felt nothing. No warmth. He was as cold as a stone wall. She knew if she pressed her ear to his chest, she would hear no beating from the organ that lay still in his breast. "I hear an emptiness as unfathomable as the depths of the ocean itself."

"You were wrong, earlier. You are dangerous, Miss Parker. Very dangerous." His voice was still a quiet whisper. When she looked up to him, she expected to see anger in his eyes. But what there was instead was grief. Grief, and hope, and the knowledge that it would surely die. The expression of a man who knew tragedy was to come and that it was unavoidable. "I should kill you now for the threat you bring me."

Before she could move, he slung an arm around her waist and yanked her up against him, pressing her there. She gasped and struggled, but it was as though a bar of steel was around her. He was immovable. He would be far stronger than she was even if he were only a mortal man. As it stood, she was pathetically outmatched.

"Stop, please—let me go—I—"

"No. I do not think I shall do anything of the sort." He

hovered his touch over her cheek. She turned her head away from him.

"Please, I—"

"Shush." His fingers hovered over her cheek, close, but not touching her. If he were alive, she would have been able to feel the warmth from his hand. "You have come here a second time to find me. You knew it would be dangerous. You have done this because you seek to know me. You wish to understand me, don't you? To what ends?"

"If I can learn more of who you are, I might be able to find a way to stop you."

"I thought we promised not to lie to each other, Maxine."

"I'm not—"

"Then it is a falsehood you tell yourself as well. You have thrown yourself into the maw of death, knowing I will spell your doom. But as you stand here, parlaying with the enemy...consider why. When you wake from this vision, find the true answer for your curiosity. I can see it plainly."

"Then tell me."

"No." He smirked. "Such things are best discovered, not told. When you admit to yourself why you came here to speak to me, I will reward you."

"With what?"

"A terrible secret I have never uttered to anyone in all my years." He hovered his fingers along her throat, drifting over her. "Oh, my dear. I think I will have a great deal of fun unraveling you. Ah. There is one thing you should know. I cannot die. Not even from your unique curse."

And with that, he touched her. His palm settled against her cheek, and she gasped. Instantly, she was shaking like a leaf. His touch was cold, but gentle. It felt unnatural, but she had nothing with which to compare it.

But he did not scream in agony. He did not collapse to

Heart of Dracula

the ground. He watched her, seemingly enthralled by her reaction. She clutched the fabric of his vest in desperation. If he had not been holding her up, her knees might have gone out. Her eyes were wide.

"You have never been touched...have you?"

"No—Please, I..."

He shushed her quietly as he slipped his fingers into her hair, his thumb resting at the hollow of her ear as he cradled her head in his hand. He tilted her up to look at him.

It felt incredible. It felt wrong. It was overwhelming. She couldn't do anything except feel *him*. His hand, his touch, his nails against her scalp. But then, there was what came with it. The feeling of dark wings spreading out against a night sky. The joy of the hunt. The beauty of the stars painted behind a crimson moon that followed him wherever he went. Beneath it was the taste of sand. The taste of an old sun, burning him.

Blood. Hunger. The joy of victory. The coldness of the grave.

Him.

"Precious girl...you can see it all, can't you? Straight through to the dead heart that sits in a cage of bone."

When his thumb began to track back and forth slowly along her skin, she whimpered. Her fingers tightened, clinging to him. She couldn't form words. She was caught up in him, in satin, in velvet, in steel, and chains, in passion, and violence. He was all those things and more.

"How eager I am to meet you in person, my darling." His voice rumbled in his chest, resonating through her. "And we will meet very soon. Then you will be mine."

"No, I—"

"You have no say in this, I'm afraid." He lowered his head to hers. All her thoughts froze. She tried to pull back from him, but his grasp in her hair tightened. "Lead the hunters to me. Light the torches, bring your weapons, and stop me if you can. You will fall. And when you do—when you kneel—it will be at my feet." His lips ghosted over hers, and she felt him smile. "And what a glorious sight it shall be."

And with that, he kissed her.

5

When Maxine awoke, lying flat on the carpet, it was several hours later. The sun was already setting. She knew she hadn't been trapped in the vision for that long. She was exhausted, and she had a splitting headache. It had taken so much of a toll on her, she must have passed out.

She had not known what to expect. But now that she woke up feeling like she had been put through the wringer of a wash basin, she also wasn't surprised. Picking herself up off the floor, she put the brooch back on the mantel—careful not to touch it with her bare hand—and went upstairs to change and crawl into bed. It was still early, and she had not eaten supper, but her head ached too badly for her to do anything else.

He had asked her why she wished to understand him and disagreed with her response. *I only wish to know him so that I may stop him.* But was it true? She thought so. But he seemed so certain she was lying that it gave her doubt. If she could discern her own motives, he said he would give her a prize. A "terrible secret" he had never said to anyone, he claimed.

Perhaps the secret to undoing him would be within those words.

When she slipped under the covers and her head met the pillow, she was almost instantly asleep. But not before she placed her fingers against her lips, recalling the brief sensation of a kiss. It had only lasted the barest second before it shattered with the rest of the memory. But it was enough.

It was the only kiss she had ever known.

And it was paid to her by a monster and a tyrant set to destroy her city and thousands of lives.

Nothing in life can ever be simple, can it?

VLAD PUSHED the lid of his coffin open and sat upright. Pressing a palm to his head, he let out a small grunt. He felt dizzy and out-of-sorts. Something he had not felt in a very long time. He could sense that the sun had finished its trek through the sky and his perpetual red moon had taken its place.

Fascinating child. Rare child. He smiled through his disorientation. He had never had his mind invaded before, not once, and he had expected to find the act infuriating. Perhaps it was the invader who made the act instead somehow charming and more than a little beguiling. He had wished it not to end.

Certainly not once he had tasted her, however brief that taste had been.

He suspected someone of her unique nature would not be able to withstand such direct and sudden contact. And what an unusual nature, indeed. He had never heard of someone who could touch their very soul to another's.

Heart of Dracula

Suddenly, he bemoaned having left his library tucked away. Soon, he would unleash his power, and with it would come all that he kept hidden. Then perhaps he would see what he could discover in his old tomes. Certainly, there must be some mention of someone with that kind of gift.

In his years, there was but one plague that remained a singular condition—one wretch that remained cursed without compare. Him. All others remained a derivative or a mutation at best.

Climbing from the coffin, he wavered on his feet before chuckling and steadying himself. *I have never been swept off my feet by a woman before. And she has done it twice in one day. I wonder, my dear Maxine, if I have left you as perplexed and intrigued? I do very much hope so.*

I will have you come to me in the end.

I think I will have you willingly kneel to me.

It wouldn't be a hard task to seduce her. He smiled as he dressed, donning his usual garb, standing in the mirror to run a comb through his black strands. No, it would not be a hard task at all.

She was not innocent or naïve—indeed, she seemed remarkably intelligent. She impressed him with her capacity for rational thought and her shrewd navigation through a difficult conversation. He had done his best to keep her off balance. He had decided quite instantly that she was adorable when she was flustered.

No, it was not because she was a wallflower or an ignorant child that he would have her easily. It was for the simple fact that he, where apparently all else had failed, could touch her. By her own admission, she had never felt a hand against her own skin. And from the way she had trembled and shaken in his arms when he let his fingers caress her cheek, he believed her words. She had been so wonderfully frightened. And not only of him.

What a tragic thing to suffer. Especially for a beautiful child such as she. He had adored the way her chocolate eyes grew wide at the sight of him. The way her long dark waves tangled in his fingers, soft as silk.

To live a life alone...

He knew what it was like to love and suffer the agony of loss. But to never know the solace of another's embrace was something not even he could fathom. He had never been shy with his desires toward others, nor had he ever been short on bedfellows, companions, or those who would share love with him for a time. The thought of being bereft of that sounded like the path to madness.

Her fear was delicious. She had begged him not to touch her for fear of harming him—he, who she had joined with others to kill! It was clear that she was a gentle thing. Kindhearted. The sympathy that had burned in her eyes when she had felt his soul had melted something in him that had been frozen solid for a long time.

Her words had cut him to the quick. He did not doubt her claim to hear the whispers of the souls around her. She had spoken to him the truth of his nature that he had never heard aloud. But it was not anger he felt at such a revelation that she had paid him.

It was hope.

She had felt the abyss that dwelled in him, and she had not turned away in revulsion. She had looked up at him with such compassion that he knew he must have her. The war—this city and his new empire—was now secondary among his goals.

You will be mine, Maxine Parker.

Heart of Dracula

Bella impacted the wall hard. She caught most of the blow with her shoulder and grunted from the pain. The ghoul who had thrown here there had been intending to tear her to pieces. She would take the wall over its claws any day.

She pulled two more knives from their holsters on her legs and glared at the slavering, drooling monster. Its teeth were all worn sharp, looking like a fish's maw more than the human it had one been. Its features were sunken and sallow. Skin hung loose on an empty frame.

Eyes that had once belonged to a person were now black from lid to lid, with only a single red dot in the center of each. It knew nothing of compassion or humanity. It only knew hunger.

The creature jumped at her again, and she dug her heel against the wall, ready to meet it with her blades.

Bam.

Its head rocked to the side with the impact of the bullet that blew out its skull. It dropped to the ground, shrieked, and burst into flame. Bella stood and watched as the thing reduced to ash. She rubbed the back of her hand across her forehead. She didn't know if it was sweat or blood on her, but she didn't much care. She was probably just smearing it around. But it was starting to run into her eyebrows.

"You're welcome," Eddie said with a lopsided smile.

"I had it under control." She smiled back at him. "But yes, thank you."

"Are you two done?" Alfonzo called from the end of the alley. "Two ghouls, and it took you five minutes. You should be faster than that."

"Yeah, yeah." Eddie walked toward their leader, and

Bella followed. She couldn't help but chuckle at Alfonzo's constant training. Even in the middle of a fight, he was always trying to teach them something. It was as charming as it was annoying sometimes.

Eddie popped open his revolver, plucked the empty shells from their holes, and replaced them with bullets from the pouch he kept on his hip. "What do you wanna do with their victim in there?"

"Are they still alive?" Alfonzo asked.

"Very much not." Bella blanched. Ghouls were messy eaters. The person looked like they had been dismantled by a pack of coyotes.

"Then leave them." Their de-facto leader sniffed dismissively. "We're not in the business of hiding corpses."

Eddie looked over his shoulder at the remains of the woman who had been the prey. At least, Bella assumed the person had been a woman. Only the tattered remains of a dress gave it away. The body was nearly unrecognizable. Her younger friend sighed and shook his head. "Eh. It just seems wrong to leave them like that."

"Someone'll find them in the morning. We have work to do. C'mon." Alfonzo gestured a hand, and the three of them headed down the sidewalk.

They walked for a while in silence before Bella spoke. "What do you think of Miss Parker?"

"I think she might be useful to us," Alfonzo replied with a shrug. "I think her power is unique. I'll take any advantage we can get."

"She seems nice. She seems to care," Eddie added. "Even if she knows she's in danger."

"She just seems so…sad to me." Bella looked off thoughtfully. "Very alone."

"What's the alternative? You saw what she can do."

Heart of Dracula

Alfonzo glanced at her. "She can hear souls. Do you think she wants to be around people all that frequently? It must get exhausting."

"That's fair." Bella tucked her hands into her coat pockets. "I suppose I didn't think of that. I—"

She didn't get to finish her thought. A snarl from the shadows nearby and a blur of motion served as her only warning. She had a knife buried into the skull of the ghoul as it hovered inches away from Eddie's neck.

Eddie shrieked and fell to the ground in shock, looking up at the twitching and dying monster in surprise.

Bella smiled down at him. "You're welcome."

Alfonzo shook his head. "Children..."

***

RIGHT ON SCHEDULE, the hunters knocked on Maxine's door. This time she was expecting guests and had made a better lunch for the four of them. It was rare that she ever had the chance to host anything more than a séance or the odd gathering. It was hardly a social call, what with their subject matter being more than a little morbid, but she found herself enjoying laying out food all the same.

The city is liable to be destroyed by an undead tyrant who kissed you, and you are amusing yourself with the crudité.

"Hello, Alfonzo, Bella, Eddie." She welcomed them inside and up to her dining room where she had set out food and drinks.

"Oh, fuck, yes." Eddie immediately went for the plate of cured meats.

Alfonzo slapped the boy on the arm. "Manners."

"I'm starving, and it was a terrible night." Eddie poured himself a glass of wine and, lifting it, made a comical show of extending his pinky finger. "There. Better?"

"Forgive him," Alfonzo said to Maxine. "He was raised by cows."

"No, I *raised* cows. Not *by* cows. There's a difference."

"Is there?" Alfonzo smiled indulgently. It was the smile of a father, teasing a son.

Maxine chuckled. "I spent many years traveling with the Roma. It's quite all right. They are hardly the vagabonds and thieves people believe them to be, but high society they are not. Make yourselves at home, please. Language and all."

Eddie was grinning in victory as he piled a plate with food and slumped contentedly into a chair. He looked tired, bruised, and a little haggard.

He wasn't the only one. Bella's arm was wrapped in a bandage that was mostly hidden under the sleeve of her dress.

"What happened to you all last night?" Maxine asked.

"Ghouls." Alfonzo sat at the table, also availing himself of the luncheon, although in a much more decorous fashion.

"One decided to try to make a snack out of me." Bella smiled as if it were nothing at all, waving her hand dismissively. "But I killed it first. Thank you so much for all the wonderful food, Maxine. You didn't need to do this, but we won't say no. We live rather austere lives, hunting as we do."

Maxine laughed this time more out of amazement than amusement. "A ghoul?"

"If a vampire feeds from a victim and kills them, they rise as monstrous, putrid beasts." Alfonzo poured himself a glass of wine and sat back. He grunted as he did, and shifted, as if he had leaned on a bruise.

All three of them looked exhausted. Flashes of blood, of snarling creatures in the darkness, and several brawls filled her mind. She heard the crack of bone and the echo of gunfire. Shaking herself from the imagery, she shuddered. She had no desire to meet anything like the creatures she glimpsed from them.

Now she was doubly glad she had made food for the hunters. They had earned it. "Why is the world not overrun by such things, then? I assume vampires feed regularly."

"They do. The simple reason we're not swarmed by ghouls is that they're careful about who they kill and how they do it. They have strict rules about their conduct." Alfonzo sipped his glass.

"How thoughtful," she replied dryly as she made herself a plate of food and sat to eat. "They can feed without killing, then?"

"That is how they prefer to exist. They either take quietly from their victims, or they convince others to live in their thrall as slaves. As...pets." Alfonzo grimaced. "Some will even trick their mortals into thinking they are valued. It is all a lie."

Maxine shook her head and looked down at her food, finding it all very hard to believe. But after her shared vision with the Vampire King, there was little she would not now take on word alone. "I talked with him last night in a vision."

A clatter of silverware. Bella had dropped her fork onto the porcelain surface, scattering a few lettuce leaves and some tomatoes across the plate. The two men were looking at her in surprise. Bella was staring at her as though she had said she had spoken to God in person and now knew the meaning of life.

"I learned very little. Shockingly little, in fact. But these things must be done slowly. It was first introductions at the negotiating table, nothing more. We have agreed that neither of us is to lie to the other, as we are seemingly incapable of doing so."

"Huh! Well, that's progress." Bella was smiling broadly. "What else?"

She recalled her conversation for them, leaving out his flirtatious comments and the kiss. It was too personal, and far too confusing, to try to explain. In truth, it was also exceedingly embarrassing. "He said he wishes to meet me in person, and that he would do it soon."

"Interesting." Alfonzo rubbed his hand along his stubble. He had clearly not shaved that morning. It honestly looked as though none of them had slept. "Very interesting."

She watched him thoughtfully for a moment before speaking. "You are considering using me as bait."

"I—no, I—" Alfonzo stammered and looked away. The poor bastard.

"Lies don't work on me, remember."

He sighed heavily and lowered his head. "Yes, fine. It was running through my mind."

She paused and drank her glass of wine and poured herself a second. "It is a good plan."

"What?" All three hunters said at once as they looked at her.

"I have sparked his curiosity. I do not think he is one to pass on things that amuse him. I think very little entertains him, indeed. Whatever—or whoever—finds themselves owning such a dubious distinction is a valuable commodity." She looked down into her glass thoughtfully, watching the midday sun glimmer off the surface. "It must be terribly boring to be immortal. He will come for me, regardless of

Heart of Dracula

whether or not I am bait." She remembered the ghost of a kiss against her lips. She shivered. The gesture was likely mistaken by the hunters as sheer horror. In truth, it was far more complicated than that. "I think he means to make me his prey. My conversation with him yesterday sealed my fate. My death is now inevitable. I would prefer that if I am to die, it be for a noble cause."

Alfonzo nodded. The look on his face was one of a man sending a soldier out onto the field, knowing he is not to return, but knowing the line must be held. "You are a brave woman, Miss Parker."

"No. I merely understand that death is what waits for us all. I have seen enough of it to know. I think you have as well, Alfonzo." She sipped her wine and put it back down, opting to pick up some cheese and a cracker from her plate.

"Indeed, I have."

Maxine shut her eyes and took a moment to steel herself. She took a breath and let it out slowly. "So." She looked to Alfonzo. "You have the bait. What is the trap?"

―――

VLAD STOOD on the roof of the building, looking out at the city beneath him. The sun had set, and his red moon had risen. With it came the creatures that hunted in the shadows. They were under strict rules about how many they could take.

Enough to sate the hunger. Not enough to cause panic.

He wanted to take this city with its populace intact.

But that was not why he found himself on the roof, surveying his soon-to-be empire. He was dwelling on his new quarry. His new prize. He knew where he would find Miss Parker. She was mortal and therefore had mortal trappings. A home, a business, bank accounts, and so on. They were trivial things, but useful. Often, he had to consort with lawyers and brokers to purchase land and new estates. It was oddly amusing for him to play at such little games. Like a parent playing checkers with a child.

He could slip into her home, steal her away, and spirit her off into some dark corner of the world where no one would find them. If she were in his cage, she would fall to him in time. All creatures kept in cages became enamored of and inured to their jailers. But that would be too easy.

He did not want a broken thing. He did not want her to crawl to his feet. He wanted her to walk into his arms, to embrace him, then to kneel because she wished to do it. These games should not be rushed. They should be enjoyed and savored.

And how much more perfect the chains she would wear when she donned them herself.

"Master."

Walter.

Vlad moved his head enough to acknowledge the other vampire's presence. His direct whelpling—one of the few who had survived the enormity of the poison that was his blood—was learning to move with true silence. He almost had not noticed his approach. "Speak."

"A suitable mortal has been found with an estate grand enough to host your gala. He is ready to throw it on any day you wish."

"Tomorrow."

"As you command. How shall I ensure that the hunters attend?"

"I know how we may lure them in." Vlad smiled to himself, a wicked plan forming. Oh, it would be delightful.

"Yes, my Lord."

Heart of Dracula

"I will need Zadok rested and sober. His gifts will be required at tomorrow's event. Inform him now so that I stand a slight chance of him being prepared in time." He let out a small growl in his throat. "Tell him he will suffer violence if he does not."

He did not miss Walter's sigh. His whelpling and right hand was a patient creature, but even he had his limits regarding the Frenchman and his extravagances. "As you wish."

"Thank you. Now...go. The line is tied. Now I must bait the hook."

———

IT WAS MORNING, and Maxine had her cup of coffee in her hand as she went down the stairs to fetch her mail. She paused. A note was lying in the middle of the foyer floor, having been slipped under the door. Leaning down, she picked it up. It was a simple piece of paper, folded over in the middle. Turning it over, it bore no identifiable marks.

She set down her coffee and opened the letter.

It was only an address written out in careful script. An antiquated script, in fact. The place it listed was somewhere on Beacon Hill behind the State House. She didn't know the exact number and couldn't quite place where it was, exactly. It was followed by a time. *8 o'clock. Tonight.*

It was signed near the bottom. Simply, succinctly, and with a single letter that left no question about who had left it. And it sent goosebumps crawling over her.

-V.

6

THAT AFTERNOON, the hunters came to call once more for lunch. She had spent most of the morning pacing around her home, a nervous wreck. She had prepared food, but she had broken two plates while doing so. She couldn't focus.

Shortly after receiving the note from Dracula, she had walked to the address to see if she could discern precisely to what she was being invited. The address was an estate. The servants outside who were placing strings of garland along the wrought-iron fencing told her a gala was being hosted that night in honor of a new dignitary come to the city. One who would save Boston from all its woes.

She had not needed to ask the name of the dignitary in question.

It would be the logical thing to climb into a carriage and ride for the horizon. She had nowhere to go, but that never stopped her before. She was accustomed to life on the road and being forced to pack up and leave.

Being an empath, and therefore "supernatural," often made her an unwelcome neighbor. In that regard, her life with the Roma had taught her well. She learned to keep to herself.

But she had spent more time in this city than any other to date. She rather liked it here. Luckily, Boston residents were private creatures. She rarely talked to the people who owned the houses around hers, even though their walls touched. It was remarkable how secluded a person could be when they wished. And how easy it was to disappear into the cracks of a city.

The larger the city, the smaller the person within it became. She was simply another face, another name, in a sea of thousands. In a village, every life is important, every event part of the story of the town. Here, she could simply blend in.

That was how she preferred it.

Her business fared better in the city, regardless. There were more clients for her to see, and more work for her to take on. More curious aristocrats who wished her to divine some forgotten truth or to speak to a "ghost." She could not summon the dead. Ghosts rarely followed the living about like invisible dogs. She was merely relaying to them what she saw in the memories she summoned from their personal effects. Telling her client what she saw was more than enough "magic" to please them and ensure she had a long list of valuable clients.

The city had its benefits. It also had its drawbacks. The noise. The congestion. Or an ancient King of Vampires came to call with wrack and ruin as his gifts.

The knock on the door disturbed her pacing, and she was almost glad for the arrival of the three hunters. She greeted them and showed them up to the dining room. Eddie wasted not a single moment before heaping food onto his plate.

"Another long night?" she asked.

"They are always long nights when a vampire lord is afoot, and we face the King of them all." Bella let out a long, exhausted sigh and slumped into a chair. Alfonzo had a slight limp, favoring his left leg, although he was doing his absolute best to hide it.

"Let me get the whiskey," Maxine muttered as she walked out of the room. When she returned, she placed a glass in front of Alfonzo and poured him a double.

"You are a saint." The older hunter chuckled. "Thank you."

"Where are you all staying? Or do you simply not sleep at all?" Maxine realized how little she knew about her new "friends." They had simply not had much time to talk about such details. There was a war brewing, after all. And it was the hunters' jobs to stop it.

"A hostel somewhere near the seaport." Eddie wrinkled his nose. "It smells like puke and fish."

Maxine chuckled and shook her head. "You should stay here with me. I have five bedrooms in this place, and I only use one of them. I have running water and flushing toilets. Probably more than what your hostel has."

"Why would you invite us in?" Alfonzo furrowed his brow, confused. "We are…you do not know us."

"You are in my city to try to save it. You will likely give up your lives doing so. And I am certainly not likely to survive any of this. If I die, feel free to sell off anything I own, assuming any of you live." She sat in a chair and poured herself a glass of whiskey. "Although you may not wish to join me here." She picked up the note that was slipped under her door from where she had left it on the table, folded as she had discovered it, and handed it to Alfonzo.

He opened it and scanned it. "When did you get this?"

"This morning. It was slipped under my front door. He knows where I live."

"Then why has he not simply come in here and killed you already?" Bella asked, blissfully unaware of the casual violence she was suggesting.

"I thought vampires could only enter domains to which they were invited?"

"Sadly, that is a myth." Bella poured herself a glass of water.

"Some nutjob vampire somewhere probably convinced himself that he couldn't enter homes without an invitation, and it got added to the legend." Eddie plucked up the bottle of whiskey and joined the rest of them in a stronger beverage. "Vampires are usually insane. Immortality seems to do that. The counting thing? Myth. Running water? Myth. Sleeping in their own dirt? Myth. Mirrors and garlic, myth. I think it amuses them to keep spreading the rumors. It makes them seem weaker than they are."

"And their fear of the cross?"

"Myth." Alfonzo sighed. "Traces to a vampire lord in Ireland who convinced himself he would burn if one touched him. But it isn't true."

"Fascinating...what of the sun?"

"That remains true, to a point. It will burn the young ones. The older the vampire, the more durable they become. I have seen some walk in the day without pain, although it weakens them and their powers."

"What of Dracula himself?"

"We do not know."

"I see." She spun her glass in her fingers, watching the alcohol swirl a little as she did. "Then to answer your question, I do not know why he did not show himself in. He likely knew I was without protection and asleep in bed. He could have done far worse than slip a note beneath my entry door." The thought made her shiver. She knew she was in danger, but she hadn't really understood how much until that moment.

"Yet he did this instead. I don't know this city. Where is this?"

"A home on Beacon Hill behind the State House. The estate of one of the bourgeoisie children of the city. When I asked the footman what the occasion was, they said they were hosting a dignitary who had come to 'save the city.'"

"Mmhm." Alfonzo let out a long, tired sigh and leaned back in his chair. "He's set a trap, then."

"It seems so." Maxine sipped her whiskey. She usually did not drink it straight, but it helped settle her frazzled nerves. "I am the bait, after all."

"He *asked* you to attend." Alfonzo held up the card and re-read it, as if it would give up more information from that method alone. "Why?"

"I see it as a command. I do not see a question mark, or anything of the sort."

"No. He could have kidnapped you, Maxine. He could have robbed you from your bed, and that would be the end of it." Alfonzo placed the note down on the tablecloth. "This is a request. He wants to see if you will walk in there willingly. Why?"

"I honestly do not know." And it wasn't a lie. Yes, she had left out Vlad's strange flirtatious behavior with her—and the kiss—but she did not know why the man who considered himself a veritable god on Earth had not simply snatched her up. "I suppose we are left to decide what we will do about the matter."

"Do you wish to attend?"

"I do not wish to die. If I go into that place, I am walking

Heart of Dracula

into the jaws of a lion. But I find myself already within the easy reach of its teeth. It is only by the benefit that the beast has not bitten down that I am still alive. I suppose I am curious as to why, same as you."

"Then you will agree to go?"

"If it benefits you three in your endeavor, yes. I fear I am following your lead in this regard. I have no experience hunting vampires."

"When it comes to Dracula, I fear we are all novices." Alfonzo rubbed his hand back over his short hair, scratching at his scalp. The poor bastard was exhausted. "I doubt the invitation extends to us. Nor would they let us in as we are. As you can imagine, we didn't exactly pack suits."

Maxine chuckled. "And I do not own men's clothing. Although," she looked over to Bella, "I have a few gowns that might fit you. It is expected for someone in my profession to dress the part of a Lady Spiritualist. I hope you don't mind wearing black."

Bella looked more than a little excited. "I have never attended a ball before."

Eddie was clearly displeased. Worry flared in him like a flame so suddenly she felt it easily from across the room. His young love burned like the sun in the sky. "This is a bad idea. Sending them both into the viper's nest. Who knows who'll be there? How many he'll bring?"

Bella shot the young man a withering look. "I can handle myself."

"That's not what I meant. I meant—"

"I'll watch the perimeter. Eddie, you'll be nearby to provide cover. When he shows himself, Bella will give us a signal, and we will storm the building. Miss Parker...do I need to tell you how dangerous this will be?"

"That I will likely not live to see tomorrow? I understand. I'll either die by vampire or potentially by being caught in the crossfire. But this must be done. He must be stopped. I have met him only the once, and I know he is as you say he is—a danger to all the lives in this city. Mine is but one. He will spend thousands if left unchecked." She drank the remainder of her whiskey in one go and put the glass down.

Eddie snickered, impressed. "Damn."

She smiled back at the boy. "The Roma taught me well."

"Clearly." Eddie was still chuckling. "I think I like you, ma'am."

Maxine winced at that. "Please don't call me ma'am. Or Miss. Just call me Maxine."

"Oh. Right. Sorry ma'—I mean, Maxine." He coughed and went back to his food and his drink. "I still think this is a bad plan, by the way."

"It's a terrible plan, you're right," Alfonzo confirmed. "But it's the only one we have. Bella, you'll go in with Miss Parker. Eddie and I will remain outside and wait until the moment is right."

"And you three will go back to the hostel, gather whatever it is that you own, and for the love of all that is holy, bathe and get some sleep." Maxine couldn't help but smile, despite the grim situation. "Your hostel smells like puke and fish, and I fear it's rubbed off on all of you. If we are all to die tonight, best not already smell like a corpse when we do it."

The three of them laughed, and she joined them. It was gallows humor. She had always had a deep streak of darkness that tainted her by benefit of who she was. It made her difficult to be around. But the three hunters seemed to share in her plight or saw it for what it was. Either way, she was glad it did not disturb them like it had so many others.

Maxine was never one to have friends. Either due to her

personal oddities, her uncanny knowledge of what others were feeling at all times, or her inability to touch or be touched, her friendships were always stilted and brief. But she had hope it might be different with these three. She knew they had seen far worse things than her in their day.

It was only a question of whether they all lived long enough.

Bella still looked over the moon with glee. Even the looming promise of death didn't seem to quell her enthusiasm. "I get to wear a gown." She laughed. "How exciting!"

"Is everything ready, Walter?"

"Yes, my Lord." He bowed his head to Dracula. This whole plan was dangerous, foolhardy, and exposed them all to needless risk. It was for those exact reasons that Walter knew he could not dissuade his Master.

"Good."

"Do you think she will come? She must understand it is suicide."

"She will come. She will bring the hunters in tow, and she will believe that is why I have asked her to attend." His Master flicked the backs of the cufflink he was pinning into his sleeve, locking it into place before moving on to the other. "Miss Parker does not realize it is for her sake that this is done."

"And what are Zadok and I to do with the hunters?"

"Kill them and attempt not to die in the process. Bring Mordecai. He does so much love to dress up and play amongst the mortals." Dracula smiled, thin and cruel. "He might find someone to entertain himself, and you may need him if things go awry."

"Surely if you are there, we will not need the assistance."

"I may be distracted, Walter. If all goes well, I will be busy with other matters."

Walter could not help himself. He sighed.

Dracula chuckled, and crimson eyes met his in the mirror. "Someday you will understand. Someday you will be as old as I and know it is these moments that matter most above all. Not the trivial hunters who stalk my shadow." He pinned the other cufflink in place and reached for the red ascot on the dresser. His Master was dressed in his finest clothing and looked every inch the royalty that he was. "They are common. They are fleeting. She may not be."

"I promise that if that day should come, I will look to you and say, 'You were right.'" Walter smirked. "I fear it will be long in coming."

"And therein lies the secret you have yet you learn, even at your age. Nothing is long in coming for any of us. All of time stretches before us. You see the span as an endless road. I see it as the tick of the clock. Once you understand the enormity of what you will experience, you will understand why I do such ill-advised and seemingly irrational things."

Walter bowed his head again. He didn't understand yet; in that, Dracula was quite right. He dreaded the day that he might.

"Take solace, dear Walter. Tonight will be exciting, if nothing else."

"That does not make me feel any better in the slightest."

Dracula chuckled and turned to him. He placed a hand on Walter's shoulder. They were nearly the same height, even though the elder vampire was far broader and filled the room in a very different way than he. Walter suspected he would always feel like a child in Dracula's presence.

Heart of Dracula

"These hunters will pose you no threat. Now, go. Fetch the others. Ensure they are ready. Ensure Zadok is sober, most of all. And pull Mordecai out of whomever he is buried inside and insist he wear pants to this affair."

Walter grunted. "It is not only because of the presence of the hunters that I loathe the idea of this night."

Dracula grinned and patted him on the shoulder before turning back to the mirror to finish dressing. "I have faith in you, dear Walter."

"I wish I shared your sentiment." He bowed at the waist and turned to do as he was told. He did not know which of the vagabonds he dreaded speaking with more, Zadok or the incubus. They were each irritating in their own right.

The scales weighed out about equal.

Letting his body dissolve into a swarm of bats, he resigned himself for what was to come. He could only pray to the gods above and below that tonight ended as smoothly as it could.

Oddly enough, he found himself sympathetic toward Miss Parker. Death had come to claim her, and not in any way she could have possibly guessed.

―――

"You look beautiful." Maxine smiled at Bella's reflection in the mirror. The young woman really did look stunning in the deep sapphire-colored taffeta gown she had chosen. It was the lightest-colored dress Maxine owned.

The public did not wish for a spiritualist to wear rose, after all.

The young woman had squawked and yelped as Maxine had tightened her corset. She hadn't ever worn one before, at least not the right way. She was still shifting uncomfortably in the steel bones. Maxine hadn't even done it up as far as it could go. She figured Bella would need to breathe if—when—there was a fight.

"As do you." Bella smiled at her in the glass. Maxine was pinning up Bella's long blonde hair into curls and a fashionable bun. The black silk gloves she wore made it more difficult, but they were a necessity. She couldn't chance an accidental brush against the young girl.

"No, I look sad." Maxine slipped a jeweled pin into Bella's hair. She looked like a princess with her blonde hair and sparkling blue eyes. Maxine always looked like a vision of death. Her pale skin stood out sharply against her dark hair, and with the jet-black silk dress she wore, she was better suited to be standing by someone's grave, not at a gala.

"Are you?"

"I feel the emotions of all those around me. Loss, grief, and anger greatly outnumber happiness in the human race. So, I suppose I do." She placed another pin into Bella's hair.

"Is that why you live here alone? With no servants? I can't imagine being around others all the time is comforting. It must be very, uh, loud. I'm not sure if that is the right word for it."

"It's a perfect word for it. And you're right." It was rare that someone understood. "How old are you, Bella?"

"Nineteen."

Only four years separated them, yet she felt as though it were forty. Maxine had always been too old for her body—she had seen too much, felt too much. It aged her soul, even if her flesh had not yet followed suit. She expected she would go gray before she turned thirty. "I saw glimpses of what led to this life, but nothing concrete enough to form a

Heart of Dracula

full story. What happened that drove you to hunt vampires, Bella?"

"My family was murdered by a pack of ghouls when I was very young. It left me an orphan. But Alfonzo found me a few years later and, hearing the story of my survival, offered to take me in. He trained me. He is like a father to me."

"How did you survive?"

Bella held out her hand, and Maxine gasped as several of the objects on the vanity—a comb, a brush, a palette of eyeshadow—rose from the wood surface. The brush flew to Bella's palm, and she grasped it as the others drifted down and settled where they had been a moment prior.

Turning her palm up, she opened her fingers, and the brush lifted to hover over her open hand and began to twirl slowly. "I have my methods." Bella smiled.

"Well, now I know why you are not disturbed by who and what I am." Maxine reached out and poked the brush where it hung in midair. It jostled a little but seemed quite intent on doing as Bella commanded.

"Not in the slightest." The hairbrush fell back into Bella's hand, and she placed it on the vanity once more. She was smiling, as if proud of the chance to show off. "What of your path to this point? You offered up your home to us, and even your things, should you die. Do you have no family?"

"None. I was driven out by my mother at a young age. My father, who was damaged by the war both mentally and physically, killed himself not long before I was born. I have no siblings."

"For someone who can hear the emotions of all those around them...you live a lonely life." Bella frowned. "I am sorry."

"It is as you have said, very loud otherwise. It is more

peaceful this way." Maxine smiled sadly and put the last pin into Bella's hair. "I am accustomed to it. Don't pity me. I have more than most could wish for." She walked over to her dresser and picked up a crimson silk choker from the stand, trimmed in black lace. Tying it around her throat, she picked up the ruby and silk brooch from where it sat on the dresser. She returned to the mirror to pin it to the center of the choker, careful to thread the pin through the first layer of fabric and not the second so that it did not touch her skin. It was jewelry meant for a man, but on her collar, it looked like a memento.

Something gifted to her by a lover, perhaps, as if to remember him by. Her cheeks threatened to warm at the notion, and she pushed the thought away before it betrayed her.

"What are you doing?" Bella asked.

She touched the ruby. Even through her gloves, it whispered to her. Wearing it was a statement. It was the lamp of a lighthouse, calling the enemy fleet to shore. It was a show she knew would not go unnoticed. "If I am to be the bait tonight, I rather think I should look the part." She would march into the jaws of death and stare him in the eyes. She would die with her head held high. "Don't you?"

7

Maxine was not certain who this "Vicomte Arthur Price" was who was hosting this event, but there were a few things she could discern the moment she walked through his door. He was incredibly rich. And he greatly enjoyed flaunting it. To call the gala lavish would be to insult the ostentatiousness of the whole ordeal.

As Maxine walked into his opening parlor, she looked up at the ice sculpture that dominated the lobby. It was a beautiful thing of carefully carved roses and other greenery. Bella gaped at quite literally everything she saw. More than once, Maxine had to take her by the elbow and pull her along.

"Why does anyone need a house this big?" Bella whispered, gaping at the soaring paintings and columns swathed in swirls of crimson fabric.

Crimson. The Count's color. It was very much on purpose, she knew.

Maxine grinned mischievously. "Because other parts of its owner are likely very small."

Bella had to cover her mouth to keep from howling in laughter. They giggled like schoolgirls, and the young woman swatted her arm as if to scold her for her commentary.

"Ah! And you must be Madam Parker." A voice broke into their amusement. Maxine turned, and found a thin, tall, blond man wearing a black brocade suit with lace cuffs that belonged to a fashion that was either just leaving or just coming in. No one else in the room wore them. "The second guest of honor this evening."

"Excuse me?" She fought back the dread that washed over her and bade her run out the door whence she had come.

"The man we honor tonight has instructed me to welcome you to my home, along with your lovely friend, and tell you to enjoy the festivities. He will be along shortly and apologizes for the delay." The man bowed with a flourish. "I am the Vicomte Arthur Price. It is a deep pleasure to meet you." When he rose, he extended his hand to take hers.

She hated being touched, even through her gloves. Especially by a man such as him. But she swallowed down her dismay and placed her hand in his. He felt like a snake in the grass to her, and she tried not to grimace. "A pleasure, as well. How have you come to meet our mutual acquaintance, I wonder?"

He bowed again to kiss the back of her knuckles. "Straight to business. A pragmatic woman. I like it." His gray eyes flickered with something fiendish. There was danger in him; she could feel it. She pulled her hand away from his when he held it for a moment too long. "He needed introductions to the good society here in our troubled city and sought me out to provide such a thing. Once I realized he

Heart of Dracula

could save us from all the dangers that stalk the night, I didn't hesitate to grant him everything he wished."

"Rumor has it he is the cause of the danger, not the salvation from it."

"Sometimes one must suffer the disease to become immune to it." He smiled sweetly. "But come, come, no more talk of this…unpleasantness." He waved over a servant and plucked two glasses of red wine from the tray and handed one to her and the other to Bella. "Have a drink. Then have several more. This night is about celebration, not death."

"We shall see. I do not think the two are mutually exclusive to our friend."

Arthur laughed. "A sharp tack you are, hm? I see why our honored visitor likes you so." He looked to Bella. "And who are you, my ravishing dear?"

"Bella Corallo. Charmed." It was clear that Bella thought of Arthur as anything *but* charming. Maxine didn't fight the smile. The girl was bright-eyed, but clearly not a fool.

Arthur took her hand and kissed the back of it, as well. "Your dance card will be full tonight, I'm sure of it. Save a spot for me, if you would." He took a step back. "But! I must go. So many guests to attend to, as you can imagine. Please, make yourselves at home. Enjoy yourselves, my darling ladies. You are both set to have quite the night." Arthur winked at Maxine as he walked away.

Something about the man felt…off. Very off. She couldn't put her finger on why, but he sent a crawling and creeping kind of dread through her. She wondered if the man weren't entirely human. "Stay away from him," she warned Bella.

"Not a problem." She sipped her wine and stared into it. "Do you think it's poisoned?"

"No. That would be too easy." She sipped her own. "But

he is dangerous. I'm not sure how or why as of yet. But there is something unnatural about him."

"Ah. And here I thought he was simply a pervert." Bella smiled. "Good to know he is also a monster. I didn't need two excuses to feed him his own fist, but now I have them. It is quite useful to have an empath around."

Useful. She'd never been called that. It made her smile again. "If we survive this, I think I would like to be your friend, Bella."

"And I yours." She was beaming again. Smiling as though she were the very sun itself. "We are in need of a negotiator. Alfonzo and Eddie are quite terrible at it, as you can imagine, and I have no talent for such things."

The thought of taking up with the vampire hunters and traveling the world defeating darkness made her chuckle. It was so outlandish that it was humorous, although she found she didn't dislike the idea at all. "They seem like fine men. Well, one man and one boy, perhaps."

"Alfonzo is a noble, determined soul. Don't let his stern exterior fool you. Time has just left him a little grizzled." They began to walk through Price's home as they talked, sipping their wine. Eddie had asked that they remain by the windows in the front of the building so he could provide support via his rifle should something happen. There was a window in the ballroom that would be perfect, and they made their way there, accepting the food that was offered to them on trays by passing waiters. Bella was ravenous, and Maxine realized the hunters might not get a chance to eat regularly.

"And what of Eddie?" she asked as they took up their post by the window in the ballroom. It was out of the main path of the guests—which was fine for Maxine, since there

Heart of Dracula

were a lot of guests—and secluded enough that she could watch and not be watched.

"He's sweet. He'll stop the horses to help a turtle cross the road. He's funny, silly, and compassionate." Bella smiled faintly. But there was a kind of remorse to her expression. A fashion of regret.

Ah. The love Eddie felt for her was not requited. Poor boy. She opted not to bring up what she knew. It would only rub salt in the wound. "How long have you traveled together?"

"I've been with Alfonzo since I was ten. Nine years, then. Eddie joined us about four years back. Alfonso has practically raised me. We both owe everything to him."

"I suppose it makes it easy to lay down your lives for a cause that has defined it." Maxine sipped her wine again. It was good and clearly very expensive. Far more so than anything she would ever purchase. She tried to enjoy it as much as she could, all things considered.

"That is true. But what of you? You have taken this all remarkably in stride."

"Everything I touch—every bauble, every knickknack, every building, I see all that has ever happened to it or within it. I see every proposal, every kiss, every moment of love. I see every tragedy, every betrayal...and every murder. I have witnessed a thousand deaths as if they were my own." She looked down at her gloved palm. "I felt their emotions as they died, and because of that...I have died a thousand different ways. I suppose that is why I don't fear it. That is why some people might even think I embrace it. I have felt the soul of this Count Dracula, and I know what is coming for me. I know I cannot fight a force of nature."

"My God, Maxine, I am so sorry." Bella reached out to

touch her but changed her mind and dropped her hand. Either out of respect for Maxine's discomfort of such things, or nervousness of her own. She wasn't quite sure. "We will fight it together. We will prevail."

I wish I had your faith. I wish I had your hope. She kept those words silent. Crushing the dreams of another was a needless cruelty. "Thank you."

"Do you have your revolver?" Bella had asked her that question at least ten times so far.

Maxine smiled and nodded once. She knew it came out of a place of concern for bringing someone untrained and untested into a situation where a fight would likely occur. "It's been many years since I had cause to use one, but the Roma were keen on all their children being trained for self-defense and hunting. I know which end to point at a thing I wish to die, though I am no marksman."

"I hope it does not come to that."

"I get the sensation that hope matters for little in moments like these."

Bella chuckled in response.

Looking out at the crowd, Maxine wondered how many of the guests were human and how many of them were not. It was hard to separate out the emotions in large groups. It all just turned into noise. It was another reason she avoided events such as these. "Are vampires able to hide in a crowd?"

"Some can, yes. Vampires are quite like people in that their powers and gifts manifest differently. Some can blend in seamlessly with humanity, while others are grotesque things that would clear a room at the very sight of them." Bella leaned back against the window frame, watching the crowd. "I do not see any I might suspect, though. Do you?"

"No. Although they all are muddled together, I admit."

Heart of Dracula

"Arthur said the Count was not yet here. Perhaps he and his prefer to be fashionably late." Bella sighed. "How inconsiderate."

Maxine laughed. "Of all things they could be, I would prefer them to remain only inconsiderate."

Bella laughed as well, and they fell into companionable silence. It was a few minutes later that a young man approached them. Maxine blinked. The man was...beautiful. There was no way around it. He had sharp features that were both masculine and also a little delicate. His blond hair was swept back, although a few strands had fallen loose, giving him a rakish air.

Eyes that were a shade of blue that appeared purple in the light of the gas lamps were fixed on Bella. Or perhaps it was the purple ascot he wore that gave him such an appearance. He was smiling, an expression that looked like it came to him easily. "Pardon me, my lady." The man bowed gracefully. "May I have this dance?"

"I—ah—" Bella stammered. "I, well—" Maxine watched as the young woman blushed bright pink. Her blue eyes were wide in surprise, and she glanced to Maxine, then back to the man, clearly unsure of what to do.

"Go on." Maxine nudged Bella's elbow. "I will be quite fine here on my own." She motioned her head out the window, knowing Eddie was there with a long-range rifle ready to assist her should something change. "Enjoy the dance."

The man smiled to her and bowed his head slightly. "Thank you for loaning me your companion." His voice was quiet, smooth, and there was something deeply seductive about him. "I promise I'll return her unscathed." He offered his hand to Bella.

Poor Bella did not stand a chance. The girl was already enamored; she could see it in her face. She put her hand in his, and he pulled her toward the dance floor where couples were waiting to begin.

Maxine watched them wistfully. There was no small portion of her that was jealous. The way they were smiling at each other. The attraction was instant and mutual. One dance turned into two. If there was a third, it would be an absolute scandal. She couldn't imagine Bella knew or cared of such social etiquette. With a sad smile, Maxine looked out the window.

It was something she could never have. A relationship. Attraction. She looked down at her gloved hands. She was always going to be as she was—surrounded by others, but utterly alone. Some days it threatened to crush her. She shut her eyes and let herself stretch out her awareness to sense the emotions of those around her. Happiness, enjoyment, and the playful excitement that came with a party. She tried to take some of it into herself, but it was a poor salve.

She stayed at her post by the window, knowing she must look bored and uninterested in the goings-on of the room. While she wished to never be alone, she hoped her expression might discourage any would-be gentleman callers desperate for a companion.

It had always worked before, and it would work again this evening.

Even without knowing who she was and what she could do, she carried the feel of death about her. She was told by many others that she was somehow inherently eerie and unsettling. Even if the living could not see the world in the way she could, they knew something very *other* clung to her like moss from the branches of a tree.

The room was filled with men, women, and those who seemed to be either a mix of the two or neither at all, each one dressed in their finest. It was a joyful affair, and Bacchus would be proud. More than once she caught sight of Arthur Price with a man under one of his arms and the other around the waist of a young lady. He clearly enjoyed the company of any gender, and he was not shy about admitting it or showing it in public. She knew it was only by his extreme affluence that his proclivities were tolerated.

The room was alive with pleasure.

And she stood alone.

After forty-five minutes of nothing, with no vampires to be seen, she had lost her focus. Bella had disappeared with her young man, likely to talk in private on some balcony. Or to go do more lascivious things. She did not judge or bemoan the girl if that was her choice. Her life had clearly been one of suffering. She should enjoy herself whenever she was allowed.

Lost in her thoughts, Maxine failed to notice a shadow that had approached by her side.

"May I have this dance, my lady?"

The unexpected voice made her jump, and she looked up wide-eyed at who had spoken to her.

The man was tall. Easily six feet or more. He had brown hair, worn swept back in the fashion of the day. He had light brown eyes that shone with warmth and a smile that matched it. He was a bit older, perhaps in his mid-thirties. He was handsome in a way that was uniquely British. His accent when he had greeted her had given that away, as well. He looked well-to-do—to be at Arthur's party, he must be—but his mien did not scream aristocracy. Nor did he ooze charisma like the man who had swept Bella off her feet.

But there was something instantly charming about him. Something that made her curious. Something that hinted of a current that ran beneath the surface of a winter lake. That there was more about him than met the eye.

Maxine was absolutely stunned and found herself only able to blink in surprise. She was leaving him with his hand extended to her and in the awkward silence of her befuddlement.

"If your card is full," he prompted with a twist to his thin lips, "I understand." Oh, he was certainly very British.

"N—no," she stammered and cursed herself for being such a child. He was a man, nothing more. He did not have the pallor of Dracula, and there was no flash in his eyes that betrayed him to be a vampire. He was a living man. "It is only that I fear I am a horrid dancer. I have not done it since I was a child. I will embarrass you."

"If you are able to follow my lead, none will be the wiser, I swear to you." She had thought him not as impressive as the young man who had come for Bella, but, as he talked, she found herself amending her opinion. There was something deeply alluring about him. Casual, but gentle. But there was something else there that she could not place. She was not one who would ever fall for such a thing, but she felt her cheeks begin to grow the barest bit hot.

Before she could really think it through, she placed her gloved hand into his. Her unease seemed to make him smile farther. It was a kind expression with a warmth that seemed genuine. His brown eyes seemed old, now that she took a closer look. *Who is this man?*

He walked with her to the dancers who were preparing for a waltz and guided her hands to the appropriate locations. The man chuckled deeply as he looked down at her.

Heart of Dracula

"If you keep that look of utter fear on your face, you may give your inexperience away."

She laughed quietly and forced herself to relax. She took in a breath, held it, and let it out, along with the tension in her limbs. "I do believe this is my first time upon a dance floor since I was not standing on a man's shoes," she admitted to the handsome gentleman.

He chuckled. "If I may be so bold, my lady?"

"Of course. I have little patience for anything else." What on Earth prompted her to say that? *Idiot! He is a gentleman from some foreign place, and you sound like a complete harlot.*

A single chuckle left him at her comment. "Good. Neither do I. Allow me, then, to observe that you carry great resolve in you. I can see it in the way you carry yourself. You are accustomed to relying on no one. But here, you are unsure, and you are unprepared for what lies ahead of you. If you do not allow me to lead, this will all go quite poorly." His playful smile had not left him.

She hadn't realized she had been pressing away from the hand that rested against her lower back. Unconsciously, she was still resisting, and he had been holding her there, as if she were out on the floor against her will. *Allow him to lead, you dimwit. Allow him to lead!* She forced herself to stop leaning back against his hand and cleared her throat. "Better?"

"Very good. And just in time." Amusement poured from him. Not mocking her, but honestly enjoying the experience. It was so very foreign to her, it left her almost as uncertain as the prospect of the dance.

The music began. There was a knowing sort of kindness in his eyes, as if he found her awkward inability to sacrifice control of the situation, even in something as benign as a waltz, somehow charming. If only. It was likely her interpretation of a man who had realized he had made a terrible mistake by choosing her for a dance partner.

She squeaked in surprise as he pulled her along the dance floor. It drew a laugh from him. She focused everything she could on simply letting it happen—letting him guide her movements. He made it easy, as there was a firm and inarguable certainty to his actions. Standing this close to him, she caught the scent of a cologne that reminded her of roses.

He was strong. Very much so. More than his thin frame belied. He pulled her along through the dance, and she wondered if she dug in her heels whether it would even do her any good. She now understood what it meant to be "swept up." If she did not consider herself to be a woman of wits, she would likely be swooning over the man with whom she now danced.

"See? There is no reason to fear," he teased as they moved, still clearly enjoying her unease. "Though you may find this more enjoyable if you stop attempting to fixate upon my cravat and look at me instead."

Maxine blinked, not having realized she had locked on to a point straight ahead of her as if that would somehow keep her from tensing up and fighting him without realizing it. "I'm sorry."

"Be not so. You are doing fine."

"No, *you* are doing fine. I am having very little to do with this!" She laughed as they twirled about.

His laugh joined hers, and he smiled broadly. "Such is the way of things. If only humanity could understand their rightful role in the world as you find yourself now."

"What do you mean?" That was an unexpected turn in the conversation, but she was eager to be distracted from her fear of ruining their dance with her ineptitude.

Heart of Dracula

"Willing surrender comes with its own joy, does it not? This Earth would be a better place if others could understand that."

She scoffed. "I reject that notion. Forgive me."

"Oft, to fight against such a thing would cause nothing but pointless harm. Take this waltz, for example. If you were to fight me now, we would topple over to the ground. And for what reason? The only way this is to be successful is if you allow me to lead. Even if you were a skilled dancer, it is the only way this moment can exist at all."

That much was true. She couldn't deny it. As much as it was entirely against her nature to allow someone else to take control, here he was, guiding her along the dance floor. But only because she allowed it. "Both must agree to the situation in which they find themselves, at all times. And besides which, a waltz is not life, as rue as we might find that to be."

"Are there no parallels to be found? Dancing is a window to the view of how men and women interact with each other. It is a glimpse of how two souls may seek the other. From approach to completion, it is a perfect gesture of the whole."

It had been a long time since she had found herself in a debate. "Well put." She conceded his point. "And as time has progressed and changed, and the social interactions between the genders have sifted, so has the dance itself. But I still insist that willful acquiescence to another is not the way of things, as you say."

He was smiling, even as they debated and danced. "Ah. Is it not? The child to a working father, the father to the foreman, the foreman to the owner, the owner to a Lord, and a Lord to a King. And that King then answers to God, does he not? The acceptance of the existence of hierarchy is all that gives authority its power. Surrender to a dance is all that gives it grace."

She let herself dwell on his statement and found she could not muster a rebuttal. She smiled up at him, enjoying a well-played game of cards, even if she had lost the pot. "Well said once more. I accept your point, as I cannot seem to find the means to argue against it." She chuckled again, realizing the irony in her situation. "Willing surrender. And in doing so, continue to prove your point."

"Stubborn adherence to a view, even once proven faulty, is the deepest plague of man. There is no sin in laying down one's sword when one is defeated." He smiled, but it was a gentle one and not prideful. He was not boasting, and for that she gave him a great deal of credit.

"I will point out," she added, "that many men and women feel trapped in their ordeal, not by their own acceptance of hierarchy, but because they are outmatched by those who do. Even when the ruler is by no means worthy of his position, the sense of singularity keeps an individual from action. Coups and riots only work by the benefit of numbers. Willful surrender to hierarchy leads to more tyrants and madmen upon thrones than benevolent ones. While I will concede that it is the way of the world, I do not agree that it is benign."

"The system of the world is not without its flaws," he agreed. "Tyrants and madmen are often the only ones willing to do that which is required to maintain power. But they all fall in their turn. Power is a spider's silk threat. Devious and intimidating, perhaps, but fragile and easily destroyed."

"Unless you are a fly."

"Indeed." He grinned, one that seemed to belie mischief.

Heart of Dracula

It glinted in his dark eyes. "I would argue that only ignorance leads one to believe they are only ever merely prey."

"And in that, I could not agree more." She found herself enjoying her debate with the man, even as much as the waltz. Sadly, it seemed both were over as the music played down to a stop. They ceased their movement and offered applause to the musicians for their work.

Maxine was surprised to find that she felt disappointed at its end. Her time with the gentleman was over. He would likely now take his fill with women who were far less discriminating than she. Less contentious, for certain.

He took a step back and bowed, and she returned the gesture with a curtsy. She had to glance at the other women in order to copy the action. Her need for assistance did not escape his notice, and his eyes glinted again in amusement with a playful devilishness. For an Englishman who looked all the world like he should be a doctor or a lawyer, he had a strange darkness to him. It was the later that brought warmth to her cheeks, and she cursed herself silently for blushing.

As they walked from the dance floor, she was surprised he did not immediately take his leave of her. As a waiter passed them with a tray, he fetched two glasses of red wine from atop it and handed her one. "If I may be so bold," he said with a twinge to his lips.

Maxine glanced across the room, catching sight of Bella. She was still with her blond suitor. It seemed they were entirely caught up in each other. They would amuse one another for some time. And still, not a sign of a vampire was to be had.

Eddie and Alfonzo were waiting outside, likely for no reason at all. She was beginning to suspect the vampires would never come. That this was all a silly ploy. She should stay by the window, but she found the thought of Eddie watching her awkward conversation with a man too embarrassing to allow.

And she did wish to speak with him more, she decided. It would be brief. He would find her unsettling like all the others and leave her be in search of more appealing company. *Bella is having a grand time. I deserve a little of the same, don't I?*

Maxine finally smiled at him faintly in return. "If you are to torture yourself to more of my unflattering blather, let us do this somewhere a little farther away from the ballroom floor." She took a sip of her wine, nearly saying the words into her glass with a narrow glance at the people who were fawning over each other and laughing.

It was so very loud in this room in more ways than one.

"What am I, if not a masochist?" He gestured his arm toward the large double door that led to the foyer. They walked from the floor until they found a spot against a railing that overlooked the entryway. There were small clumps of people here and there, doing the same as they— looking for a quieter place to socialize away from the hustle and bustle of the ballroom.

You're here for work, not pleasure, she reminded herself as she leaned on the railing, looking down at the people below them, laughing and enjoying themselves. *There will be vampires here tonight. Don't fool yourself into thinking otherwise. And they are ones who want you captive or dead.*

But she had reason to be distracted. Her company was enthralling, she had to admit. There was something in his warm eyes that made her want to stand closer to him. He drew her in. It was not like her to feel such a way about anyone, let alone a stranger.

"There is a darkness that comes over you when you look

Heart of Dracula

at others," came the warm voice next to her. "What is the source of that, I wonder?"

Because I can feel in them all the pain they have suffered or caused others. Because I do not belong among them. She shook away the wave of emotions that crashed over her, pouring in from all those that surrounded her. There were too many to separate. They became like rain in a storm—a collection of solitary drops that blurred into one. She pushed it all away.

"We have known each other for the space of one dance, we have not even exchanged names, and you can see that much of me?" She looked down into her glass of wine and at the reflection. She wasn't angry at him. Some part of her was pleased that he was as observant as he was handsome. "I'm impressed."

"Many would see that darkness and mistake it for an inhospitable demeanor—"

"And many do," she confirmed.

He chuckled. "But I see it as something else."

She turned to look up at him. The way he said it made her both leery of him and charmed at the same time. There was a darkness in him as well; she saw it plain as day. It was part of his very being, his very nature, hidden behind the welcoming exterior. Something terrible must have befallen him at some point in his life and left him changed. It was stamped into the fabric of his very soul. Perhaps it was that quality that drew her in. She had never been afraid of the dark. "What do you see, I dare ask?"

"Unhappiness. The belief you see something that you will never have." He sipped his wine, casting his gaze down to the group of people beneath them. A hardness stole over his features for the first time. Hardness, and something like contempt. "You are enticingly beautiful, young, and breathtakingly intelligent. There is no reason I can see to think you would be so cast out from their world. Yet here you stand."

"You say 'their' world. You exclude yourself as well."

He smiled at her. He seemed to enjoy their repartee, and it gave her hope that this might not be a fleeting amusement for him. "I do. Allow me to introduce myself." He took her gloved hand and bowed to place a kiss against the back of her knuckles. "I am Jonathan Harker. A pleasure to meet you."

8

"It is a pleasure to meet you, Mr. Harker. I'm Miss Maxine Parker." She chuckled. "We rhyme."

"That we do. It must be fate." He smiled and looked back down to the crowd. "It is clear you dislike being around crowds. Although, for my sake, I'm glad you acted against your instincts and are here tonight. Without such, I would have been deprived of your candor, intelligent words, and your stunning beauty." He released her hand which was still in his after he had kissed her knuckles.

She hadn't realized she had neglected to pull it out of his grasp until then. It made her flush again, and she answered her shyness with a sip of wine. It made him chuckle.

She faced the railing to try to hide her cheeks that were still too warm. "I hate to guess, but I take it you are from England?" She tried to desperately speed up the discussion to avoid her making a further fool of herself.

"Yes, I do figure the accent does give it away."

"Well, allow me to welcome you to our dismal city. I fear you have come at an odd time. Things...have become strange of late." She glanced out the window in the foyer to the moon that hung in the sky outside. It was red, as it had been every night in the past month. It painted the world around it in shades of crimson. It was unsettling before she knew why it had become that way. Now she knew who was to blame.

"I have noticed. What an odd phenomenon, the moon turning red and never changing shape. Does it frighten you?"

"I admit so, yes. I think only a fool could look up at that and not find it somewhat alarming." *Not to mention the disappearances and the death.* No need to make herself less appealing. She wouldn't need to try before long.

"Then you are wise." He let out a thoughtful hum. "It shall pass. I have heard rumors of events such as this occurring before. They have lasted for a few months at a time at most, then it ends."

"I do hope it passes quickly."

"I think it shall." He moved closer, and she felt the warmth of him beside her. More proof that he was not a vampire.

The flirtatious movement almost made her weak. It was so rare for her she had no defenses against it. It took her a moment to speak before she was certain it wouldn't leave her a few octaves too high. "What brings you to the city, Mr. Harker?"

"Please, call me Jonathan. And the same that brings me to this party, I am afraid. There is someone here I would like to meet, and I decided, rather unfortunately, that this was the best opportunity to do so. I think they are a bit skittish, and there is safety in a crowd. I would have far preferred a restaurant or my parlor. But, *c'est la vie*, their needs demand, and here I am."

"How exhausting." She sipped her wine. "I fear I find

Heart of Dracula

myself in a similar state. I have come to acquiesce to someone's oddly eager attempts to meet me."

"And the feeling is not mutual?"

"No. I do not think this person brings me anything but ill will."

"Well, then, I hope we both have come to find another reason to call this evening a success, even if our primary motivations are not nearly so pleasant." His hand ghosted by her cheek, and she jolted. She pulled her head back out of his reach quickly. He withdrew his hand. "Forgive me. I did not mean to startle you."

"It's all right. I simply—" She broke off at what she saw.

There was passion in his eyes.

It was unmistakable. While she was hardly an expert, there was nothing else it could possibly be. It burned in him like a pyre. He leaned closer to her, and she was certain he meant to kiss her.

She stepped away quickly. "Jonathan—forgive me, but—"

"I thought as much." He sighed. "You are spoken for."

"No, I..." She swallowed. "It's not that." *It's worse. If you touched me, I would kill you. At best, I would ruin you as I crashed through your mind and left you only a drooling madman.*

"The jewel at your throat rather boldly states a man's claim upon you." He pointed at the ruby brooch in her choker. "I had hoped it was a *memento mori* and that was the reason for the morose veneer I see in your eyes."

"I am not—you misunderstand." She touched the jewel at her throat. She had begun to become inured to the constant feeling that poured from it, the more time she spent near it. "I do not belong to anyone."

"That you wear the brooch of a man at your neck tells a very different story." Jonathan did not seem angry. He did not even seem disappointed. There was a strange and dangerous heat in his words and in his brown eyes. "It tells a very different story indeed." He took a slow step toward her, and he ghosted his fingers over her cheek again. He didn't touch her. Something in his gaze kept her pinned there, unable to move. She felt trapped in a spider's web.

"I—"

"Introducing Lord Walter Northway." The door attendant interrupted her words.

It was then that Jonathan's expression shifted to irritation and anger. Maxine took a step back, as if a spell had been shattered, and she turned to look at the figure who walked into the room.

If ever a person were to scream that they were a vampire, it was the man who walked into Arthur Price's house. He was immensely tall and thin. He had short hair the color of fire and moved with a fluidity that belied an unnatural nature. He looked for all the world like a corpse, and he viewed the room with an emptiness that echoed the coldness of the grave. His skin was as pale as ash.

She felt his presence in the room in the way one might know sickness had come to a home. He was a plague. She shivered and drew back from the railing reflexively. The first vampire had arrived. While it was not Dracula who had come for her, she did not discount that the man was likely any less dangerous. "And so, it begins."

"Pardon me?" Jonathan asked from beside her.

"There is going to be trouble here tonight, Jonathan." She turned to look up at him and placed her gloved hand on his wrist. She squeezed it gently but insistently. "You need to leave. I don't want to see you harmed." She grieved their time was over. "This has been wonderful. It truly has. But my business here this evening is dangerous

Heart of Dracula

—very dangerous. Heed my warning and go, please, before you are caught in the middle of it. The last thing I want is..." She sighed and shook her head at her useless attempts to explain herself. "You have been very kind to me. Very few people have paid me the attention that you have this night. Genuine or ingenuine as it may be, I thank you."

About twenty expression fought across his face, each one vying for supremacy. It flickered between surprise, incredulousness, amusement, and several others she could not name. Where it landed was where she had not expected—a gentleness that could have been mistaken for affection. "Of course. I cannot argue with that." He took a step back and bowed. "I hope to meet you again, Miss Parker. I hope you escape your danger safely."

"Thank you." She smiled sadly. It never would have worked between them. She was not fit for a normal life. She was not fit for companionship. He seemed intrigued by her unabashed nature and did not seem to find her too eerie or unsettling to be near. She had appreciated that he had been happy and ready to debate with her, an action seen by most as unseemly for women. But he had no place in her world. What kind of relationship could they have, where they could never touch?

He turned to walk down the stairs toward the entrance. That was enough of an indication to her that he was heeding her warning and leaving the party. The vampire would ignore him, she was certain. Mr. Harker was simply another guest to them. Knowing he was safe, she walked back into the ballroom to find Bella.

She found her by the wall, swooning in the presence of the beautiful, amethyst-eyed gentleman. "I hate to interrupt."

Bella blinked, as though she was waking from a dream, and looked to her. "Hum?"

"They're here. One of them is, at any rate."

Bella sighed and looked more than a little disappointed. She looked up to the young man and smiled. "I am sorry, but I must go. You should leave. Things are about to get... uh...messy."

The gentleman didn't seem quite sure what to say to that. "Will I see you again?"

"I can only hope so." Bella reached for his hand and took it. "This has been wonderful, Mordecai."

"The feeling is mutual." He smiled and picked up her hand to place a kiss on the back of her knuckles—a slow one.

Maxine looked away for the sake of propriety and cleared her throat.

"Goodbye for now, then." The gentleman finally took his leave. Bella was smiling, and it was clear she was besotted with the man.

She was also watching the man's rear as he walked away from them.

"Bella, please focus."

"Oh. Yes. Sorry." She shook her head and turned to face her. "So, you say a vampire has—" She broke off and her eyes went wide. "Oh."

"Greetings, Miss Parker. Miss Corallo. I hope the evening finds you well."

Maxine turned about to look at who had interrupted them. The tall, red-haired vampire, who was looking down at her with matching crimson eyes, the same hue as those Dracula owned. Good glory, if there were ever a creature on the face of the planet that might wear a sign about his neck that read *"Hello, I am a vampire,"* it truly was him. He was

Heart of Dracula

uncanny by his very nature. The room quieted at his passing. It was as though the others could sense something was awry. She hadn't figured there were two men like Vlad Dracula, but here she was with proof.

She pulled the revolver from her purse and leveled it at his head, pulling back the hammer. The crowd nearby gasped and retreated quickly from them.

Good. She did not want anyone caught in the crossfire.

The vampire did not flinch.

"What has he sent you to do? This Vampire King of yours? Kill me?" She kept the defiance strong in her voice.

"Were it so simple." The man's expression was stoic and empty, but she felt an ounce of annoyance and regret in him all the same. "I am afraid not." He bowed his head in greeting. "I am Walter Northway. I am to take you to my Master. Please come with me quietly."

"I think not. And what of her?" She motioned her head at Bella without lowering her gun or taking her eyes off the vampire.

Walter shrugged dismissively. "She is to live or die as she sees fit. If she interferes, she will die. If she does not, she may live to see tomorrow."

Bella stepped up to stand at Maxine's side. "You will not take her."

"You are surrounded and outnumbered."

"How so? I see only one of you." Bella scoffed.

Walter's stoic expression twisted into a smile. But it was a sad one. "Look again."

It was as though a curtain was suddenly pulled away. Like her bedroom had been cast in the murky darkness of morning only to have the sunlight stream in. Although perhaps the analogy was backward. For it was not life that was added into the room, but life that was taken away.

The guests in the room.

Every single one of them.

They were all *monsters*. Pale faces and glinting eyes watched her from faces that were only a moment ago filled with the color of life. Or were now no longer human at all, but twisted creatures of every nightmare a man could have. Horned things, scaled things, furred things. Vampires and demons. A carnival of things both living, dead, and undead surrounded them.

Maxine took a step back in shock and bumped into someone. Whirling, she saw the Vicomte Arthur Price. But as she watched, the illusion fell away, and someone else took his place.

He was beautiful, sharp and wicked features accented by lupine yellow eyes that sparkled with a deep hunger for violence. He had dark blond hair that was swept back from his face but did not fully subdue its curly nature. He would look innocent, if not for the fiendishness emblazoned on him. He took a bow with a deep flourish. "I am sorry for the trickery, my beautiful darling. I am Zadok Lafitte, at your service. They call me The Illusionist. I fear now you see why. You cannot fight. You cannot escape."

Bella pressed up closer to her. She did not know the magnitude of the telekinetic's power, but she did not fathom that she could take on a room full of creatures like this. "Maxine..."

They were doomed. "I know."

"Oh, don't be so afraid...Come with us, *ma chere amie*, and you will find there is nothing to fear. Come with us, and the huntress walks free," Zadok crooned. He had a voice like velvet and quicksand—beguiling and dangerous. The promise of safety that would swallow her whole.

"I repeat—no. Go back to your Master and tell him that

Heart of Dracula

he shall have none of me. Tell him to leave me be." She pointed her gun at Zadok now. She knew she didn't stand a chance, but she was not going to go down without a fight.

"I fear Walter was right. Would that we could, my sweet dove," Zadok purred and stepped toward her. She pointed the gun at his head, and he lifted his hands in a show that he meant her no harm. His glittering yellow eyes caught her attention…and that was her mistake.

She felt it but could not fight it.

It snared her. Something wrapped around her mind like the coils of a snake. Terrible but warm, so very warm. Each time she struggled against what invaded her, it grew a little tighter. *Surrender,* his eyes said to her. *It will be bliss.* Her fear faltered, stuttered, and gave way. He murmured to her something in French that she didn't quite catch as the words were too quiet. But their meaning was clear. Promises and platitudes, soothing and alluring. *He isn't going to harm me. I am safe. This is how it should be.*

She lowered the gun.

"I told you she would not come willingly." Zadok stepped toward her, and she watched him, rapt, unable to look away. He reached out to touch her, and she was helpless to stop him.

"Zadok. Remember. You are not to touch her. She could destroy you."

Zadok growled in frustration and glared a hole into the taller vampire. Still, the spell did not break. "Why am I never allowed to have any fun? I—"

The sound of a shattering window and gunfire interrupted them. Zadok gurgled in pain, lurching as blood bloomed through the front of his white shirt.

Crimson poured down his chest as he collapsed to the floor. And with that finally went whatever reverie he had placed her in. She shook her head, feeling dizzy. With a frustrated snarl, she raised her gun to Walter and fired.

He vanished as the bullet was about to hit him.

The door was kicked open by a heavy boot, sending it crashing into the wall. Alfonzo marched in, in a long white coat emblazoned with a gold cross on the front. He carried a sword. An honest-to-God broadsword. The monsters turned to face him.

More gunfire, and another broken window.

The room descended into chaos.

"Stay safe!" Bella pulled a knife from her purse and ripped a slit down the side of her dress, yanking the tulle underskirt off. Maxine knew her gown would be ruined, and she hadn't cared. They had planned for this. Hidden in the skirt had been a dozen blades. They flew up from the fabric and began to dash through the room at the woman's command, tearing open throats and punching through ribcages. Monsters screamed as they died. "Stay safe, Maxine. Run and find somewhere to hide!"

She did not need to hear the instruction twice. Maxine went to run but found a hand had snatched her ankle. She looked down at the French vampire who had grabbed her.

Zadok was gurgling, coughing up blood that pooled around him. But he was not dead. In fact, the wound on his neck seemed to be…closing itself. She raised her gun and pointed it at his head, intending to put a few bullets through his brain to see if that could kill a vampire.

She wasn't quite sure if it could, but she was eager to find out.

Zadok vanished in an explosion of rats. Maxine jumped back, startled as the sea of scrambling animals screeched and fled out the door to the foyer.

Now she had one task ahead of her. One goal. Escape.

Heart of Dracula

If only she could be so lucky.

WALTER SIGHED as he heard the mayhem from inside the building. The hunters were formidable. He had sent a pack of ghouls to distract the gunman on the roof, but they all now lay as dust on the street. "Master?"

"Keep the hunters at bay. No one is to touch Miss Parker. She is mine. They may threaten and draw close, but none are to lay a claw on her."

"Yes, my Lord."

"Good. Now…if you'll excuse me."

And with that, Walter summoned his rapier to his side and entered the fray.

HER PROGRESS out of the building was harrowing but eventually successful. She had emptied her revolver in the directions of monsters and had ducked into a nook to reload. Her fingers shook as she put the bullets into the chambers of the cylinder and clicked it back into place. The door was a dozen or so feet away. The monsters seemed intent on killing Bella and Alfonzo. They hardly glanced at her.

They know I'm not a threat.

"Do not run, Miss Parker." Walter, the tall vampire, stood in the foyer with a long silver rapier in his hand. "It will only make matters worse for you."

She aimed and fired at him, and he vanished into fog before the bullets could land. Like Hell she was going to listen to him! She made it outside and, without stopping to look around her, ran up the sidewalk as fast as she could in her heels. She turned and fled, leaving the chaos of the fight behind her.

She had made it one city block before the fog came.

Fog the likes of which she had never seen before. It was thick, impenetrable, and she could barely see the crimson moon overhead through its opacity. It rolled in like a cloud, pouring around the buildings like liquid.

She couldn't debate its sudden arrival for long. A snarl came from the darkness. She held her gun high, pointing it into the murky shadows. Two eyes glinted back at her, thin, animalistic slits. Something crawled from the shadows. Something that was not vampire...and was not human. Something that seemed lesser than both. She took a staggering step backward at what she saw.

This must be a ghoul.

It appeared to have once been human *and* vampire but had befallen some great misfortune. It was gaunt and gangly, the flesh around its bones sunken and rotted away. All its teeth were far too long and pointed as if filed or worn to dangerous tips.

It snarled at her. She watched as blood, thick and black, drooled from its maw.

She screamed. She turned and ran into the fog, not caring what direction she headed. Simply away—away from the thing that looked as though it would eat her flesh from her bones. Walter had warned her that running would only exacerbate the situation. He had not been lying.

She tore through the fog in a wild panic, turning this way and that, barely able to see a few feet in front of her face. She heard the thing in the darkness...and heard that it was not alone. The ghoul had come with friends, and they were chasing her.

It was then that she rammed fully into someone who

appeared too quickly from the fog for her to stop herself. In her panic, she staggered back and raised her gun. But it was neither a ghoul nor a vampire that stood before her. It was a handsome man in a long peacoat, watching her in surprise and amusement.

She furrowed her brow. "Jonathan?"

9

It was not Walter or a ghoul as Maxine had feared. Instead, it was the oddly charming gentleman she had shared a dance and a drink with barely an hour ago. The poor Englishman who had found himself caught in the middle of mayhem. He was cast dramatically in the flickering light of the amber glow of the gas lamp overhead.

He raised his hands in surrender, and she realized she still held her gun pointed at his chest. She lowered it and shook her head apologetically. "I'm sorry. I don't know how you found me in the fog, but you should go."

"I decided I could not leave you there to defend yourself alone in good conscience." Jonathan glanced down to her gun. "Although it seems you have the situation handled."

"Not really. Not I, at least. I will be all right, though. Mostly..." Who was she honestly trying to convince? The gun was useless against monsters like them. But it made her feel better regardless—any shelter in a storm.

"Mostly?"

She let out a breath. "I know this is a lot to absorb, Mr. Harker, but there are creatures in this world that aren't

Heart of Dracula

human. They prey on mankind. I fear one of them has their sights set on me. He sent his friends—his minions—after me."

"Do you know why?"

"No. I know what I have done to inspire him, but I do not know what he wants from me."

He cast her an incredulous look with one eyebrow raised. But over which half—her ignorance over the vampire's mission or that there was a vampire at all—she did not know. "I do not care if you believe me." She laughed sadly. "I merely need you to leave before you're harmed."

A crash and several inhuman roars inspired her to whirl, pointing her gun off into the darkness. The boom of gunfire and the screams of monsters were close, far closer than the distance she had run. Either the fight was moving after her, or between the fog and her fear she had gone in circles. It was a fifty-fifty chance at the rate her evening was progressing.

She kept her gun pointed aloft into the darkness. The screams in the shadows were not the sound of any beast or man she had ever known. Ghouls, perhaps. Or worse. The things at the gala that she had witnessed were beyond her imagination.

Harker pulled in a breath of air in surprise. "You aren't lying, are you?"

She glanced over her shoulder and winced in regret. This was probably a great deal for him to witness. His brown eyes were wide as they scanned the shadows. She was sympathetic. This was all very new to her too. "I know, and I'm sorry. Attribute this to having too much to drink and go home. Go, before they see you with me and attack you."

Another roar and a crash, and she turned her focus back on the battle that was coming closer, not at the man behind her. A figure lurched from the darkness, and its glinting, terrible red eyes gave it away. Another ghoul was coming for her.

It leapt through the air, and she opened fire. She put a few bullets into its chest and head before it landed in a heap some five feet away from her. It hissed and tried to claw at her, its fangs distended, its lips drawn grotesquely away from its rows of sharp teeth.

She waited for it to get to its feet. She waited for it to lurch upright and continue its goal of tearing her apart. She jumped back in surprise as it suddenly and abruptly burst into flame, howling as it was reduced to dust.

Strange. I did not do that. I suppose I shouldn't look a gifthorse in the mouth.

"Do you know what is after you?" Jonathan asked from behind her. His hand took her empty one. Glad for her gloves, she squeezed it gently and felt him hold hers tighter in return. She gave the man credit for not being a blathering, weeping idiot by now. Most people would have been reduced to an incoherent child at the sight of what he had witnessed.

"A vampire." She kept her back to the poor man caught out of his element as she was still desperately scanning the darkness for any figures in the fog. "There are several of them. I will…do my best to make sure they will not hurt you. They are after me. If it comes to it, I will give myself up."

"You would sacrifice yourself for a man you do not know?" She barely caught the oddly sentimental tone in his voice, as if something had touched him very deeply. But she had no time to try to pry into his statement, as she was worried about the very real threat of the vampires in the darkness.

"They are not going to give up. They will hunt me no

Heart of Dracula

matter where I run. I see this now. You have been very kind to me this evening, Jonathan Harker. I will not have your blood on my hands. It seems they knew I might come prepared."

"There is no need to be concerned. Mr. Harker has been dead for several years now." The hand that held hers shifted as he moved closer to her back. His voice was next to her ear, and she could feel his words pool against her skin. It sent a chill down her spine—his breath was *cold*. Something shifted in the sensation of him at her back, like a curtain was drawn away from his soul. She felt the energy of him turn *dark*.

She whirled to face him, yanking her hand from his. He allowed it. She took a step back and pointed the gun now squarely not at Jonathan Harker...

But at Vlad Tepes Dracula. The man had melted away like the illusion of a dream and left the terror that she had seen in her vision, a nightmare made real. He towered over her. Long black tendrils hung loose around a pale face. Crimson eyes glinted in the torchlight, flickering like embers in the darkness. His skin was the color of white ash. All sense of life around him had fled.

Of course.

I am a terrible fool.

She had let herself believe anyone had been spending time with her of their own volition. No...he had merely been masquerading as a man. Hiding himself by means she didn't understand. "Magic?"

"Of course." His voice had changed back with the illusion. It had become the deep, velvety rumble she remembered from their shared vision. "A simple illusion. I chose Mr. Harker for I believed you might find his demeanor..."

His eyes flicked to her gun and then back to her. "Disarming."

He was a terrifying sight. Seeing him in the waking world, he was all the more overwhelming. His eyes had taken on a wicked gleam as they watched her, promising terrible things.

She shivered as she took a step away from him. This man dripped power. It filled the air around him and forced her breath to come short and shallow. It was as though invisible, dark wings snapped wide around her. She needn't touch him to sense it. "I am impressed you managed to keep yourself hidden from me. You played me. And you did it well."

"I am flattered."

"The question remains, though, why?"

He bowed elegantly with one hand folded out in front of him, the other at his back. "I was greatly enjoying my time. Were you not?" His tone was coy as he straightened, an amused smile on his pale lips. She could see the barest glint of too-sharp teeth that hid behind them.

"I don't generally enjoy being toyed with."

He went to respond to her, but she didn't give him the chance. She opened fire. The bullets reached the space where he was—where he had been—and passed harmlessly through empty air.

"Now, now..." That voice that seemed to vibrate through her on some strange level came from behind her as he scolded her like a child. His hand grasped the gun in her hand. She turned to face him as he lifted it over her head, pointing it harmlessly into the air. She was nearly out of bullets, regardless. "There is no need for any of that. You know it will do you no good. The ghoul would have killed you, had I not ended his life first. I do hate to be disturbed."

Heart of Dracula

She cried out and had to let go of the gun as he crushed it in his hand like it was made of paper. He tossed it aside, and she heard it clatter to the ground. He reached for her, and she took a staggering step back. "Don't! You can't touch me, remember?"

"I would like to test that theory. Come here, my dear." He held his hand out to her. "If you are right, I die, and your problems are solved. If I am right...you will belong to me." A small, snide smile spread over him. "Either way, I win."

She furrowed her brow. What did he mean by that? She didn't have time to dwell on his statement. He reached for her again, and she turned and ran. Vlad laughed behind her. She knew it was pointless, but for now, she was free. There wouldn't be another opportunity like this one. She took off running in the direction of what she hoped was her home.

It had only been a few hundred feet before she heard wings beating in the night air.

A great deal of wings.

And they were headed in her direction.

She couldn't help but glance back. The sight of the swarm of huge black bats, swirling in a cloud above the fog, made her breath catch in her throat. Catching sight of the thousands of the animals, dark and innumerous overhead, showed that he hadn't lied. She realized in that moment that she had no idea who—or more correctly *what*—she was up against.

The bats dove toward her, and she turned to run again. She couldn't move fast enough. She screamed as the creatures overtook her, and her world changed from fog into a sea of black wings and claws that scratched at her.

Maxine struggled and fought—swung her arms against the things around her—but it was hopeless. Something else had taken over. There was only sensation of movement and the ground leaving her feet. She felt tumbled end-over-end as though she had been rolled down a hill.

When it ended, she fell to her knees and felt grass, damp in the dewy fog, under her. *Grass? Where am I? What happened?*

Her world was wheeling around her. She felt disoriented and dizzy. Still, she tried to push herself up, even as she tilted dangerously and threatened to crash back down.

A hand took her elbow and lifted her, planting her on her feet. Firm, but not harsh.

She knew who it was. She turned, looking up at Vlad as he towered over her. His lips formed a line that promised wicked and cruel things. His glinting crimson eyes shone with a deeply sinister amusement. She pushed away from him and took another step back. She glanced around herself for an escape, but she could barely see more than five feet in the dense fog.

"And where will you run? Even if you could escape me on foot, you know not where I have brought you." He was right. She had no idea where she was, and she had already tried to outrun him once already and had failed miserably.

"What do you want from me?" She tried to sound firm and angry. Honestly, she sounded frantic more than anything, even to her own ears.

"That, my dear, is both a very simple and very complex topic..." He lifted his hand to her. She looked at it, to him, then back to him incredulously. He insisted. "Give me your hand."

"You're mad if you think I'm going to—"

He cut her off as he stepped toward her. The simplest action from him choked the words in her throat. If she couldn't run, what *could* she do? Punch him? The idea was

Heart of Dracula

laughable. The hunters were likely too far away to aid her now. He must have known that when he had brought her here.

"Maxine..." His dusky growl brought her gaze up to meet his red eyes.

That was her mistake.

She should have learned. She tried to look away before it was too late, but if Zadok had been alluring, this man was inescapable. Something seemed to snare her in its grasp like talons, and the whole world dropped away. Nothing else mattered.

There was only him, and her, and this moment in time.

He stepped around her, circling her slowly. She stood there, hovering, feeling as though she was wrapped around his fingers or dangling from puppet strings.

"I am many things..." His voice was quiet and deep, a sensual rumbling sound in his chest that made her eyes slide half closed. "But mad, I am not. Not as of yet."

Her body didn't feel her own. She commanded it to whirl, to slap him, to punch at him, but none of those things manifested. Instead, she stood perfectly still as she felt him slide his hands along her shoulders, slipping along the fabric of her dress.

He ran a hand over her hair, pulling the pins from the curls that kept her hair in a bun, and let the tight spirals fall loose along her back. He let out a low hum and combed his fingers through the strands. He had sharp nails that felt like claws, and they dragged along her scalp like a comb. No amount of willing herself to turn around was working. He had come close to touching her, but he had not done it yet.

She couldn't even command herself to speak and could only make a soft whimpering sound at his nearness. She shivered and felt goosebumps spread. He repeated the gesture. Her eyes slid shut, lured by the feeling of those sharp points against her skin. It felt so good, even though she knew it shouldn't.

A dark chuckle reverberated in him as he leaned his head in close. Cold breath pooled against her. "What a rare thing you are. So strong, and yet so fragile. And to never have been touched at all? This will be quite delightful, my treasure. You do seem to enjoy the sensation *very* much."

He turned her to face him slowly, and he reached to the crimson choker at her throat. He pulled the brooch from the fabric and pinned it to his lapel. "I appreciate the commentary. I would hate you to think I overlooked it. You wore my color. You wore my jewelry. You paint yourself as my property, seeking to lure me into a trap. How did it go, I wonder? Has this worked to your satisfaction?" He reached behind her neck and untied the string that held the choker in place and tossed it aside. "You have lured me in, I will say that much." He leaned toward her neck, and she felt his breath there against her. She knew what he meant to do.

"Please—I—" she gasped and tensed, her panic pushing through his control of her. "No!" When she shoved against him, she felt the spell snap. By her struggling or his release of it, she did not know.

He banded an arm around her lower back and pulled her flush against him. She felt as though she were in the grasp of a force of nature. He might as well have been a volcano or an avalanche. Crimson eyes bored into hers, and all her will to fight was robbed from her once more. She railed against his hypnotic spell, but she could not break it. She felt her limbs go slack, surrendering to him. *No!*

"I feel you fighting me. There is much strength in you, little empath. I cannot wait to taste you."

Heart of Dracula

He hovered his hand over her cheek. She whimpered. "Please—don't—don't touch me, you can't."

"If I do and you rip out my soul, then so be it. You will be the victor where all others have failed. If I don't...oh, Maxine," he grinned. "Think of the fun we will have."

"Wait—"

"No." And with that, he laid his palm against her cheek.

She quietly cried out as she felt the strength in him pour over her. Not only the power in his firm hand, but inside his very being. She felt him crash over her like a wave. She struggled to maintain control, but she was slipping. She tried to hold back the tide, armed only with a teacup as she was.

She shivered as he cradled her cheek in his touch, stroking her skin with his thumb.

"My, my. What's this? A last bulwark?" He hummed. "Look at you, trying to stay in command of your gift. Do you seek to protect me?"

"No—"

"You are protecting yourself, then? Does this pose you any danger? I think not. I think you simply wish to avoid adding anyone to your list of victims. Tell me, how many people have you killed?"

"Stop, please," she begged. Strings like yarn were stretching thin in her fingers. She couldn't withstand him. She struggled to hold on. "Stop touching me. I can't...I can't control this for long."

"Then don't. Let go. You cannot harm me, little empath. I can feel you there, inside my mind. Mortals may not have the power to withstand you, but I am no mortal." He leaned toward her throat once more. His lips grazed her throat.

She pressed her palms against his chest, finding the sudden will to fight. He was going to bite her—to drink her

—perhaps to kill her. She couldn't let that happen. "Please, no!"

He laughed, a low, dark sound that vibrated through her. He lifted his head to look down at her. His hair brushed against her in its soft, dark tendrils. "Still, you struggle against me. I am impressed. You know you cannot win."

"I know, but…" It didn't stop her from trying. "Please." She could only beg him. There was nothing else she could do.

"You will feel my kiss this night, Maxine Parker." Crimson eyes were lidded as they watched her, the desire in them undisguised and burning as bright as the red moon in the sky. "But I will reward you for your bravery—for your conviction."

She was shivering in his grasp, trembling. She had no words.

His lips ghosted across her cheek. There was a sound from him then, something strange an inhuman—like an animalistic, bestial purr. Like a great predatory animal was before her, hungry for the kill. It was not a vague metaphor. It was the truth.

He hovered his lips by her ear. "I will have all of you in time, Miss Parker. You have sealed your fate with me this night. How I have delighted in you…how I know I will continue to do so. Do you fear my bite?"

"Yes." It came out as little more than a terrified whisper.

"Then I will take my kiss from you another way instead." He shifted to hover his lips over hers, a hair's breadth between them. For that brief second, it seemed as though all of time stopped. Her heart hitched in her chest. "Let go, Miss Parker."

Then the gap was closed.

He kissed her.

Heart of Dracula

His skin was cold to the touch. He had no body warmth of his own, but the heat behind his embrace drove all discomfort out of her mind. One of his hands slipped to the back of her neck and held her, cradling her head in his grasp. The arm around her waist pulled her tighter against his chest. Even from this, she could tell how unbeatably strong he was.

A growl left him as he kissed her. He took from her all that he wanted, and he wanted it all.

Despite herself, despite what she should feel, she moaned against his lips.

It was her first kiss.

Her first real kiss.

And it belonged to a vampire.

Her mind reeled for purchase against the onslaught of what he was levying against her. She should be screaming in panic. Instead, her hands were against his chest, clinging to the lapels of his black peacoat. She could not find the strength to push him away.

She had never felt anything like it before in her life. She would have fallen if he was not holding her so effortlessly in his arm.

But then, it changed. Reeling from his embrace, her grasp of the reins of her power ripped from her fingers. More than the kiss rampaged through her.

He tore into her mind like a wildfire.

Like a stampede of wild beasts, her empathic gift linked them together without warning. She felt him there inside her mind. Felt his desire and his need for violence. Their souls touched, and in that moment, she saw the crimson moon above. She felt the spread of enormous dark wings upon the cold wind, blotting out the stars above.

The feeling of freedom—of the joy in the hunt.

But more than all the rest, she felt *hunger*.

She saw a mountain range. She saw miles and miles of trees that stretched up to stars that she did not recognize. She saw sand, burning in the blistering sun. The taste of blood in her mouth, bitter and poisoned. She saw death. Bodies in the mud, soldiers left to rot where they fell.

She felt the loneliness, the crushing emptiness that surrounded his heart that now felt like hers. She felt as that loneliness turned into ice. She felt the pain recede, and a cold like the grave took its place.

The years...

There were so many years.

She felt the loss—the grief. Tears streaked down her cheeks as a pain unlike any other seared through her like an iron brand and marked her soul for the rest of eternity.

Abandoned by God.

And now a god on Earth himself.

When he broke off the embrace, she was breathless. She felt the dampness on her cheeks and knew her tears were real. He looked down at her, his eyes narrowed in irritation and curiosity in equal measures. "Prying child, I stand corrected. It seems I cannot protect my mind from you."

She couldn't speak. She couldn't fathom what she had seen. It was only flashes of imagery and emotion. It was too scattered—none of it made any sense. But what she could understand was the grief, the pain, and the emptiness. And the *years*. She reached up and placed her palm against his cheek. The pain had been his.

It still was. She felt him as though what burned in his heart were her own feelings.

Something crossed over his features again. Something akin to surprise flared before it dulled into a softness edged in need. "Careful opening doors. You may not like what you

Heart of Dracula

find." She pulled her hand away from him. He winced briefly, as if he did not intend to scare her touch away.

His moment of vulnerability was tucked behind a stern, hard exterior as quickly as it had come, and he straightened his shoulders.

"You are a curious thing, Miss Parker." He cradled her cheek in his hand. His touch was cold, even in the dewy fog. She shivered. He placed his thumb against the hollow of her chin below her lip, and she felt the press of his sharp nail against her tender skin.

Then came an order she could not deny.

"Sleep."

10

Death.

And the feeling of cold skin against hers.

"If you are right, and I die, then your problems are solved. If I am right...you will belong to me. Either way, I win."

Death. It echoed in his words. In his touch. In his kiss.

Her dreams were filled with it. Blood mixing with the mud of a sprawling battlefield. Flashes of imagery filled her mind. Wading through the thick muck. Bodies within it, some moaning in agony, some lying still. Fingers and limbs jutting from the ichor like roots of a tree.

She felt something worse than apathy for those lying in the mud. This was delight. This was pleasure. This was *joy*. The feeling of the thrill of the kill. The love of bringing death, pain, and suffering.

Flashes of throats being slit. Of screams in the night. She saw a figure in full armor, driving a massive blade through the chests of enemy soldiers. Blood dripped from his sword and from his archaic leather armor. It was an ancient vision of times long ago. She had long since learned to keep herself as a separate observer in moments like these—and not

Heart of Dracula

trapped within the eyes of the person whose memory she was witnessing. It was far less traumatizing.

Especially in cases such as this.

She did not recognize the man in the armor at first. His helm was removed, and his hair was short, blond, and matted in blood. But when he turned to look at her, she saw his crimson eyes, and saw the soul inside.

Vlad.

He wore a different face, but there were some things that could not change.

A man in steel armor came for him, raising his sword, meaning to cleave Vlad in half. But he deflected the blow easily. He drove his hand—his very hand, sharp nails and all—through the throat of the man who stood before him. He tore out the man's flesh and watched as he crumpled into the mud, a bloody heap. A dying carcass. Nothing more than *meat*.

"Hello, little empath. We meet again so soon."

She gasped as she felt him there inside her mind. Their souls had touched when he kissed her. He had broken down the barriers she had so carefully placed as though they were nothing but paper screens.

The figure had not talked, but she heard the vampire's voice all the same. She watched as he lifted his bloody hand to his face and snaked his tongue out to lick a line of crimson from the back of his fingers. She shuddered.

"Are you so eager to see me?"

His voice was taunting her, even as she couldn't find the strength to respond, watching the warlord as he smiled wide in sick pleasure, his teeth stained red.

"Do you even know it was you who called me here? I heard you whisper...and I answered."

"No, that's not true." She took a step back, nearly stumbling in the mud, and bumped into something behind her. The dream shattered and shifted, changing around her like oil in water. When her world reformed, she stood in a private study. A fireplace roared by one wall, filling the room with warmth and amber light. She could smell the burning wood. It was a comfortable, familiar smell, but it did nothing to quell her fear.

A hand splayed across her stomach, fingers spread wide, pulling her against what she had bumped into. Not what—whom. It was Vlad, and he felt as immovable as stone.

"What have you done to me?" she whispered.

"I left you asleep in your bed, beautiful child." Amusement was thick in his voice. She entertained him, and she was not quite sure she was glad for it. A sharp-nailed finger trailed through her hair, tracing over her scalp, tucking her hair behind her ear. It brought a shiver out of her even before she felt cold breath against her cheek. "And I lay in my coffin alone. I slept only to hear your call in my dreams. And so, I have come."

"I have not called to you."

"I thought we promised not to lie to each other. You disappoint me, Maxine."

"Then if I did call to you, I have not meant to do it." She shivered again. She felt so cold. The fire did nothing. It wasn't real, after all. His other arm wrapped around her, pulling a long swath of fabric with it. A thick black cape with crimson lining. It was as though he meant to warm her.

"Now that, I do believe." He let out a quiet and thoughtful hum. "Tell me something, my dear...have you come to realize why you seek me out? Why you touched the stone though you knew it to be dangerous, or why you answered my invitation to the gala? Why you whispered to me now? Why I know you will answer the invitation I have left upon your dresser?"

"No."

"For someone so aware of the emotions of others, you are ignorant of your own."

"That is true. I will not deny it."

"Why is that?"

"My emotions have never mattered, vampire." It was a personal confession, but they had made an accord, after all. And it felt impossible to lie to him in this place, even if she thought she could. "Therefore, I have never bothered with studying them."

"Oh, child..." He slowly ran his fingertips over her cheek. She pulled in a sharp breath through her nose and went rigid in his arms. It was all too much. "Such a lonely thing you are. That is why you whisper to me in your dreams. There is a void deep within your heart, an emptiness that longs to be filled. And it is the very same you feel in my own soul. You see a reflection of yourself in my shadow. That is why you are drawn to me."

She opened her mouth to deny it. She wanted to say he was wrong. She wanted to tell him he was mistaken or, at the very least, was misunderstanding her. But she found she could not. With a sense of defeat, she shut her mouth and said nothing at all. It was true. From the moment she held that gem, she felt something in him that drew her in. Her shoulders slumped. Damn him. *I am likely too late for that.*

"Not to mention...I believe I am the first soul to ever touch yours and not feel your wrath. Is that not so?" When his cheek pressed against hers, she felt her eyes slip shut. She found herself pressing into him, seeking more of that which she had never had.

Touch.

Simple contact.

He hummed in approval, turning her slowly in his arms until she was pressed against him, chest to chest, her fingers finding the lapel of his clothing. She gasped in surprise. He wore another version of himself, it seemed.

His face had barely changed, but his hair was a stark white that flowed around his shoulders in sharp contrast to the dark fabric. It gave him a much older air, and his clothing was far more antiquated and austere, as though he were an ancient King in some dusty castle.

Perhaps he was.

Perhaps he had been.

"Who are you?" She searched his crimson eyes for the answer and saw only the depths of his years looking back at her.

"I have been many names and many faces. Countless personae have come and gone. But you can see through that easily enough, can't you?" He lifted his fingers to her cheek again, brushing over her skin. "You can see through to something deeper."

Tears stung her eyes. She felt them slip loose.

He shushed her gently and, using the pad of his thumb, stroked them away. "Why do you cry?"

"I'm frightened."

"Of me?"

"Yes, of course. But..."

"But?"

"I am more frightened of your touch. Of this." She had promised not to lie to him. "That I seem to wish for it."

The look on his face softened to one that seemed filled with a strange kind of warmth and affection. As if she had once more melted something in him that had been frozen for a long time. "You have no need to be frightened of me. I

Heart of Dracula

mean you no harm." He leaned down and kissed her forehead. The sensation was so foreign to her.

"What do you want from me?" She had asked before, and she asked again.

"I have left you another invitation to meet me alone. This time upon your dresser. Answer it, and I shall answer you." He tilted her head up to him with the crook of a finger underneath her chin. "Now, my darling, I have told you to sleep, and you disobey me. You need to rest."

As his lips lowered her hers, she let her eyes slip shut. He kissed her, and the dream faded away.

———

Maxine awoke with a start, sitting straight up in her bed.

Her bed.

She put her head in her hands and tried to still the spinning. Her vision was reeling around her. Even with her disorientation, there was no mistaking where she was. She knew the smell of her room, the feel of the mattress beneath her. This was, without a doubt, her home.

Dracula had carried her into her house and placed her in her bed. That answered a few questions she had suspected she knew the answer to, but now had confirmed. Yes, he not only knew where she lived, but where she slept. And no, there was nothing stopping him from coming and going from her abode as he pleased.

"Damn it."

Maxine slipped her hand along her neck and didn't feel any puncture wounds. He hadn't fed from her. He had kissed her and commanded that she sleep. And she had dreamt of him—no, with him—and he had once more calmed her restlessness.

Why did he bring her home?

Why?

It wasn't that she was not glad for it. She expected to find herself in chains in a stone cell. But it made no sense. He had her. Why had he let her go?

Then she remembered his words in her dream. He said he had left her an invitation upon her nightstand. Looking over, she saw two objects that were out of place. A single red rose, and another piece of paper folded in half, identical from the outside to the one that had been slipped under her door.

She reached for the rose and the envelope and brought them into her lap. The rose was beautiful and in full bloom. She had the sudden and inexplicable urge to find a glass of water for it.

Maxine could not remember ever receiving a flower from a gentleman, let alone one like that. She twirled it in her fingers, being mindful of the thorns, and thought it over. The Vampire King was flirting with her, that much was painfully obvious from the number of times he had kissed her alone. But he was also hunting her.

It was quite likely that to someone like him they were the one and the same.

Regardless, she trusted him as far as she could throw a horse and carriage. Placing the rose down on her lap, she opened the envelope.

She had hoped for a letter explaining his intentions and his actions. She hoped for an apology for his violence and his impositions upon her. Instead, it was a simple card on the inside that read, *"Marliave, eight o' clock. –V."* Beneath it was penned another line in a simple postscript. *"Kindly leave the hunters at home."*

She couldn't help but laugh once at the postscript. She

Heart of Dracula

shook her head and folded the card back up and slipped it into her dresser drawer. She lay back down on the bed. She shut her eyes. She felt exhausted by everything that had transpired. And sore. There was a deep stiffness in her legs from running in shoes that were not designed for such things.

She cringed as one of the bones in her corset dug into her ribs. She was still in her full dress. The vampire hadn't stripped her. While this was uncomfortable, she was far less embarrassed than if he had undressed her, and she found herself debating which one would have been worse.

She climbed out of bed and went to change into her house dress. It was as she was brushing out her hair that she heard footsteps on her stairs. She went to go grab her pistol from her drawer before she remembered Vlad had crushed it. She picked up a hairpin, long and sharp, and brandished it like a knife.

Moving out onto the stairwell, she braced herself for what she might see. A vampire. A monster.

Three very tired, very bloody, very injured vampire hunters.

"Oh."

They all looked up at her, in various states of shock. Alfonzo was the first to recover. "Maxine?"

"It seems so."

"You escaped!" Bella smiled through the pain. Blood was streaked down the left side of her face. She had a series of cuts on her right arm, and there were trenches cut into the bodice of the gown she had worn. Luckily, it seemed the corset had served more than a fashionable purpose—it seemed to have spared her being gutted. "How did you get away?"

"I...didn't." She shook her head. "I don't know how I'm

going to explain, but I will try once you are all cleaned and mended. Come. It can wait until you've all been patched up."

"I don't like the sound of any of this." Alfonzo grunted. "But I won't argue."

Eddie looked down at his feet. "I think I'm bleeding on the rug."

———

"I DO NOT UNDERSTAND WHY, my Lord." Walter watched his Master where he stood before the window of the home he had rented for his time here in Boston. It was a stately thing, smaller than his manor in England, but it served his purposes well enough. "You had her. Why did you release her?"

Dracula clasped his hands behind his back. "She is intelligent enough to understand what has befallen her."

"And you think she will accept your invitation?"

"She will."

Walter did not miss the amusement in his Master's voice. It continued to bring him great dread. Walter cringed and shut his eyes. The fight with the hunters had not gone well. While both Zadok and Walter survived, many of their ilk had died. And the three humans still breathed. "The hunters survived, and you decide to toy with her. You could have her and save yourself complications, but instead you insist on these idle games. Why release her to her own home when you could have her in your grasp? You would repeat the London debacle all over again."

"This is not about taking my prey, Walter. This is about something far more important than that. She shall come to me."

Heart of Dracula

"What of the hunters?"

"She will not tell the hunters of our meeting tonight. She will come alone."

"You are so certain?"

His Master turned his head to glance at him over his shoulder, lips pulled into a cruel smile accented by a flash of sharp fangs. "Yes…I am."

———

MAXINE WAS happy to find that most of the blood on them was not theirs. She helped tend to their wounds, wrapping and cleaning what she could. She had no means of stitching them up, but she did her best.

"Thank you once again for your kindness, Miss Parker." Alfonzo's tone was gentle as he held a patch of gauze to a slash on his shoulder as she wrapped a bandage around his bare chest to hold it in place. He was a maze of scars that looked like they had been given to him by teeth, claws, and every manner of weapon a man could devise. The poor man. This was hardly the worst scrap he had been in, by the looks of things.

"It is my pleasure. I am sorry I could not be more use during the fight itself."

"Now, please, can you tell us what happened?"

She didn't really know where to begin. She did her best, recounting her false encounter with "Jonathan Harker" and their dance, through to Walter's appearance and the crowd being nothing but monsters.

Alfonzo sighed. "Harker is dead. Has been for some years now. He died in London. Along with my cousin and several of Dracula's victims."

"I'm sorry to hear that." Maxine sighed. "Sadly, I did not know that when he introduced himself to me."

"And there was no way you could have known. You are not to blame for this. Any of this."

Maxine smiled lightly. One detail still troubled her. "How is it that an entire crowd of monsters appeared to be human?"

"The French bastard. You met him. Zadok Lafitte. He's an illusionist. He can control the minds of people around him. We saw only what he wanted us to see."

"Then why not kill us while we were unawares?"

Alfonzo shrugged, winced as he remembered his wound, and pulled on a clean shirt carefully before leaning back on the sofa. "Vampires toy with their food. We're a game to them. Keep talking."

She told the rest of the story...leaving out the kiss once more. All she said was that he hypnotized her and touched her cheek.

"I thought you couldn't be touched?"

"I can't. I didn't think I could. Not without destroying or maiming the other person." She looked down at her gloved hand. "It seems it works differently for him or his kind. I saw into his mind...into his soul."

"What did you see there?"

"Death." She laughed dryly. "A great deal of death. And...he has changed his face and his name over the years."

"What?" Alfonzo furrowed his brow. "What do you mean?"

"I think he is far older than you know." She shook her head. "I'm not sure yet. I can't confirm it. It's only a theory."

All at once, the three hunters looked deflated, their shoulders slumping. The idea that they might not know the truth of who they were fighting settled on them like physical

Heart of Dracula

weights. It hurt her to see. "I have not learned anything of the war he wishes to wage upon the city. We did not have much time to talk."

"Why did he bring you home? Why go through all that mess only to…drop you off in your bed?"

Maxine took in a slow breath, held it, then let it out in a rush. She knew the answer; she hated having to say it out loud. "He wants me to realize the trap I am in is far larger than any chains he would sling on me or any cage he might keep me in. He brought me to sleep in my bed to show that I cannot run or hide from him. I am still his prisoner all the same. In his own right, I think it is a show of mercy to let me run about my jail with some sense of freedom."

The room was deathly silent.

Not enjoying the awkwardness, she continued. "Even if you were to try to sneak me from the city limits, I believe he would follow me. Our souls have touched. He…is in my dreams now. It is…it is already too late for me, should he wish it."

"I'm sorry." Alfonzo shut his eyes and leaned his head back against the wall, rubbing a hand over his stubble. He didn't argue her point. He knew it was true.

"What do we do?" Bella frowned. "We can't let this happen."

"Tonight, we hunt. Eddie, you'll stay with Miss Parker to protect her."

"No." Maxine shook her head. "I don't think he intends to hurt me. I would be dead, or bitten, or a ghoul, if that's what he wished. Putting Eddie with me is guaranteeing he be considered a complication that would need to be removed."

"She's got a point." Eddie seemed less than excited about

being in the vampire's direct path. "But, Maxine, what if he comes for you?"

She paused. Now came the difficult choice. To tell them about his invitation or not. If she did, they would follow her and likely die because of it. Dracula would not take kindly to interlopers in what she assumed was meant to be a private parlay. If she didn't tell them, she was lying to the first attempt at friends that she had experienced in many years.

Lying would save their lives.

But it would still be a lie.

While the three of them had barely survived a tussle with the vampire Walter and Zadok and their forces, she knew a fight with Dracula was a very different thing entirely. She had no doubt he could destroy them without trying, especially if he felt he had reason to.

"He might come for me. And if he does, so be it. He is toying with me as you said, Alfonzo. I amuse him because of my gift. He is enjoying tormenting me."

And so, she lied.

The two younger hunters looked to Alfonzo, their mentor and leader. "What do we do now, boss?" Eddie asked.

"We hunt once the sun goes down. We hope Maxine may continue to use the vampire's fascination with her to suss out more of what he is planning. It is better to have him distracted."

She nodded. She could do that much. The creature needed to be stopped, no matter the strange pull he had over her. No matter the fact that he could touch her.

He meant to destroy the city.

It was just as she had told him in her dream.

Her conflicted emotions mattered for nothing.

11

It was seven thirty in the evening when she stepped out her door, intending to walk to Marliave, the only true French restaurant in the city of Boston. It wasn't a long trek from her home in the Back Bay to its location on Boswell Street, after all.

Locking the door behind her, she turned to walk down her steps and pulled up short at the sight of a man standing at the bottom of the stairs. She recognized him—the tall vampire from the previous night. His red hair was swept back from his face. He stood perfectly still, far more so than a mortal person might be capable. It did nothing to help his eerie appearance with his crimson eyes.

A shining black carriage sat behind him at the street corner. Unsurprisingly, at its head were two large black horses. The driver had a top hat pulled low over his eyes and a dark scarf pulled up over the bottom half of his face. When he turned his head toward her, she gasped in surprise. The man had no eyes, only empty sockets where they should have been.

The identity of who had sent the carriage was certainly not in question, vampiric escort or no.

She brought her focus back to the creature standing at the base of her stoop. She forced the fear she felt back down. It threatened to take her whole stomach up her throat with it. He did not seem to mean her any harm. He was merely standing there watching her. Waiting. "Walter Northway, was it?"

He bowed his head. "Yes, Miss Parker."

"Has he sent you to fetch me, then?"

"Yes, Miss Parker." He repeated himself with such a lack of emotion that it was nearly comical. She wanted to laugh but held it back. It was likely not wise to laugh at a vampire. Walter stood aside and held his arm out to gesture to the carriage. It opened, pushed from the inside by someone she could not see in the shadows. "If you please."

"I had hoped to walk. I would enjoy the time to sort my thoughts."

He let out a breath. It was the only sign of annoyance she caught from him on the outside. But she could sense from him more than he let on. Dread. Misgivings. He believed this whole endeavor to be steeped in foolishness. Something told her he resented more than simply having to take the carriage to retrieve her.

"You think this is a mistake."

He looked up at her, confusion and shock crossing his features. "I...said nothing to that effect."

"You needn't speak the words around me." She watched him curiously. He was old. It was hard to say precisely how many years he had existed in this world. He predated the style of clothing he wore. "Your Master did not warn you, did he?"

Heart of Dracula

His jaw ticked. "No." And it was clear he begrudged Dracula the fact. "I am not warned by him overmuch."

"I was told you were gutted by Alfonzo Van Helsing. It seems you lot heal quickly."

"That we do." He paused. "Will you ride with us, Miss Parker? If not, I fear I will have to accompany you regardless."

She considered her options. Walking to the restaurant with a vampire at her side seemed to defeat the purpose of her desire to make the trek by foot. She could hardly convince him to leave her be. She was not intending to declare war against him or his species this night. It would end poorly for her. It would be no more effectual than a toddler railing against the injustice of their curfew.

There was no sense in denying him. She nodded. He made no motion to express his relief, but she felt it palpably enough that she chuckled. He was an emotive thing buried underneath his stoic exterior.

"What is so terribly funny?"

"You resent being your Master's errand boy. You want nothing more than to have this business with me concluded." She watched him with a wry smile. His look of shock had returned. "In that, we are agreed."

"I see the rumors of your psychic ability were not fraudulent as I had assumed."

"No. I cannot read your thoughts. I am an empath. I can read your emotions. The rest is for me to intuit." She crossed the sidewalk to the carriage and glanced into the open door. Another man sat inside. Zadok, looking quite pleased with himself. She cringed.

"He has emotions?" Zadok huffed a laugh. "What phenomenal news!" He scooted across the bench and patted the seat next to him. "Come, my beautiful thing. Join me."

"Two elder vampires for a single mortal girl? Isn't that a bit of an overreaction?"

"Dracula informed us you were our most important priority this night. Especially since there are three hunters lurking in the shadows." Zadok rubbed his hand against his neck. Bella had told her that she had slit his throat during the brawl. "I think it is a valid concern."

"I am alone." She stepped up into the carriage with Walter's assistance and sat on the seat across from the blond, yellow-eyed, smiling vampire. He was a vicious and sadistic thing. It did not take her gift to tell her that. His expression did the deed well enough.

"Mmhm." It was clear the grinning vampire did not believe her. He stood from his seat and moved to sit beside her. There was no avoiding him.

Walter climbed inside, shut the door, and rapped on the wall closest to the driver with his knuckles. The crack of a whip sounded from outside, and with the lurch of wheels, they were off.

"You did not speak to the hunters of your appointment with our Master?" Walter watched her warily from the bench across from her. It was clear he did not believe her.

"I did not."

"Why?" Zadok purred. "Did you want to come, then? Do you desire to be our Lord's new plaything?"

"No." She glared at the blond vampire and shifted farther away from him in her seat. "Under no circumstances do I want anything of the sort."

Walter tilted his head slightly as though trying to solve her like a puzzle. "Then why? It is foolish to come at all, let alone without telling the others."

"If I speak to the hunters of his invitation, they would follow me, even if I requested that they not. If Dracula

Heart of Dracula

sensed them nearby, he would kill them for their intrusion. Am I wrong?"

"No," Walter confirmed.

"And he is far more formidable a foe than both of you, even combined, am I correct?"

"Yes." The redhead conversed in simple absolutes, it seemed. He was not a conversationalist. She preferred it over the leering creature sitting at her side.

That left one last question. "If I refused to come at all, what were your instructions?"

"To go inside and drag you to his lair," Zadok provided, his voice sultry as the thought of it clearly brought him great pleasure. "Kicking and screaming."

"I suspected as much. You see why I have come peacefully. And you see why I have not told the hunters. I only wish to avoid violence. For me, for the hunters, for the city as a whole."

"It is a hopeless endeavor. But I commend you for your efforts," Walter replied, and she was once more surprised at how old he felt to her. Far older than even the Vampire King himself. All she could feel from him was a tired weariness over the whole ordeal, where his elder was still driven by passion. "It takes a wise soul to understand they will fall to something they cannot hope to defeat."

She looked out the window to the street as it rolled past them. His words were true. She was facing a power that could command monsters and turn the moon an eternal, full, and unflinching red.

What am I against a creature such as him?

"Tell me something, vampires." She let her fingers trace along the fringe of the curtain that decorated the wall. "Why do you serve him?"

"Our reasons differ." Zadok chuckled, shifting lower in

his seat. He draped an arm over the back of the upholstered surface, inching his touch closer to her shoulder. She leaned away from him. "Myself? I enjoy it and the benefits his cruelty afford me. Walter does it from a childish sense of loyalty, as Dracula is his sire." Zadok paused, as if waiting for her to ask what the word meant. She was well enough versed in the breeding of horses to catch his meaning. Vlad had made Walter directly.

She nodded once in understanding.

The blond-haired, yellow-eyed Frenchmen smiled broadly in response. "Tell me. Is it true that I cannot touch you? Usually, our lord threatens me with violence if I play with his toys. But with you, he said there were far more dire consequences than the usual dismemberment I suffer."

"He is being quite literal. If you don't wish me to tear out your soul from your carcass and sending it skittering into the void, no, you can't touch me." She looked to him pointedly. "On second thought, go on and try."

Walter chuckled.

Zadok recoiled from her. "What kind of monster are you?"

She smiled at his look of horror. "I could not rightly say."

"Why has our Master taken a toy he cannot touch?" Zadok asked Walter. "That's madness, even for him."

"It seems *he* can touch me."

Silence. She shouldn't have said that. Both vampires were watching her in curiosity and confusion, reflected in yellow and red tones. She looked away from them and sighed. "His soul is immovable. Even from me, he is immortal. It is for the best. If I tore out his soul and left him an empty shell, I dislike thinking of what kind of wandering spirit might come to inhabit something with that manner of power."

Heart of Dracula

"An unsettling thought indeed," Walter muttered.

"He can touch you. And you have never known the embrace of a man or a woman?" Zadok cackled. "I see why you climbed so willingly into this carriage, my beautiful thing. You'll climb as eagerly into his bed before long."

She shot Zadok a withering glare.

The vampire only howled in laughter. "Oh, what a look! No wonder he is infatuated with you. How I wish I could have you for myself. I would teach you a man's touch in all its glory."

She looked to Walter. "How angry would Dracula be if I ripped his soul out of his body?"

"No. You will do no such thing—" Zadok protested.

Maxine and Walter ignored him. The redheaded vampire thought it over. "I think not very."

"May I, then?"

"I would ask that you not." He smiled thinly at her. "As tempting as it may be."

"I resent that, old friend." Zadok folded his arms across his chest and propped his feet up on the bench across from them, crossing them at the ankles. "You would miss me."

"You would be disappointed to learn how very little I would do anything of the sort."

She fought a smile and lost. She turned her gaze back out to the window. "What is it that he wants from me?"

"Well—" Zadok began.

"That is not our place to say," Walter interrupted him sternly. It was clear that Zadok was to keep his mouth shut on the subject. "You may discuss it with your Lord."

"He is your Lord, not mine," she protested.

"Oh?" Walter watched her, devoid of emotion, and she realized how fruitless a sentiment it was that she clung to. She had come here for lack of any other choices. If Vlad wished her in a cage, she would be in one. If he wished her dead, she would be so.

Who was he now, if not her King?

Willful surrender. His words to her during their dance rang in her mind. It disgusted her that she could not see him for what he was in hindsight. But he had hidden from her flawlessly. She had trusted her gift to warn her of an intruder, and it had failed her.

Zadok trailed a hand over her shoulder, ghosting over the fabric. It seemed even though he had decided not to touch her skin, he was still intent on playing with her. She flinched and pulled away, but there was nowhere for her to go in the small carriage. He shifted closer to her, his leg touching hers. "Do not be afraid, my beautiful. He does not intend to hurt you."

She glared at him and pushed his hand away from her. Or rather, she tried. He returned it to her shoulder a moment later, undiscouraged. "What did you do to the man you pretended to be last night?"

Zadok laughed and ended it with a grin, a reminder of the sharp fangs that he owned. They were not long enough to cause the wound she saw without leaving the mark of other teeth—they must retract like a cat's claws. "Arthur... lovely boy. He was quite willing in whatever harm I paid him, I assure you."

"Please stop touching me."

"You do not scare me."

"I should."

"I do love a little danger. As do you, I think. Or else why would you be here? I will tell you this. Our kiss brings pleasure the likes of which you have never known. Tell me, Miss Parker...since you cannot touch anyone, are you quite skilled in pleasuring yourself, then?"

Heart of Dracula

"Enough, Zadok," Walter hissed from across the carriage. "I needn't remind you how displeased our Master would be with this indiscretion of yours."

The blond vampire sighed heavily and slid away from her obediently. "Yes, yes...Why must you ruin my fun, Walter?"

"Someone must."

Zadok grumbled.

And with that, the carriage came to a halt. She recognized Boswell Street. The wooden sign for Marliave swung in the breeze from its hooks. Walter pushed open the door, stepped out, and offered her his hand. She was glad to be away from Zadok, and she eagerly followed the red-haired vampire.

Walter bowed to her, climbed back into the carriage, and shut the door without a word of goodbye. With the crack of a whip, they left her there. Technically, the church bells had not yet struck the hour and she was early. But she knew he was waiting for her regardless. With a shuddering breath, she tried to steel herself against what was about to happen.

It was time.

12

The sound of laughter, glasses quietly tinkling, and of silverware meeting porcelain greeted her as she stepped through the door. Along with the smell of food, the warmth of the room complimented the elegantly decorated interior. Boston had only the one real French restaurant, although many different establishments drew inspiration from their cuisine.

Despite the murders and the disappearances in the city, the restaurant was crowded. It was filled with people, and the feeling of their emotions washed over her. The comfort that came with company. The enjoyment of not being alone.

But they felt like stars circling a black void. One she could sense waiting upon the edges of the room like a cloud. He was here. She did not doubt it. He was like the rushing river underneath a bridge.

The dining room was on the smaller side. It felt, for lack of a better word...intimate. Different from the bustling grandeur of the Parker House, and far more refined than the Oyster House or the Green Dragon. It felt distinctly European.

Heart of Dracula

It should have been a rare treat to come here. Instead, it filled her with nothing but nervous anticipation and dread. She wondered if she would live to see the morning. Hell, she wondered if she would live to see nine o'clock.

"Mademoiselle," greeted the *maître d'*, a very polished looking gentleman standing behind a small counter by the door. He was as French as the décor and as well-kept. "Welcome, welcome! I believe I know who you have come to meet." He gestured with a white gloved hand as he began to walk into the restaurant. "The *monsieur* has been expecting you."

"I'm certain he has," she muttered.

"Pardon?"

"Nothing, never mind." She waved him off. The man, seemingly perturbed at anything that missed a beat in his expected routine, turned back to leading her through the restaurant.

A table by a window was their destination. The sight of the tall figure standing there with his hands clasped behind his back sent her heart beating into a faster tempo after skipping a few in its eagerness to double its efforts. She pulled up her steps and froze like a deer spotting a hunter.

"Is something the matter, *mademoiselle*?"

"Very much so." She did not take her eyes off the man—the creature—who had yet to turn to face them. She had been in his presence before, but it always seemed so brief and hurried. This was going to be a much more drawn-out affair. "There is nothing you can do about it. Thank you. You may go."

Heeding her dismissal, the head waiter bowed and, without another word, left her to her plight.

The figure at the window stayed stoic and unmoving. If she hadn't known better, she would have figured him for a ghost. He looked so very detached. He was a silhouette cut against the lights of the street and the crimson clouds beyond. He looked out at the passing people, carts, and horses that crossed in front of him.

She wondered how much of his existence he had spent watching the living. Last night, when he had kissed her—the thought made her cheeks grow warm—she had felt so many years stretch out behind him. So much time lived within his soul that she found she could not fathom it.

"A city so young and full of life...it is charmingly naïve in its hope for a new nation. It will mire in death soon enough."

Maxine was not certain whether it was his voice or his words that cut her to the quick and made her hair stand on end. They came from him in a bass rumble, and with them came such unwavering darkness.

"More quickly now that you have come." She was honestly surprised she found her voice at all. "Each morning I read that more have been taken. You are to blame for these disappearances?"

"Of course." He finally turned to look at her, his crimson eyes glinting in the candlelight of the establishment. "You answered my invitation."

It was an obvious statement, and she knew what he meant by speaking it aloud. He wished it known that she understood why she was here. He wished to skip the pretense. She appreciated that much. "You made your point perfectly clear, Count Dracula. What manner of blade you hold against my throat I do not know, but its presence there is undeniable."

A wicked smirk twisted his lips. "Do not tempt me. Although I find knives are so...impersonal."

She could not keep the warmth from her cheeks, and

Heart of Dracula

she turned her gaze away from the creature in front of her. The room was filled with dining couples, business partners, and friends. Joining them now was a monster...and whatever she was. "Why did you choose this place?"

"I thought perhaps you would appreciate somewhere with the safety of a crowd. As I am unlikely commit any rash acts or do you harm where I may be discovered." He moved toward her. She locked up as he did. She had become comfortable with his distance, but now he seemed to wish to change it. "And I am eager to enjoy an authentic European meal. I do miss it. The cuisine here in America is...lacking."

She took a single faltering step away from him. By all the Gods, he was *tall*. He stepped closer to her, and she felt so very tiny in his presence. The power that filled the air around him washed over her like the fog had done the previous night. Without realizing it, she had clutched her hand to the center of her chest over her heart, which was now thudding painfully loud.

She wondered if he could hear it.

Judging by his smile, the answer was yes. "May I take your coat?"

She stammered an embarrassing sound before she managed to swallow it all down. This was a negotiation—a parlay. She needed to remain calm. She nodded. Her resolve lasted a brief second. She jolted and went stiff as he circled behind her like some great shark and placed his hands on her shoulders.

He lowered his head to her ear. His cold breath on her skin made her shiver. "You were brave to come here."

"As I said, I have little choice..."

He slipped her coat from her shoulders. She stepped forward, eager to put some distance between them. She turned to watch as he hooked the dark gray fabric on the wall. Crimson eyes caught her gaze. "There is always a choice."

When he moved toward her again, she took a step back too quickly and bumped into the edge of the table. A knife and fork clattered to the ground loudly.

Not a single person turned to look.

She watched the room, curious and afraid in equal measures. There was something wrong here. *Very* wrong. With a rising sense of dread, she looked back to the vampire before her. "This place is no safer than any other, is it?"

"What do you mean?"

"If I were to hurl that glass against the wall, not a single person would hear it shatter, would they?"

Vlad smiled, pleased. He crouched to pick up the fallen silverware and placed it back on the table. "Sit, Miss Parker. Let us talk." He pulled her chair out for her.

"No. Not until you explain to me what you have done here." She narrowed her eyes at him, trying to sound firm. "I will not knowingly walk into a lie. Did we not make a promise, after all?"

"That we have. Forgive me." He raised his hand and, on cue, all conversation ceased. Maxine looked out at the room. The true horror of her situation was now laid out before her. She thought perhaps he was merely hiding their presence and keeping them unseen and unheard.

No. It was far worse than that.

Everyone in the room—absolutely everyone—had simply stopped. Stopped everything. They were standing or sitting, whichever they had last been in the process of doing and were staring blankly ahead like so many dolls in a window display.

Maxine's heart thumped in her ears almost painfully as

Heart of Dracula

fear flooded through her system. He had everyone in the room under his control and dangling from his fingers like puppets. Each and every one of them was in his thrall.

When he spoke, it startled her. "I had hoped to spare you this."

She would have withdrawn farther, but she was already up against the edge of the table. She had nowhere to go. Not just here within the restaurant, but in a far more global sense. "Spare me what? The truth of my inescapable circumstance?"

"Yes."

She shook her head and struggled to find her footing in the sinking sandpit in which she had found herself. She swallowed down her fear. She refused to let herself devolve into panic. Raising her chin, she met him head-on. "No. Pay me any unkindness that you wish, Count Dracula, but do not mask your cruelty behind a guise of kindness." She swallowed and forced herself to take a deep breath. She knew she was to die someday. If it came now, like this, it made no difference to what waited for her at the end. "I have seen and felt a thousand deaths as if they were my own. I have felt far more than my life's share of tragedies. Do not think me so naïve or fragile. I assure you I am neither."

Dracula bowed his head to her. "Forgive me. I am accustomed to dealing with those of a far less...pragmatic demeanor than what you possess. And, may I remind you, my dear..." His crimson eyes caught hers again, making her heart stick in her throat. "To you, I am only Vlad."

He snapped his fingers.

And with that, the room sprang back to life as if someone had released the gears on a wind-up toy, letting it resume its actions without any knowledge of its pause in time. Maxine let out a breath.

"Please." He gestured to her chair. "I ask you to entertain my invitation to dine with me, a ruse though it may be. It was not my intention to scare you. Quite the opposite, in fact."

"Are you certain you wish to dine *with* me and not *on* me?" It was meant as an insult.

He certainly did not take it that way. Instead, he took the barest step toward her. "Patience…" The sound was barely more than a low rumble in his chest. It seemed to resonate inside her, and she shivered. "Now, sit. Please."

Overwhelming. There was that word again, the one that sprang to mind in his presence. What would she prefer, to fight with him? To be shackled and chained? Kidnapped by his cohorts and thrown at his feet?

Was dinner not preferable?

She nodded weakly, not truly having any other recourse. Turning, she sat in the chair. He pushed it in for her as she did. He took his seat at the corner, choosing not to sit across from her but close. It was intimate. It put her nerves even more on edge than they should have been. With a simple beckon of his finger, a waiter came forward and poured them both a glass of wine.

Red.

Naturally.

"Before we go too far, I must ask you something." She picked up her glass of wine and sipped it. She was glad for its presence. It would make this all that much more tolerable.

"Of course." He was holding his wineglass in such a way that he could watch the light of the candle on the table reflect off the surfaces. His thumb ran along one of the ridges in the cut crystal stem, and she found herself entranced by the motion. He was graceful and dexterous for

Heart of Dracula

someone his size. She had to snap herself out of it and turn her focus away from him and out the window to the people crossing by instead.

After gathering her wits again, she looked back to him before speaking. "Tell me—how did you manage to keep a straight face while I not once, but twice, attempted to save you from your own creations?"

Whatever question he was expecting, it had not been that. Perhaps he expected something banal or predictably related to her current situation. His moment of surprise turned into mirth, and he laughed. A real, authentic sound. One that seemed as though he had not done such a thing in a very long time. After his laughter faded, he watched her with a tender look in his eyes. "I found it immensely endearing. I do not think anyone has come to my rescue in many thousands of years. You must forgive me, for it was a rare fantasy that I could not stomach to shatter in the moment."

"And I don't believe anyone has ever described me as endearing in—" She stopped talking as her mind pulled to a full stop. "Pardon me. Did you say *thousands* of years?"

He nodded. "You sensed this when you went rummaging about in my mind uninvited."

"To be perfectly clear, you were the one responsible for that, not I. I warned you of what I was capable and what would happen when you touched me. You did not listen."

"Touché."

"Regardless." She was not certain where she found the gall to argue with the King of Vampires. She found it far more enjoyable than her terror. She would hold on to her indignity as much as she could. "I was not certain what it was that I saw. Merely flashes of places. A sense of time stretching on to the horizon. I had no knowledge of numbers." She watched him, fascinated and horrified in the same moment. He was older than the church. Older than any civilization, living or otherwise. "You are the first of your kind," she guessed.

"Yes."

Neither of them said anything for a long moment. He seemed content to let her grapple with the magnitude of her situation in silence. She was the vague prisoner of the King of Vampires...and a creature older than she could possibly fathom. She reached for her wine and downed the glass in one go. She coughed. "I believe I will need more."

He laughed again and gestured for the waiter to refill her glass. When the young man was gone again, she sat back in her chair. Tears pricked her eyes unexpectedly, and she fought hard to swallow them down.

This is hopeless.

She squeaked, startled, as he touched her face. His emotions rushed over her as he did. Regret. Hope. Amusement. Pleasure. Hunger. Sadness at her fear. His soul brushed against hers, but she felt it go no farther. A touch, but nothing more.

He had reached across the corner of the table and placed the crook of his finger underneath her chin, lifting it to look at him. His red eyes were boring into hers, staring deep through her, and for a moment she was afraid he might put her under a spell once more. "Do not despair." His thumb trailed along her cheek. The touch was tepid, but it bothered her surprisingly little. The pad of his thumb was that of someone who had worked with their hands. He was a warrior, after all. "You are strong, Miss Parker." He sat back again, removing his hand from her face, and watched her with a strange and eager expression. "That is such a unique sensation."

Heart of Dracula

She shivered and sat back. "I wish you wouldn't do that so candidly. It is unnerving. Each time you do, I..."

"You what?"

"It will sound like nonsense."

"Try me." It came out as a low and hungry growl.

She swallowed. There was no point in hiding. "I feel the night sky itself. I feel...time. So much of it. It stretches on like the sky, and in it are a hundred million stars, a facet of every life you have ever known. I see a forest, I see a desert, and I see countless fields of bodies. I see an ocean of existence. It is...disconcerting." She stared down into her wine. "I warned you, it is nonsense."

"It is anything but."

She looked up at him, and he had a strange expression on his face. It was as though he had been stabbed in the chest. She furrowed her brow. "Vlad? Are you well?"

The expression fled, and he was his aristocratic, arrogant self once more. It was a shield, she realized, armor that he wore, reflexive as a second skin. He watched her through lidded, crimson eyes. "I promised I would tell you a secret if you came here tonight, did I not? That I would speak to you of a truth I have not told anyone in all my years if you admitted you are drawn to me. Can you admit that you come here willingly, not simply for the fact that you believe you have no choice?"

They had made a promise not to lie to each other.

And his words were simple truth.

She nodded once, barely. To him, she could admit what she would not say to the hunters or to his vampires. And not simply for the reason that Zadok had insinuated, either. While she was overcome each time he touched her, it was not for that reason alone. The feeling of the night sky—of him—of crimson velvet and satin, of violence and passion...

it was alluring to her. It seemed to take her by her own soul and pull her in. "I am."

"Then I will tell you what it is I wish for. What I desire more than anything else in this world. It is the reason I undertake all that I do. All the death, all the wars, all the torment I might pay you and others."

She watched him, eager for his answer.

"Take off your gloves, Miss Parker."

"I..."

"Please. Humor me."

She swallowed again but did as he asked. She pulled the black silk from her hands and laid them on the table.

"Give me your hand." He reached his out for her, skin as pale as white ash. His pointed nails looked as dangerous as they always had. She hesitated, and he asked again. "Please."

Carefully, she laid her hand in his. She pulled in a breath at the sensation. At the feeling of him against her. Skin to skin. Soul to soul. He lifted her hand until he had his palm to hers, her fingers against his as if through a pane of glass. His fingers were long and powerful, and they dwarfed hers. He laced his fingers into hers.

Finally, he answered the riddle. "I wish to either live...or to die. I care not which."

There came that hunger once more. A hunger not only for blood, but for *life.* For love, for happiness, and for solace. He wished to *feel* alive. Across from it was balanced with a hunger for the grave. For true peace. For rest that he had been denied.

"I am neither alive nor dead." His voice was quiet. "When I said I had hoped my life might end when I touched you, I was not lying. To die is the greatest gift given a man, and it has been denied to me. I am spurned by the living and rejected by the dead. I am alone."

Heart of Dracula

"You have others like you. Walter and the others."

"No. They are merely children of my poison. A perversion of both my curse and their former lives. They can die, Maxine. They can be destroyed. I cannot. Not even by you."

"I...I'm sorry."

"You pity me?"

"It isn't pity. It is sympathy."

"I am a murderer and a monster. Dozens in this city have died by my command. Thousands of your neighbors will be in the ground before my work is done. I have killed millions in my centuries. I will kill millions more. It is simply who I am. Do you feel such sympathy now?"

"I am aware of what you are, vampire."

"Are you really?"

"The lives you have spent are the rain in a storm. Simply because I have not stopped to count the drops does not mean I do not comprehend the weather."

"Such a poet you are." He pulled her hand toward him, and she watched in fascination as he kissed her fingers slowly, one by one. "My precious Maxine. You have not yet asked me to spare your city."

"Would you do it if I had?"

His lips twisted into a smile against her thumb. "No."

"Then do not scold me for not wasting my breath."

He chuckled and turned her hand to place a kiss against the sensitive spot in the center of her palm. She pulled in a hiss of breath through her nose. She shivered, and goosebumps crawled up her arm. He smiled at her reaction. "Do you want me, Miss Parker?"

"That is not an appropriate question."

"Yet I have asked it all the same. And we have an accord." He kissed her wrist, over her pulse, his lips lingering there for a long time. She watched him, her eyes wide, her pulse racing, knowing he must be able to feel it. He parted his lips, and for a moment, she was terrified that he meant to sink his fangs into her skin. Instead, he rolled his tongue along her vein slowly.

Her face exploded in heat. She must be beet red. She yanked her hand away from him, unable to take it anymore. She buried her bare hands in her lap. "Enough."

He chuckled darkly. "Very well. But only because the meal has just begun."

"No, I mean you are to stop—" She paused as another young gentleman arrived with food. The first course. She sighed. "I mean that you should stop such advances altogether."

"Why?"

"Is it not enough that I have asked you?"

"You are afraid of what I make you feel, Miss Parker. It is cowardice that inspires your words, not revulsion."

"I am not a coward."

"Correct. You are not. And it is for that reason I refuse your request. It is a temporary fear. Like jumping from a cliff into a pond. It will pass once you realize you will survive the fall." The vampire laughed and sipped his wine. "Eat, Miss Parker. Please."

It was an arrangement of cheese and cured meats. It all looked quite tempting. They fell into another long stretch of silence as they ate. Finally, she worked up the nerve to ask a question she had spoken twice before and been denied both times. "I fear I must now ask you the question to which I know I will loathe to hear the answer."

"Please do. If it is what I believe, I find myself quite eager to finally reveal it."

The way he said it made her shiver. She knew that this was some manner of line that she was about to cross. Something was about to begin with her next words, and it was something that she could not avoid. After stepping past this boundary, all things would change.

She felt herself teeter on the end of a cliff. But the words must be said. She must take the jump. She swallowed down her fear and tried to meet her fate as best she could. *I do not fear death. I will not let him change that. I will not give him that power.* "What is it you want from me?"

"Oh, my darling Maxine." He purred the words out in a dusky rumble. She felt goosebumps spread over her skin. "From you, I will have all that you are."

13

SHE FELT the warmth drain from her face at his words. She knew she must be staring at him in horror. His expression was juxtaposed perfectly to hers. Where she was frightened, he looked pleased. Where she felt small, he looked regal. He watched her with all the aristocracy of a hungry tiger—perfectly aware he was at the top of his food chain and eager to act upon it.

She folded her hands in her lap, clenching the fabric napkin between her fingers. "I am afraid I do not know what you mean."

"Oh, but it is clear from those beautiful features of yours that you do." He smiled and tilted his head barely to the side, a stray tendril of dark hair falling across his pale cheek. "But if you wish for me to provide specifics...very well."

He lifted his wine glass and pondered it. "What I wish from you is quite simple, Miss Parker. I will have not only your fealty, but your undying loyalty. I will have your blood. I will take your body, your heart, your mind, and your soul. I will have all that I desire of you...and I desire it all."

She shifted back in her chair and found herself sorely

Heart of Dracula

tempted to run from the restaurant. But where would she go? Where in the city could she hide? He was a demigod as old as civilization itself. He would follow her now wherever she might run. "And do you plan to take all this from me?"

"If I must." He grinned slyly at her. "But I admit I prefer to be given that which I want."

"And why would I be inspired to do anything of the sort?"

"For the very reasons you answered my invitation to dinner. You know it is pointless to fight me. Far more importantly…you do not wish to do so at all, do you? Give me your hand once more. Feel that which I can give you." He held his hand out to her again. "Touch me."

"No."

He watched her, patient as a parent watching a child who fights against the inevitability of their curfew.

She cringed. "I think I despise you."

"Yes, yes. You are not alone. Your hand, Miss Parker, if you will."

With a pained noise, she gave in. He laced their fingers once more. The sensation of his soul washed over her, and she shuddered, feeling it intertwine with hers all the same. It did something to her. It pooled a heat in her body that wanted to join them in more physical ways. It called to him, begged for him, pleaded for more.

He had asked if she wanted him.

The sad and revolting fact was that, for better or worse…she did.

"I want to take everything from you, yes. But I do not come to this negotiation as a tyrant. I come as a merchant willing to trade. I can give you the one thing you have never dreamed possible—a connection with another."

The image of claws in the darkness flashed through her

mind. She had to shut her eyes to let the visions play out. Teeth, sinking into her. Her blood upon the ground. Snapping bones, shredded tendons. Another carcass in the mud. More meat on the table. "I would only be your prey."

"No." New visions took over. Instead of blood upon the muck, it was satin sheets. It was teeth, but they scraped and toyed. They worshipped and teased. They bit...but she felt pleasure at their touch, not pain and terror. "I will not kill you. I will not hurt you."

"I am not special to you."

"You may think that, but you are wrong. You very much are." Dark wings spreading over the night sky, immense and ancient like a dragon. She found herself lost in the enormity of it all. "You can see me for what I really am, Miss Parker. In a way no one else ever has. You are my mirror. Your emptiness calls to my own. I am compelled to seek you, just as you are to me. You are already very special to me, Maxine...I do not think I shall ever let you go."

She opened her eyes, meeting his crimson gaze. "Everything slips from your fingers like sand."

He frowned. "Yes. You needn't remind me. All falls away from me in time. Even my immortal children like Walter and the rest succumb to madness or death in time. I am the only thing that is immortal in this world. I am the one soul cursed with true eternity." His grasp on her hand tightened, and he looked at her fingers twined with his. "What happens, Miss Parker, when you touch someone who is not I?"

She was glad to change the topic away from the enormity of his words. She pulled her fingers from his slowly. It was not in rejection. It was not because she did not want to maintain the link between them—in some strange way, she did. After a long moment, she formed the proper words.

"It is as though their soul is a soap bubble in my hand. I can protect it for a time. But it will falter. It will pop. I cannot control it. And when it happens, I take a piece of them into myself."

"What...?"

"Not only their memories or their emotions. I rob from them a piece of their soul." She rubbed her other hand over her heart, the reminder of an ache that had long passed but remained fresh. "It fades over time, but they are a deep wound that is hard to heal. It leaves a scar like it would in my flesh. I am still plagued by their dreams. For a time, it as though we were never different people."

"It sounds terrible."

"I worried it would drive me mad. Even the slightest touch, and I can absorb some of another's soul. It is for that reason I avoid it so."

"I feel different to you, then?"

"Yes. Your soul is unique. Instead of a soap bubble, I find myself holding a cannonball instead."

He chuckled. "I am a heavy lead weight, thank you, Miss Parker. Quite flattering."

"That is not what I meant!"

"Oh? I am a heavy lead weight whose only use is the destruction of life and property, then?" he teased, a mirthful and wicked smile on his lips.

"Yes, I do think that is far more accurate." She glared at him and sighed heavily. "You are bent on destroying this city, after all."

"I am."

"Why?"

"I must."

She watched him curiously. "Explain. What do you mean?"

"I am more than the curse of my soul, my dear. I am haunted by every life I have ever killed. You saw the beasts that attacked your friends last night at the gala? They dwell within me. I am to leave nothing but death and destruction in my wake. I can keep them at bay, but they hunger. They whine. They are incessant and loud. From time to time, I find myself inspired to feed them. And so, I take a city or two as my own, and let them do just that."

She sat back, watching him, stunned. "I am not sure I know quite what to say to that. You say you are not merely plagued, but you claim to be the illness itself."

He lifted his glass to her in a silent toast and sipped it again. "I tried to convince them to take up crochet or knitting, but I fear they did not listen to me."

She put her hand over her eyes and sighed.

"I thought that was quite clever."

"You are monstrous."

"And?"

She shot him a look and found him smiling, laughter in his eyes. She couldn't help it. She chuckled. He did the same. When they quieted, he was still smiling. "I do not wish to frighten you. I do not wish to harm you. I hope for the day you will run into my embrace, not away from it."

Her face went warm again, and she looked down at the table. "Why? I know what you now want from me, but why do you *wish* these things from me? To what end? What would I become to you?"

He opened his mouth to answer then paused. It took another second for him to speak. "I will respectfully decline my answer for the time being."

"Loyalty brokered by terror is a fragile thing. It shatters on the first display of weakness from he who holds the end of the leash."

Heart of Dracula

His smile broadened at her words. Something glinted in his crimson eyes. "How lucky for me that I have never shown such a thing as weakness, then. And I do own quite a number of leashes if you do care to try one on."

"I will also respectfully decline." She shut her eyes and rubbed the back of her neck. It was tense, and the knot there was threatening to give her a headache. He was not helping the tightness.

"Remove your hair pins."

"What?" She looked to him and furrowed her brow. "Why?"

"I prefer your hair down." He paused. "Please."

Maxine swallowed thickly and did not move. She glanced to the rest of the people in the restaurant but remembered they cared nothing for what she said or did. If she stood atop the table and screamed for help, they would carry on blissfully aware.

"You hesitate. Why? You have already touched my hand twice so far at my request."

"Yes, for my own curiosity's sake. This is different." She kept her gaze averted from him. "I am of the distinct impression, Count Dracula, that you are not the kind to give up an inch once it has been given."

"You will call me Vlad." He chuckled darkly, pleased, and reached out to touch her cheek and turn her face back to him. She jolted at the contact. She was not accustomed to it, and it was jarring each time. "I returned you to your bed unharmed. I had you in my grasp. I had your lips against mine. I could have taken you, yet I did not. Why do I then let you roam free now? Why do I sit to converse with you? I could have you on your knees." He grazed the tips of his sharp nails over her skin, and she shuddered in response. She knew she was blushing by the warmth that washed over her. "And such a beautiful sight that will be, my Lady of Souls."

Her blush deepened, and she pulled away from him. "I do not know the reason behind your actions."

"Because as you said, fealty by terror is a fragile leash. I do not want to break your knees—I want you to bend them. I want you to kneel of your own accord."

"And why would I be inspired to do anything of the sort?"

"Because you wish it."

She pulled out of his grasp. "No. I do not."

"Are you so certain?"

"I am." She paused. "We could trade. My life for the life of this city."

He seemed intrigued by that. He watched her curiously, ponderously, then shook his head. "No. You would hold it against me all the same. You would bemoan my cruelty in time, claiming the only reason you succumbed to me was under duress. No, my darling. You are drawn to me, Maxine. In time, I will have you."

"My blood and my body, very well. I admit those might be inevitable. I have never known a man, and you have a distinct advantage in your unique ability to touch me. But—"

"Is that the only reason you desire me? Oh, Maxine, again you lie to me." He *tsked*, smiling wickedly at her.

She continued as if he hadn't interrupted her. "But do you think you can win my heart? My soul? Do you think honestly believe you can if I choose not to give them?"

"You will offer them to me in time."

"I am not so certain. You threaten the lives of everyone in this city. Thousands of lives. I have felt what it is to die, Vlad. I do not think you understand how deeply I wish to prevent

Heart of Dracula

this fate for others, especially if I can help it. I want to know you, Vlad Tepes Dracula. I wish to understand you. But I cannot do so while you plan to murder thousands."

"I seek to feed my wolves. Do you bemoan for the fish you have eaten? Do you weep for their families? You are short-sighted. You think mortal lives to be valued higher than the rest. Humanity is a plague upon this Earth, and culling a few thousand is a paltry thing. You will continue to spread, to eat, to destroy, until this world has shrunk and there is not enough for any of you. I am doing you all a service."

"Horrifyingly enough, I think you believe what you say."

"I do."

"And what happens when you are done feeding your wolves, and the livestock in the city are all dead? When you have made a metropolis of ruins, what then?"

"I will leave."

"And will you leave me here in the tomb you have made? An empty corpse? Tell me what you would have me be to you in this world of bones and ash you would wreak upon this city. Speak to me of why you desire all this from me, and perhaps I will listen."

"No. Not yet."

"Then agree to my trade. My life, for this city."

"You are convincing, Miss Parker. A truly skilled negotiator. I am tempted to take you up on your offer, and I am not a warlord who is easily dissuaded. But you do not wish for what you ask."

"I believe I very much do."

"Very well. I will trade this city for you."

She smiled.

Her victory was only momentary. He grinned. "Strip yourself naked and kneel at my feet."

"What?"

At her look of horror, his grin faded to a cruel and austere smile. "You have your wish, do you not? You can spare this city. You offered yourself up to me. Do you not want to make the trade any longer?"

He was right. The feeling of being commanded to do something to save lives was mortifying. She had been foolish to think it would be anything else. "I…"

"You find yourself disgusted already by the prospect of obeying my commands. Did I not say as much?"

"You did."

"If you truly pledged yourself as my slave in return for this city, I could demand you kneel between my legs and pleasure me. I could have you bend over this table, and I could take you right here in front of all these witless fools. And to spare your city, you would be forced to do so. This is what I wish to avoid. It is this look on your face that you wear right now that I do not wish to see. Loyalty built on fear is fragile, but loyalty built on trade is a lie. To that end, I will ask you one last time. Do you wish to make such a bargain? Can you do it without it being built upon a falsehood?"

She shut her eyes and felt her hopes fade. She had failed. "No."

"Good. It is a child's bargain that you wished to make, nothing more."

"Do not insult me."

"I am not. Believe me, I am not. Kings, Emperors, and Pharaohs have offered me all the same. You are far wiser than they. You admit your mistake so readily. Fealty cannot be bought. What I want from you can only be given, not taken."

"I will not stop trying to find a way to spare my city."

Heart of Dracula

"And I will not ask you to. You have taken the hunters who seek to end my life in under your roof, and I have not once asked you to spurn them, now, have I?"

She paused. No, and she hadn't even realized it until he pointed it out.

"I do not fault you for your nature. I ask that you do not fault me for mine. Now...please, remove your hairpins. I find this modern hairstyle disappointing when it comes to you."

She reached up to her hair and pulled the pins that kept her long, wavy hair in its loose bun on the back of her neck. She let it all tumble loose. Placing her pins on the table next to her plate, she resumed eating, despite her stomach being tied in a knot. "There. As you requested."

"Now you are upset with me for that I beat you in this game of chess."

"Yes. And I suppose it is *childish* for me to feel that way. I suppose I shouldn't be surprised I have been outplayed by you."

He sighed. "No. This is not how this evening is to go. I will not have you despondent and hopeless."

"How am I supposed to be, faced with what I now know? That you will have all of me, to what ends you will not say. That my city is doomed, no matter my fate? How am I supposed to feel?"

"I can be a gracious and giving creature, Maxine Parker, should I find the inspiration."

"And do I inspire you?"

"Oh...very much."

His insinuation sent her face rushing in heat. Something shifted in the room again, and she looked up to find him gone. Missing. His chair had not been pulled away. The mystery did not last for long as a hand settled on her shoulder.

Gasping, her hand flew to one of her hair pins. She brandished it like a weapon.

He laughed quietly, a sound that was both sinister and dangerously alluring. He leaned down over her, and she felt his lips graze against her ear. His hand slid into her hair, combing through it, before gathering the strands in his fingers and holding it in his grasp. "You would think to stab me?"

"I have little other recourse."

"Draw my blood, and I will have to spend yours in return." He let out a low hum, and a sound like an animalistic purr joined it briefly. His lips ghosted over her cheek, and he tilted her head, baring her throat to him. "Go on, then. Please defend yourself."

"Don't—"

"I wish to taste you, my beautiful little empath. I wish to feel you on my tongue. I find the wine a poor alternative." His other hand ran slowly down her arm before it reached her wrist and took the pin from her hand. She was shaking too much to fight him. She did not resist as he placed the adorned metal stick back on the tablecloth.

When he kissed her throat, she gasped. She writhed in his grasp, and she could not deny that his touch set her on fire. It sent a heat coiling deep inside her that threatened to consume her. And there was nothing she could do to resist it. He was inevitable. He was a force of nature. He wanted her, and she suddenly realized she did not wish to tell him no.

She wanted him.

What he could do to her.

The feel of his soul sent hers begging for more. For a different kind of union.

But she was terrified of it all the same. "N...Not here, please."

"Ah, I see. You are shy. You do not want witnesses as you feel my kiss for the first time." He chuckled and placed his lips against the skin of her neck where it joined her shoulder. She jolted beneath him. "They will not remember a single moment of this."

She scrambled for excuses. She struggled to find any reason he should stop. "I—I—"

"Although I find I must agree. This place lacks a certain...mystique. Your first experience with my true kiss should be a memorable event." He straightened and released her hair. "I will grant your request. This will not happen here. But it *will* happen tonight, Miss Parker."

She was trembling as she watched him disappear from her view. Like a dark shadow slipping over the room, he reappeared in his chair as if nothing had happened.

It would happen tonight.

She knew there would be no convincing him otherwise. Her hand traced her throat at the spot where he had kissed her, as if she would find something. "Where will it happen instead?"

"Somewhere more suitable." The statement was so vague that she shot him a pointed glare. He laughed at her expression. "I find I prefer your ire to your fear. Fascinating. This is not a normal occasion for me. Tell me, Miss Parker. Do I frighten you?"

"Yes."

"Yet you find the conviction to argue with me. To debate the nature of loyalty. You vie to sell yourself to me in trade. You ask for concessions from me. You want me. I can see it in your eyes. But you also want to kill me to save your city. I find it a heady and intoxicating mix. You belong to me, and somehow I find myself uneager to ruin you."

"I do not belong to you."

"Another lie you speak unwittingly." His lips pulled back in an expression that was both a sneer and something animalistic, showing his pointed teeth. "You come to me not simply to avoid violence but because you desire to know me. You said it yourself."

Now it was her turn to be angry. "You do not own me."

"Ah, but I do."

She glared at him. "There is nothing you can say or do to convince me that I—"

Glass shattered beside her outward onto the street. The window in its frame exploding was the first thing she grasped had happened. The feeling of a thousand wings battering at her, at tiny claws scratching at her skin surrounded her. Vlad had exploded into a swarm of bats, filling the restaurant and surrounding her.

The feeling of movement, and she was swept away once more.

Maxine screamed. Rather, she tried. No sound came out. She realized she was not being carried by the bats—no, she was as they were. A thousand pieces of herself. He had changed her form even as he had changed his own. She was helpless but to feel tumbled about as though she were falling and flying in the same breath.

When the world rebuilt itself around her, she would have collapsed to the ground, save that she was already lying on something that felt like cold stone. Her head spun and reeled. She felt nauseated. Slowly, piece by piece, bit by bit, the world stopped its wheeling about.

She sat up slowly and looked around to try to discern where he had brought her. She groaned. Vlad had promised to bring her somewhere that suited her better. He had a wicked sense of humor.

She was in a graveyard. It was a snide statement on her fate, perhaps. Or his state of being. The graveyard was one of the older colonial ones in the center of the city. It was surrounded by the buildings on three sides, and trees lined the yard between her and the street. She knew no one would see her.

Or him.

A hand twisted in her hair and pulled her back down to the stone. Forceful, but not violent. She gasped as she looked up at the Vampire King. He towered over her, standing at her head, crimson eyes glinting in the dim light from the moon and the gas lamps at the street. He was barely discernable from the tree above him in the darkness. He leaned closer, emerging from the shadows like a nightmare.

"A shame you will have missed dessert." He grinned devilishly. "But I shan't."

She screamed and struggled, swatting at his hand, and tried to roll off the stone. She was lying on one of the stone tabletop tombs in the cemetery that marked the entrance to a larger underground vault. The grit of the weathered granite dug into her as she fought, but she could not care less.

And as quickly as her fight began, it ended. He released her hair, but suddenly—appearing there all at once—he was atop her. Supporting his weight with an elbow next to her head, his hand was on her cheek.

Her eyes met his, and she felt him slip into her mind like venom from a snake. He shushed her, soothed her, and silently promised her there was nothing to fear. His thumb traced a pattern slowly over her cheek before drifting to rest against the hollow of her chin beneath her parted lips.

The feeling of his soul against hers worked stronger than any hypnotism he could have ever used. He needn't use it to calm her any longer. Something else now held her in his thrall. Something far more poignant and longer lasting than his illusion now kept her in his clawed grasp.

His desire.

"Do not be afraid. You will enjoy this, I promise you." He lowered his head, ghosting his lips over hers. "Make no mistake, Maxine Parker. You may struggle against me. You may fight me. But you...*are mine.*"

And with that, he kissed her. He took her with the same passion, the same need, the same driving hunger she had felt the night before. But now, he seemed to know he would have what he wished for in the end. He took his time.

Her mind was free of his control. But she could not push him away. Part of her knew she couldn't budge him, and the other part didn't want him to stop.

His tongue flicked at her lips, and she willingly granted him entry. Her eyes slid shut as she felt him wash over her like an ocean wave. As he claimed her mouth, he slid deeper into her mind. The lines between them became blurred. All at once her lips were against his, and his were against hers.

She felt her fear. She felt her desire. She felt her fascination with him, how her back arched and pressed her up against his chest. She heard herself moan through his ears. Wanton and furtive, afraid and angry, unsure and bold.

"I want her, and I will have her. She will love me."

The thoughts were not hers. But they might as well have been.

Vlad?

He broke off the kiss, growling in his throat like a hungry

Heart of Dracula

beast. It allowed her the blessed chance to breathe. "I will learn to curtail that gift of yours in time." He smirked. "My little prying child. You may hear more than you wish you had."

His lips descended on hers again, uncaring for what would follow. He slipped closer to her, his body filling the space between her knees as she spread them for his presence. Clothing separated them, but he was over her, surrounding her, inside her mind, his tongue dancing with hers as he explored her.

Her hands were tangled in his coat and vest, and she moaned again. She writhed beneath him as she felt his desire mingle with hers. It was too much. She was too warm. She sought more of his touch a in the need to cool down.

He chuckled, and his hand drifted from her cheek down to her throat. Her heart was pounding beneath his touch.

"So many years of sorrow in such a young body. So much sadness. Such a rare jewel. So beautiful. So curious. Mine."

His thoughts were still hers. They turned toward her, addressing her. *"You hunger for this as much as I, don't you?"*

He broke away from her again and tilted her head to the side until her cheek rested against the cold stone beneath her. Her chest was heaving as she greedily filled her aching lungs with air. She wished she had not done up her corset so tightly.

When his tongue slid up her throat, she whimpered and writhed beneath him. Her hands were on his chest, but they were not pushing him away. They were clinging to him like a raft in the ocean. She was going to drown in him. She wondered if she would die happy that way. He was nestled against her hips, and she found herself pressing up into him, seeking the feeling of his weight against her.

His lips lingered by her ear. His breath was no longer

freezing. Somehow, it was warmer than before. A puzzle she registered but had no time to think on, as his dusky and rumbling voice filled her thoughts.

He hummed approvingly and let his tongue flick against her ear before he murmured to her. "I will take a moment to point out it was you who pulled me close."

This heat inside her body was her own fault, then. His lips found the hollow of her throat below her ear, and she gasped, arching up into him. She did not bother to deny that which they both knew.

He meandered his kisses down her throat, his lips now hot against her. She slid her hand to his neck, and there beneath her fingers, she felt a pulse. Slow. Thick. But it was there.

His heart could beat.

"We are creatures of hunger. Three things may inspire a vampire's heart to beat. Lust for violence, for blood, or for flesh." She felt him smile against her as he settled himself lower over her, his chest against hers, his lips now at that spot where her neck joined her shoulder. "And, in rare joyous moments, more than one."

His hand grasped her hair, holding her head still, and he rolled his tongue over her skin once more. She moaned and whimpered in fear in the same breath. "Wait, please—"

"Shush, Maxine...be still." He kissed her throat again, slowly, again and again. He was luring her down from her instinctual panic. The hunter was coaxing the deer closer to him with a beckoning hand. It was a lie, but she could not resist it. Little by little, she felt her panic slide away as he lavished her throat with slow, tender, loving kisses.

"That's it," he praised her and moved to cradle her head in one of his hands. "Look to yourself, my beautiful child, and tell me you do not desire this. If you can say the words to me without a lie, I will leave you be." His fingers threaded into her hair, stroking her skin. He returned his lips to her throat.

This feels like bliss.

She could not speak the words. No matter how much she *should,* she could not. He was right. She had pulled him closer. She had arched into his touch. God help her, she wanted to feel his kiss.

With a shiver, she took a deep breath and let it out, forcing herself to go lax in his arms as she did. Shutting her eyes, she turned her head and bared her throat fully. *This is willful surrender.*

He moaned, a sound that rumbled through her like the call of a bell might resonate the stones around it. And with that, something sharp pierced her throat.

Maxine cried out.

14

His fangs pierced her throat.

The noise she made was broken off nearly in the same instant. The pain had been total, but it had been brief. For the breadth of the barest second, everything seemed to hang suspended in the air.

Then everything throbbed.

Everything moved with the tempo of her heart. Of his dead heart that should not beat, spurred to life now in time with hers. It stole her rhythm, and it became his own.

She felt him there, his fangs still deep in her skin. But something had risen to take the place of the agony she should have felt from the deep wound. Instead, she could only feel something that was far more dangerous. Far more insidious.

Far more damning.

Pleasure.

Overwhelming, total, and utter pleasure.

Her body was alive with it. Consumed by it. Her breath came short and shallow in her chest as she lay there beneath him. His weight was against his elbow near her

Heart of Dracula

head, and he caged her in on all sides. Escape had been impossible.

And now, it was undesirable.

All her will to avoid this had ended the moment his teeth had pierced her skin. Now, heat rushed over her body like she had been doused in a hot bath. It burned in her, reached into her core and lit it on fire.

Tha-thump.
Tha-thump.
Tha-thump.

Like the beat of a drum, she heard her heart in her ears. But with each moment, with each pounding sound, she felt him *pull* from her. *Take* from her. *Drink* from her.

And he was in no hurry.

And still, his thoughts coaxed her. His presence against hers whispered that he would leave her alive, unharmed, and barely the worse for wear. It was not about leaving her a drained husk. This was not meant to kill her. This was not meant to harm her.

This was a lesson.

It was to show her what he had promised her. He had sworn she would enjoy it. And now, in the face of it, she could not deny that he had been right.

The hand she had placed against his throat was now tangled in his hair, holding his head to her throat, begging silently for more. For him to sink his teeth deeper and take her fully. Each time he pulled from her, she felt a wave of bliss wash over her. She had never known anything like it. She surrendered to it once more. Surrendered to him, and whatever he sought to do with her.

Then he began to purr. It was a low noise, deep in his chest, and she felt it more than it reached her ears. A low, soothing, enticing rumble that vibrated in her and made her wish to sink farther into his grasp. It made her wish he would take it all from her. If she were to die like this, certainly there would be no better way to greet the reaper. It was animalistic, inhuman, and utterly foreign.

It should scare her. He was consuming her. And she wanted it.

"Yes. Let go, my beautiful." Those thoughts were not hers. They belonged to him. Mixing with hers, becoming tangled up in them and indistinguishable. *"Surrender to me. Surrender to this. Give me all that you are, and I can give you everything in return."* Still, that beastly, terrible, and wonderful purr continued in his chest.

She felt a burning need that roared forward with alarming fervor. She wanted him inside her everywhere. Everywhere he could be, she needed him to be. Her mind, her blood, and now her body. Hunger consumed her thoughts.

As she bent her knees, drawing him deeper between them, she moaned as she felt proof of his own desire pressing against her through their clothing.

He growled against her throat, loud and primal. *"Patience."*

She did not know which one of them he was scolding. Perhaps both.

Tha-thump.

Tha-thump.

The pleasure did not cease or dampen. It threatened to empty her mind of all other thoughts. He was all that existed to her in this moment.

The spread of dark wings against a night sky. Stars she did not recognize over a forest of evergreen trees. A castle in some lonesome mountain range. The burning sun overhead as everything had been taken from him. Grief, and pain, and loss, and *time* filled her. Hunger and desire. Lust for life, desire for death. *Passion.*

All that he was, she was.

And she embraced it all.

Kiss me. Please. I need you.

His fangs slid free of her throat. She felt him pull his head away from her enough that he turned her to look at him. Crimson eyes were glittering with pleasure and that all-consuming intensity she had felt. He was not immune to what had passed between them.

But he had heard her thoughts. He had heard her command.

And he obeyed.

THE POOR LITTLE thing had fainted.

To be truthful, Vlad was not entirely surprised. Gifted with power such as she was, she was still a mortal child. She had endured much in the past two days, and it was clear she had not slept or eaten very much in the time that had passed. And he was not easy on her. He pushed her at every opportunity to see what might happen. And it had been very worth it. Oh, what he had felt from her as they embraced!

He could feel her soul in the darkness of his, pressed against him like a lover in the shadows of the night. Like honey and apples. Like the crisp fall wind. Like *life* itself, the moment before it blazed and fell away.

He did love the autumn months. They were a celebration of both life and death. The glory of what came before and the reminder of what would follow. And she was just that. She was a warm hearth, and he was so cold.

He could feel her need, her desire, her curiosity, and her compassion. And such a compassionate thing she was. Drawn to comfort the monster in the darkness, even as it snapped its teeth at her. *My creatures will adore you. They will worship you. You will be a balm to us all. I vow it.*

Even as his fangs had been buried in her throat, even as he had threatened to take her life, she was the invading army. He felt her there, inside his mind, pervasive and total in her presence. No one had stepped inside his thoughts in all his years. Let alone some bright-eyed, fiendishly intelligent girl. She rummaged through his memories, dredging up sights he had long since forgotten. He was nothing but an unlocked warehouse to the child. Even as he drank her blood, he was *her* victim.

It triggered in him a desire that transcended wanting and now was firmly *needing*. She needed to be his. And he would have her. She was a dangerous toy to play with, and it did little to dissuade him. Indeed, all the opposite. She could undo him, and that thrilled him.

You think you cannot destroy me, my darling. Oh, no. You can. My soul still sits in your hand. Too strong for you to destroy unwittingly, yes. But you could still cast me upon the stones if you wished, cannonball as I might be. He tried not to laugh and kept it to a quiet chuckle. Yes. His little empath was far more than met the eye.

Not that what met his eye was displeasing in any way.

And now he was certain she wanted him. Her pleasure had echoed in his, reflecting at him like a candle in a mirror. Their minds had twisted together and joined as one as he had fed from her. How she had writhed beneath him, as her desire became tangled with his and became too much for her to battle.

It was delicious to watch her succumb to not only her

passion, but his. Even as she had pulled open the darkest corners of his mind to peer inside, the gates had opened wide both ways. He was not certain how much of her lust was truly her own or for how much of it he was to blame. If she had not fainted, he was certain he could have taken her here on the cold stone of a stranger's grave and she would have begged him for more.

Sadly, she had not been able to withstand all he levied against her. A setback or an opportunity, he was not sure.

This is a game best played slowly.

But he would not complain with what he had won already.

What a joy it would be when he could strip away those layers of fabric one by one and take her as he wished to do. As his body demanded he do in this moment, throbbing painfully as it did, trapped in the confines of his clothing. It was so rare that his heart ever beat at all, but it was not that particular organ that felt as slighted as the other. But he would not have her for the first time when she was unconscious beneath him. He wanted to watch her face as his conquest was complete.

It would not be complete, though...of that he was now quite convinced.

It was not her body that he now realized would be the greatest challenge, as it was for most. For most, the body fell last—the mind surrendered first. For her, he knew it would be the opposite. It would be her heart that would remain closed to him. And farther than that, it would be her mind that would be the ultimate prize. If she could love him, would she ever not feel regret for doing so?

Those would be the battlegrounds of their war. And what a wonderful fight it would be.

He had heard her command echo in his mind. *Kiss me.*

She had demanded it from him. And who was he to resist such a thing? And so, he had granted it to her in full. Released of his bite, the pleasure that had been forced over her like a poison had faded, and with it she had become overwhelmed.

He had kissed her until she slipped into unconsciousness. Now he lay with his head on her chest, listening to her heartbeat, careful to keep his weight from crushing her.

Beautiful child. Wonderful child.

He had barely taken more than a few mouthfuls from her. She would not even be dizzy come the dawn. He grinned to himself and turned his head to plant a kiss against her collarbone. She was so very warm. So very soft. He growled in his unsated desires and tried to take solace in those that had been fed this night.

You are mine, Maxine. The threat he had paid her had not been an idle one. It had not been a vain statement to scare her. It was the simple truth.

This surprising child—this mistress of souls—belonged to him now.

And no one would pry her from his hands.

———

Maxine was dreaming.

She would have expected a nightmare. Flashes of being chased by a ghoul through the streets, perhaps. The cruel laugh of a Vampire King, threatening to steal her and consume her.

"You are mine, Maxine."

The words echoed in her mind, the dream whispering close to her ear. But it was not a cackling laugh from the shadows. It wasn't a threat. It was a promise.

Heart of Dracula

She moaned in her dream. Her hands twisted in crimson sheets. He was there above her, caging her in, dark tendrils of hair draping around his alabaster features and brushing over her skin. She felt him there between her legs, lying against her, as he had been atop the tomb when he had fed from her. When his fangs had been buried in her throat.

But now, one thing had changed.

He was hilted deep in a very different way.

It was a dream. Only a desperate fantasy of her sleeping mind. The world around her was fuzzy and unreal. Intangible at the edges, like a watercolor painting left in the rain. But what was close to her—near to her—was very real.

His lips claimed hers, and she whimpered. Her stomach twisted in excitement. Despite her entire inexperience in the act itself, that didn't stop her body from dreaming up what it might be like. From imagining the primal truth that creatures knew and desired. That was before one counted the memories she had gathered from others. Those dreams of other lives had shown her what it was like to experience intimacy from both partners' perspectives.

But she had never known it herself. It had been an impossibility.

Until now.

When his lips trailed to her ear, she felt something change. Something shifted. The dream became...sharper. Clearer.

She was not alone.

"My, my...What a pleasant surprise."

She went rigid and tried to push him away. Embarrassment rushed through her. But his hand caught hers. He carefully pressed it to the silk sheets beside her head. She stammered. "I—"

"Shush." He kissed her, silencing her protests, and she

cried out as he pressed his hips into hers, deeper than she had imagined the dance might possibly go. Her body might not know what it felt like—but his did. Taking from his memories, she felt the pleasure tear through her.

She moaned as he withdrew slowly, nearly all the way, before repeating the gesture and filling her. He was slow. Gentle, but unstoppable. Unwavering as he stretched her and withdrew. Moving with the same patient tempo as when he had fed from her, he was once more proving to her what he could offer her.

Pleasure.

And by the gods, it felt astonishing.

With each easy stroke into her, she felt the tension melt from her limbs. She felt him lure her to open to him, easing her fears, just as he had done before his bite.

When she once more lay beneath him willing and supple, only then did he break his kiss. Crimson eyes watched her, heavy-lidded and thick with passion. With his own pleasure. There was a slight twist to his lips. "You never cease to amaze."

"This is only a dream. An illusion. You're not here. You're —Ah!" Her words cut off as he sank himself deep into her, somehow farther than before. She didn't even know it was possible. She knew she had lied when she had said it. He was in her mind. He was in her dreams. He was in her body. He was everywhere.

"This is a fantasy. One I would be happy to make real, my beautiful Maxine." His voice was a dark, dusky rumble as he pressed into her, a little harder than before, but still no faster. Her mind reeled with what it did to her. She was squeezing his hand in hers. "Don't be afraid. Don't fight it. You have nothing to fear from me."

"This isn't my fantasy," she gasped.

"Oh, but it is. You called me here. We are sleeping, and I felt you call for me. And here I am." He pressed inside of her, and she moaned. She turned her head away in embarrassment. "No, Maxine. Do not turn away from this. There is no shame here. Dreams are honest. They are a window to the soul. In this place, there is no hiding from what you really are. What you really need."

"I shouldn't—"

"It doesn't matter." He pressed into her and withdrew nearly all the way again.

The friction was bliss. The feeling of him inside her was more than she could have ever even hoped. "You're my enemy."

"No, Maxine. I am not. You wish I would be such, but it is hardly that simple. Accept it."

"I can't—"

"You can." He leaned down and kissed the hollow of her throat beneath her ear. "You can, and you shall." Still he moved in her, never faltering, never speeding. Deep, consuming, tearing away all the shadowy parts of her soul and making them his. She struggled to keep hold of some private parts of her mind, and he growled over her. "Feel me, Maxine. Stop shutting me out."

"I can't shut you out…"

"You are stronger than you think. Let me in. Let me touch you."

He pressed again. She arched her back, his bare skin against hers. She cried out as he seemed to reach a part of her that she had never known existed, and it sang for him.

Just as her body had opened to him, she felt her mind follow suit. She felt his soul rush toward hers and he was filling her in more ways than one. She heard his desire, heard his hunger, heard his *need* for her. He wanted this as badly as she did. More so, if it were possible.

An image of him lying her down on her bed once more, fingers trailing over the wound on her neck, played in front of her eyes. A second rose joined the first in the glass vase upon her nightstand. He had left her there to sleep in her own home. But how he had wanted to take her. To steal her. To do *this* to her.

But he was patient. He would wait.

His hand released hers to trail down her naked body. His touch was hot, his blood pumping in his veins. Lust was what drove it forward, he had said—for blood, for violence, or for flesh.

"Do not be afraid of this." His voice was a breathy whisper by her ear. "Embrace it. Embrace *me,* my beautiful one."

She could only whimper beneath him as he pressed himself into her, and she felt him there now to the hilt. He throbbed, surged, and she could feel something hot inside her body. A growl left his throat, eager and feral.

He felt impossible inside of her. Too much of him, too deep. She felt split wide, broken in two, left helpless in his hands. She whimpered as the feeling of him was too much. She came undone, feeling ecstasy threaten to wipe her mind empty of all thoughts. Of anything that was not *him.* It was only a dream, yet she had never felt anything like it before in her life.

"I will come to you tomorrow. We shall speak, then perhaps we shall make this fantasy real. But for now...rest. And know that I sleep now in my coffin with a smile upon my face."

And with that, her dream faded away.

15

The morning came.

And with it came the sunlight. It streamed through her curtains, and she let out a small grunt as they were still apart, sending the light streaming into the room. She was exhausted. With a sigh, she gave in to the pointless inevitability of staying in bed.

She let her hand trail over her throat and felt a slight sting. There was a wound there, but it felt no more serious than a mosquito bite. *He is one Hell of a mosquito.* She climbed out of bed and was glad to find herself once more still dressed. It meant nothing had happened.

While we were awake.

She swore in her mind at her own weakness, her own desperate need for affection. She had never been touched by a man, and her mind was all too eager to dream up what it would be like. Vlad was as quick to show her.

Walking to her mirror, she turned her head to examine the bite. Two small red marks on her throat. They did not look inflamed. It looked as though she had missed with her hairpin, and nothing more. Yet the hunters who were potentially sleeping in her house would know the marks for what they were.

Hiding them with a scarf seemed like an obvious ploy. How on Earth was she going to explain this? She sighed. Changing out of her dress once more, she threw on something far more comfortable to wear and laced up the bodice in the back.

All things considered, she felt...okay. She did not feel more tired than she would after any long night out. She felt overwrought emotionally, but that was to be expected.

"He came and asked me to dinner. I agreed, because I am trying to learn how to stop him," she said to her reflection. She practiced the words as if that would help. "He bit me. I did not drink his blood. He returned me here to his house because he...is enjoying the game of seducing me."

She cringed at the sound of it. "To be frank, I think he knows he's already won. He simply likes dragging out the victory."

No. She would not be telling them anything of the sort. She would tell them of dinner. She would tell them of what she learned about his true age and his motives in destroying the city—unleashing more of the creatures like she had seen at the gala. But she would mention nothing to them of his desires for her.

Or her desire for him.

She finally looked to the nightstand. There, in the vase she had placed the first rose, sat a second. No note joined it this time. She let her fingers trace over the delicate petals.

She reached out and picked up the little music box that sat as a perennial watchdog upon her nightstand. It was a simple thing, carved out of wood with an opal pattern inlaid in the lid. It was simple, but she loved it more than anything

Heart of Dracula

else she owned. Truth be told, it was her only prized possession.

Opening it, she watched the little ballerina spring up from under the lid. It played a bittersweet, melancholy tune. A waltz. It always brought a sad smile to her face. She shut the lid and replaced it on the stand. Something else caught her attention—something far more important. The smell of food.

The hunters were indeed home, and one of them had cooked. Her money was on Bella. Her stomach rumbled, and she chuckled. Her stomach did not care for her reticence in explaining her evening to the hunters. It wanted food.

It won.

———

"He...*what?*"

Maxine winced at Alfonzo's shout. Bella and Eddie were watching her with wide-eyed shock and dismay. She pulled aside her hair for them to see the marks on her throat. She decided to begin with that and get it over with before one of them noticed mid-meal.

"You seem...fine." Bella blinked, astonished.

Maxine nodded. "He did not take much. He was proving a point."

Alfonzo's jaw was twitching. "The point being?"

"That he could, I imagine." *That I wanted him to, moreover.* She opted to leave the second half silent. "I do not believe he intends to turn me."

"He intends to corrupt you all the same." Alfonzo was pacing around her kitchen now. "He lures you out to dinner with him. He feeds from you. He returns you to your bed for a second time. He will come for you a third time. This is his game. He chips away at people."

"He's done this before, then." She wasn't surprised. Eddie was putting together a plate of food for her. "Oh, Eddie, stop. It's quite all right."

"No, you've fed my dumb ass several times already. Here." He put it down on the table and gave her a knife and fork. "Eat. Al's gonna be mad for a while."

"I have every right to be mad." Alfonzo grunted.

"Not at her." Eddie glared at the older man. "We got her into this mess. She's not a hunter. She's doing her best. So, calm the fuck down, sit down, and let her talk."

Maxine was astonished at both the display of his backbone and the show of support. He had been fairly quiet up until that point.

"I need a smoke." Alfonzo walked out of the room, and she heard his heavy steps as he went down the stairs toward the back door into the courtyard.

It wasn't until the door shut that she sighed. Bella smiled gently at her. "Don't mind him. He is upset and troubled by what has befallen you, and he is expressing it in a bad way. He blames himself for your fate. He has said as much. Now that the vampire has…laid claim to you, he is angry at himself."

"This isn't his fault."

"Nope. It's all of our faults." Eddie picked up his coffee and sipped it. "We came to your door. We brought the brooch. We started this."

"He was already in this city. I would die from one of his monsters if not at his hands. You might have sped up the inevitable, but I think…I think this is my fate. I think this is meant to be."

Bella frowned at her plate. "I do not think I believe in fate if it means this is the outcome."

"We do not get to choose what it has in store for us. I have time, all the same. I can still be of some use to you three."

"It's not about use, Maxine." Eddie rubbed his hand over his disheveled brown hair, making it worse in the process. "You're a friend. You've taken us in. You've shown us kindness. Fed us. You aren't a tool to us."

Maxine smiled and reached out a gloved hand to rest it on his wrist. "That means more to me than you can know. I am not one who has friends. It makes this worth it." She returned to her food, grateful for the pile of sausage and scrambled eggs. It was precisely what she needed. "Alfonzo is right. Vlad will come for me again."

"Do you know when?"

Another lie to spare them. "No."

"Alfonzo wants us to try to find his lair during the day. We're going to split up in an hour and head out into town for the rest of the night, I think." Eddie got up to refill his coffee. "Do you want one of us to stay behind with you?"

"No. It's all right. One of you can't stop him." *He is thousands of years old. I am not sure all three of you can stop him together.* "Better you try to find him while he sleeps. If he comes for me, I will try to learn all I can as to where he might be when he is vulnerable."

Alfonzo came back in and seemed much calmer for having had his cigarette. He sat at the table at his plate of food. "I am sorry, Maxine. Eddie is right. My anger isn't at you. This is not how I wished this to go."

"I know. I am sorry I am too weak to fight him."

Alfonzo didn't hesitate when he took her hand and squeezed it. She was glad for her gloves. "No. You are not to blame. We are responsible for putting you in this scenario. He is at fault for being the monster that he is. He is preying on you, Maxine. You have nothing to be sorry for."

If you only knew how mutual this seems to be. She smiled sadly and nodded, looking down at her plate. She picked up her fork and went back to eating. "Thank you, Alfonzo."

"We won't be back until tomorrow, I expect. If he comes…when he comes…" Alfonzo trailed off, not knowing what to say to her. "I'm sorry."

She nodded and did her best to smile again. "Do not blame yourself for this. My life is not on your hands, hunter. I do not outweigh the thousands you are trying to save. I promise you."

"You are a kind soul, Maxine Parker. You do not deserve this."

"People rarely deserve anything that happens to them."

She told them the rest of what she discovered—his true age, his designs on the city. They listened in curious silence, with Bella peppering her with questions, before she was out of the appropriate portions of the story. It was not long after that when the hunters cleaned their plates and left. She spent the rest of the day lost in thought.

There was something deeply wrong with her. It was her confusion over the subject of the Vampire King that sent her to her room just before sunset, digging out a small silk bag from her trunk. The black fabric was opaque, meant to protect from the light. It was a superstition, but then again, so was most of her life.

Sitting at her table by one wall, she opened the bag and drew out a deck of cards. They were well-worn and well-loved. They had been a gift to her. A parting gift from the Roma. Tarot cards.

She was not a psychic. She was not a soothsayer. She

Heart of Dracula

could not see the future. But she could see into the hearts of the people around her. Yet her own always remained a mystery. How cruel a gift it was, to see the truth of all those around her yet to be blind to her own.

Vlad had seen that clear as day.

She sat back in her chair and began to shuffle the cards idly. She let her mind pore over her recent troubles. The Vampire King had found her, and it seemed he wanted far more than her flesh. He was more dangerous than any wolf in the woods. Where one might sink its teeth into her bone and marrow and merely eat her for dinner—the other wanted so much more.

But to what ends? Why? For the simple thrill of the hunt?

Last night he had laid her out upon a tomb, in a yard of the dead, and had drunk her blood. She should be horrified at the notion. But it brought a warmth to her cheeks, and she could only recall the deep and burning pleasure it had brought over her. The fire it had sent pouring through her veins like liquid metal.

He might have taken from her, but he gave to her in return. It had felt like nothing she had ever known. For the first time in as long as she could remember...she had not felt alone.

And oh, how she had wanted him to take more, if it meant she could have what she discovered she wanted. But it was wrong. He was a vampire! A monster set to destroy her! He had killed an untold number of people in his *thousands of years*. She should not want him.

But her dream had shown a very different truth.

Stripped away from all the weighty chains of conscious thought, all that was left was how she felt. And Vlad was right. She was terrified and excited at the thought of his presence in equal measures.

I'm nothing to him. A diversion. Something to be used and thrown away. Even though what I feel for him is wrong, the real issue at hand is that while it may be requited, it is temporary for him.

Yes. That was a better shelter. Any branch over her head in the storm to protect her from the hail that threatened to destroy her armor and her will to fight was a worthy one to take up. She did not know him. She could not trust him.

He likely had dozens of women around the world. Some living, some undead, some trapped in between, all answering his beck and call. He was thousands of years old. He left a bloody trail in his wake. She would simply be another notch on his bedpost.

She placed the cards on the table before her. Cutting the deck with her left hand, she put the bottom on the top. She spread it out in an arc in front of her on the cloth tabletop.

As she shut her eyes, she let herself focus on everything and nothing. Hovering her hand over the cards, she began to drift it over the arc of cards an inch or two above the surface and waited. She was searching for the warmth that felt like a candle beneath her hand—a card whispering to her that it was the one. It was the message that should be told.

She did not read cards like most did. She had never met another who used them in this fashion. Most dealt from the top or cut the deck into several piles and chose cards that way. But this was how *she* did it. And the method worked, so she never saw the need to learn another.

Perhaps it was because she cared nothing for telling the future. Her readings instead focused on gleaning a deeper understanding of the now. A glimpse into the heart of the present and the past. And that was what she so desperately needed right now.

I am hunted by a vampire who has promised to consume the whole of me.

And I find myself desirous of it.

He means my ruin, and all I want is to dance with him once more.

One by one, she pulled the cards as they called to her and stacked them atop each other in front of her. Each one in its turn called to her, and she slipped it from its brethren to tell her what it knew, until she had ten cards.

Swiping the remaining cards into a neat stack, she set them aside. As she was about to lay out the first card, a sound froze her, her hand hovering over the first card in the pile. A music box began to play behind her. A tune she could never forget.

Turning in her chair, she saw a figure standing by her bedside, a small wooden box in his hand. Her stomach twisted in anticipation and terror. *Think of the Devil, and he appears.* "Vlad. I—I wasn't expecting you."

"I said I would visit you today, and the sun is just now setting."

His voice, deep and rumbling, never ceased to make her shiver. "You do not fear the sun's rays?"

"Most of my kind would die with its touch. For me, no. It carries no such threat." A pointed nail hovered close over the tiny, slowly twirling ballerina in its forever pose. "I have been curious about this box and would have opened it, but I did not want to wake you either time." He watched the little figurine spin in fascination. She would ask him to put it down for fear he might break it, but he seemed quite gentle with how he was handling it. And the look on his face was faraway and oddly wistful.

"It is quite valuable to me."

"I assumed as much." He seemed uneager to look away from it. "Why?"

"It was a gift to me from my father. The only thing I have of him." At his silent question, she sighed. "He fought in the war. I am from Virginia, and he was a landowner. It was expected that since he had no sons to send to die, he would go instead. He returned but was injured and subsequently very ill. Mentally and physically. He killed himself before I was born, but he had the music box commissioned before he could not withstand the pain any longer." She smiled sadly. "I think he wished for me to be a ballerina."

"All fathers wish their daughters to be beautiful."

"And look what came of me."

"You are beautiful, Maxine." Yet he did not look away from the music box. "And it is astonishing to me that you do not see it."

"I can't imagine he would approve of me now. My mother certainly did not agree with what I became."

"Life is cruel."

"Did you know your parents?"

"If I did, I do not remember." He shut the box delicately and set it back down on the nightstand. "I do not remember most of my past."

She furrowed her brow at him curiously. "Truly?"

He let out a quiet hum and turned to face her. His expression was unreadable. For once, it did not look as though he meant to consume her whole. It was a welcome change of pace. "I am thousands of years old, darling. Do you expect me to hold all of it within my head? That might truly make a man mad, indeed."

She stood from her chair as he swept across the room to her, his hands folded idly behind his back. He glanced down at the cards on the table then looked to her with a raised eyebrow. "You are no psychic, you said."

"No. I read the present, not the future."

"And for whom were you reading?" He gestured a hand around the empty bedroom. "Do you have a lover hiding in your wardrobe?"

"If I did, I would think you could smell him." She smirked up at him.

He grinned at her riposte, obviously pleased she still had the strength of will to spar with him. "Indeed. And he would be dead for it within seconds."

"For what?"

"Touching what is mine." He sat in the other chair at the table. "For whom were you reading?"

She bristled at his claim of ownership again but shoved it aside with a sigh. She sat. "Myself." She shuffled the cards she had pulled back into the deck. She wasn't interested in sharing such private things with the vampire. The gods knew she shared enough intimate things with him already. "I find myself in need of guidance."

"Whatever for?"

She shot him an incredulous look. "I have stock in the wheat industry." She layered the sarcasm on thick. "Why do you think, vampire?"

He laughed, a low and resonant sound that was pleasant and unnerving both at once. A flash of sharp teeth reminded her of what he had done the previous night. In that one small expression he had called her bluff, and she felt the color drain from her face.

Seeing her expression shift, his own settled into a sly and cunning smile. "Never spare me your jabs. I enjoy your fire."

"Try not to kill me, then, and perhaps you'll have more of it."

"Killing you was never my goal."

"Turning me, then?"

"I fear that if I turn you, your gifts will be lost to you." He tapped a finger on the table as he watched her thoughtfully, his other hand curled underneath his chin. He looked all the part of a mastermind playing a game of chess. And she felt less like the opposing player and more like a part on the board. "No. I will not turn you unless you ask for it."

"I suppose for that I am grateful. You do not wish to kill me, and you do not wish to turn me. What do you wish for, then?"

"You know. You heard my thoughts. You stole them in our private moment last night."

"I was a bit distracted." She glared at him.

He smiled. "Then I am glad you did not retain them. I will keep my secrets a little longer. Tell me something, Miss Parker. How many souls have you destroyed with your touch?"

She hesitated.

"Please, Miss Parker."

With a sigh, she shook her head. There was no point in hiding. His body count was far higher. "Eleven."

He let out a low hum. "And how many deserved it?"

"None. No one deserves the fate I bring them."

"How many of them were murderers? How many of them had done terrible deeds worthy of destruction? You saw their souls laid bare. How many would you *personally* deem unworthy of life?"

"None. It is not my place to say that someone is irredeemable."

"Not even murderers?"

Heart of Dracula

"Murder is an unnatural act for anyone. It is not in the self-interest of the species to commit such blatant acts of violence. While it is in human nature to do so, it is never without great cause. Mental illness, emotional duress, depravity brought on by extenuating circumstances, or when required by society such as in war. Look deeper past the degenerate nature that inspires such an act, and you will find someone worthy of pity."

"And what of me?"

She was still shuffling the cards and looked up at him for a brief moment. "You are not human."

"I was, once."

"Were you?"

"I was not born a vampire."

"Do you remember what made you this way?"

He let out a long breath. "No."

"What do you remember?"

"The same as you've seen. Sand, the burning sun. Blood. Monuments to ancient gods...and wrath. I believe I destroyed a city the day they made me." He sneered. "It was my first, but not my last."

She did remember those visions quite well. Grief and agony. Someone being taken away. She saw a bowl of blood, thick and poisoned. Being forced to drink it. A card slipped from her hands and fell face up on the table.

The Tower. Tragedy and disaster. She cringed and picked up the card and put it back into the deck. "I'm sorry."

"For what?"

"For what you've suffered."

"There is not enough sympathy in the world, I'm afraid." He let out a long, low growl, then schooled his features back into a softer expression as he looked to her. "I appreciate the sentiment. It is rare that I receive such kindness." He watched her for a long moment. "Read my cards, Miss Parker."

"Why will you not tell me what you wish me to be to you?"

"Perhaps the cards will tell you all you need to know."

She narrowed her eyes at him accusatorially. "You're toying with me again."

"Indeed I am. Amuse me."

"I am not the ballerina in my music box. I do not dance for your amusement."

A thin twist to his lips and that devious, hungry look in his crimson eyes returned. "Do tell."

She sighed in frustration and placed the cards down on the table in front of her. "No, Vlad. I will not read for you. I will not be ordered around by you."

"You belong to me. Now and forever. From the moment you touched my brooch, until the moment you are dust."

She cringed.

"Never forget who and what I am, Maxine. Never."

"Why would you not wish me to forget?"

Crimson eyes slipped shut. "Everyone else does."

Something about his words sliced her deep. They were unexpected. They were honest. She could feel his emotions rolling off him in waves. Grief, anger, loneliness. But resilience. A certain kind of bullheaded stubborn pride. He was not ashamed of those deaths. But there was a bitterness about them that confused her. "What do you mean?"

"I have nothing more to say on the matter at the moment."

He was a difficult man. She pinched the bridge of her nose and tried to resist the urge to throw a lamp at his head. He would disappear before it struck him. Perhaps he was right. Perhaps her cards would show her something. She

Heart of Dracula

looked down at the deck of cards on the table and picked them up. She shuffled it one more time and placed it in front of him. "Are you right-handed or left?"

"Left."

Of course. She let herself smile. "Cut the deck in half with your right hand, wherever you like, and place the bottom on the top."

"Why?"

"You asked me to read your cards, didn't you?"

With a low hum, he did as she asked. She took the deck again and fanned it out into the arc in front of her. Shutting her eyes, she hovered her hand over the card and began to sweep along the path, searching for the ones that called to her in turn.

"Tell me something, Vlad. Is there anything I could do that would convince you to spare this city?"

"No."

"Is there anything I could do that would convince you to spare the lives of the hunters?"

"No."

"Then why is it they are not dead, and this city is not already in ruins?" She paused in her progress and looked up to him.

He was watching her, curious and amused. "I am distracted."

"I can stall for time, then. Good."

"Is that the only reason you so peaceably agree to see me? Are you a treacherous little succubus after all, luring me into your dreams with the promise of your sweet embrace, only to trick me?"

Her face bloomed in warmth. She glared at him viciously. It did nothing but make him laugh. "Do not mock me."

"I am not. I think it is quite charming how you try to hold up the bastion flag and convince me the only reason you dreamed of yourself in my bed is because you seek to 'stall for time.'"

"This is wrong. All of this is wrong. On many levels."

"Oh, do tell."

"Even if I were to accept that I desire you—"

"You do."

She shot him another vicious glare and earned a cruel chuckle in return. "How many women do you keep in your 'employ,' Vlad?"

"You say that as if I am going to pay you." He raised his hand when she went to shout at him, cutting off her tirade before it began. "None. Have I kept companions in my years? Yes, of course."

She paused for a second as she thought over her words. "Do you remember all the people you have killed?"

"No." He raised an eyebrow at her, as if wondering where the conversation was headed. "Do you remember all the meals you have ever eaten?"

"Are we only that, then? Meals?"

"Yes."

She winced. There was a cynical air to him again as he watched her. This was the cruel King of the Vampires that most of the world saw. A deeply haughty, aristocratic, tyrannical thing. Not what she had known to date. What she had seen was a passionate and surprisingly approachable thing. She found she disliked this version of the man.

Seeing her reaction, he softened. The coldness faded. "Forgive me. It is easy to be that which others expect me to be."

"What do you mean?"

Heart of Dracula

"I am only ever what others wish me to be. The villain, the tyrant, the demon, the monster."

"What of those who serve you?"

"Even to them, they only see a piece of me. To them, I play the father, the lord, the friend, or mentor. Your kind are not always merely livestock to me. Sometimes, you become more than that. Sometimes you become family."

"Like Walter and Zadok."

"Indeed. I care for them deeply. Even the Frenchman, as hard as that may be to believe."

"But you say they do not know the whole of you?"

"No one ever has. I am as old as the human race itself. I have been many things in all those years. I have played my part for them all. It is exhausting."

"And what of the companions you said you've had?"

"To them, I have been a lover, a betrayer, a saint, and much more. I have been the gentle husband or the cruel prince. Whatever they have wished me to be. Each saw a facet of me in turn, and only that, like all the rest."

She went silent. She could press him for more, but she didn't. She was beginning to suspect he was giving her the answer to the question she had been pondering. *Why me? And for what ends?*

Suddenly, she was not certain she wanted to know the answer. But it was too late now. "I do not wish for you to pretend to be any facet of yourself, vampire. I do not want to know only a part of you. Only the whole, as much as I am capable of it."

"For that, I am immensely grateful. More than you may know." He gestured to the cards. "Please, continue."

She went silent and finished pulling the cards. Stacking the remainders, she began to turn them out into the layout she preferred. An adapted Celtic Cross she had changed for her needs.

The Ace of Cups. Death. The Emperor. The Hanged Man. Three of Wands. Seven of Swords. Five of Wands. The Devil—she tried not to laugh—followed by the Hermit. Lastly came the Ten of Swords.

She looked down at the cards and felt something was missing. There was more to be told. She picked up the deck again and, rifling her finger down the side of the stack, pulled out another card and placed it next to the last one, the foreboding Ten of Swords.

The Lovers.

She sighed.

16

She stared down at the cards and felt nothing but dread. She heard the chair across from her click, as if it rocked briefly on its legs. She looked up and found it empty. Once more, he had disappeared from it without moving.

The mystery of where he had gone again did not last. His hand touched her cheek, cradling her face, as he tilted her head to look up at him. "I am no Roma spellcaster. But I know what that card means."

"I—it doesn't—"

"Yes, it does." He hummed and stepped closer to her. The scent of roses washed over her. "Shall we speak of our shared dream, Maxine?"

She pulled away from him, desperate to keep the feeling of him from overtaking her. Once it did, she was hopeless. She would be unable to deny him anything he asked. "I haven't yet finished your reading."

He grinned, seeing her very transparent attempt at a dodge for what it was. He motioned a hand toward the table. "Well, then...after you." He vanished into nothing more than a shadow, and she watched in fascination as he reformed in his chair. "Or would you rather save it for later? I know of something else we could pass the time with instead."

Her face was warm, and she knew she was blushing. She studied the cards in front of her. Anything to keep from looking at the dark and smirking vampire across from her.

She tapped the two cards in the center of the cross. The first two she had drawn. The Ace of Cups who sat crossed by Death. She decided there was no dancing about the subject. "What I am going to tell you may be unkind."

"I would want for nothing else."

He wasn't listening to her. She tried again. "Stop me if I go too far, if what I say becomes too personal."

"Nothing you could possibly do could ever be too intimate for me." His purr was seductive, filled with insinuation and entendre.

She glared at him and tapped the two cards crossed in the center again. Very well—if he wouldn't heed her warning, she'd teach him to be more mindful. "You fear loss. It keeps you from feeling anything at all. That is what consumes you. For someone who can never die, death is all that surrounds you. You have lost everything you have ever come to care about in your thousands of years, and it leaves you crippled. Afraid and unwilling to ever let yourself feel anything legitimate again."

The playfulness left his expression, but he said nothing. He leaned back in his chair and watched her. For all the world, he might have been a statue.

"This position is your consciousness." She tapped the card over the two crossed in the center. "All that weighs on your mind that you are aware of. Here we have the Emperor,

Heart of Dracula

and never have I seen a card so fitting for a man. You think yourself Master of all that you see. All that you touch is yours to own. A tyrant."

"In the upright state, it is meant to symbolize structure. Rightful authority, does it not?" His eyes narrowed with his words.

"You know the tarot?"

"I know a great deal of things about a great many subjects." He watched her, his expression once more unfathomable. "I am very old."

She nodded once. Of course. She was foolish to think he didn't understand the cards himself. "I choose not to read cards reversed or upright." She shook her head. "I believe every blade is double-edged. Every card has two meanings."

"Then how do you know if your Emperor is benign or malign?"

"It is determined by its context—the cards around it. Like all the rest of life, nothing can be viewed alone in a void."

"And what do you see?"

"I see as I told you." She placed her hand flat on the card in question. "A man who thinks he owns the world around him. You conduct yourself accordingly."

"But you do not believe in my power. Why is that?"

"Because neither do you."

"Bold accusations."

"Is it? This card." She tapped the Hanged Man, who sat beneath the crossed cards. "That which lies within your subconscious. That which influences you without your recognition." She looked down at the figure who was hanged by a tree from his ankle, his hands unbound but crossed behind his back regardless. "A man who chooses to trap himself within his pain. A martyr of his own making. A man who suffers because he cannot see that he has the power to free himself. You are not a god—you are not an emperor—you are powerless in your own fate. Or so you see yourself."

Vlad was silent, watching her. Waiting. Giving up nothing. *He is a man who takes an inch and never relinquishes it,* she reminded herself. *As such, he believes the same of all those around him.*

She tapped the position to the right of the crossed cards. "The Three of Swords. The influences that are leaving your life. Looking ahead. Travel. Trying to see the future. You wanted to leave all you were behind you."

"I left London. It did not suit me."

"Not across the ocean, but away—away from all the pain you've known." She tapped the position to the left of the cross. "To this. You have not come in good faith. The Seven of Swords. Deception, trickery, and tactics. You are trying to scheme your way through your future. You tried to leave your past, only to repeat it."

"Ah, now you make the soothsayer's mistake. You assume your way through the gaps."

"I am no soothsayer."

"And it shows. I agree I have left the past and looked ahead. I agree that I have come here with deception in mind. But you connect the two in ways you should not." He picked up the Seven of Swords, plucking it from underneath her fingers. He turned the card about, pondering it. "Deception. Have I deceived you, Miss Parker? Have I not shown you all that I am from the very beginning?"

"You danced with me as a mortal man."

"A blink of an eye. A single evening's diversion. A game."

"Do you play games often?"

"At every opportunity."

Reaching for her card, he handed it to her, and she replaced it where it had been. "And now we reach this." She moved her hand to the first card in the righthand upright path. Four cards in a row. Four cards that people delighted over but were far less weighty than the six she had already read. "The future is like a lighthouse. The farther away the object from the lamp, the harder it is to read. The less certain its location. Do you understand?"

"The future is still mine to change."

"The future is still changeable," she corrected. His egotism was unflinching, but it was consistent. "But yes." She shook her head and resisted the urge to slap him. Barely. "The Five of Wands. Conflict and rivalry. Strife awaits you."

"With whom? You?"

She picked up the deck of cards, rifled her finger down the side of it, and pulled out a card where she felt the urge to stop. The Page of Wands. "No. Someone else." That card was not her. One of the hunters, perhaps. But she was not certain which one.

"Then I do not care."

She sighed. Of course, he ignored her warning. She moved on. She tapped the next card. "This card represents how people view you. How you are seen by the world around you." She touched the Devil. "Do I need to elaborate?"

He laughed. "No."

She moved on to the next. "Your hopes and fears."

"In one card?"

"That which we hope can also be that which we fear, in

its absence. And now you see why I do not read cards inverted." She looked down at the card in question. "The Hermit. You hope to find guidance, you hope to find your inner truth, but you think you may be lost. You worry that you are without redemption. You fear that in the end, all that you are is meaningless."

Vlad was silent.

So, she moved on. "The future is twofold." She tapped the two cards that sat beside each other. The Ten of Swords and the Lovers. "Defeat—utter surrender. Surrounded on all sides, beaten and broken. Or...love. The choice is yours what road you will take."

She moved to swipe the cards away, but his hands stopped hers. Pressed her hands down against them and refused to let her clean the table.

"Love with whom? Who awaits me at the end of that path?"

She sat back and watched him warily. "I don't know."

"Ask the cards, if you do not know." He motioned to the stack of cards. She hesitated. He urged again. "Ask."

She picked up the deck, rifled her thumb down the side, and placed a card in the center of the table. The Moon.

"Who does that represent?" He pressed her. She suspected he knew the answer.

Her face grew warm, flushing. She shut her eyes. "I don't know."

"You lie. Say it, Maxine. Tell me who waits for me at the end of that road, should I take it. Who waits to welcome me from the jaws of defeat?"

Her heart wrenched in her chest, and she sank lower in her chair. "I—It would presume too much to—" She put her hand over her face and tried her best to hide it. That card

Heart of Dracula

had always represented her for as long as she had read them.

His hand touched her wrist. He was no longer sitting but standing over her. Once more his chair had not moved—he had not pushed it away. Fingers curled underneath her chin and tipped her head up to look at him. The sense of him rolled over her. Restrained, but close. The more she touched him—or rather, the more he touched her—the less out of control it became. "Do not hide from me, Maxine."

"I am not—" She could deny it, but it was true. She *was* hiding. Hiding her face. Hiding everything. She looked up at him and met his crimson eyes and stopped her protests. Once more, hypnotism was not to blame. It was simply the fathomless depths of red that had done the deed.

"You have no need to shy away from me. Not now, not ever." He leaned down and placed a kiss against her forehead. "Come. I would like to walk with you. Sunset has come, and the city is beautiful at this time of night."

"I will need to get properly dressed."

He chuckled, looking down at her housedress. She felt her face grow warm again under his scrutiny. "No need. Throw on a coat. No one will know the difference. Otherwise, I will be happy to assist you." That wicked smile returned to his face. "If so...do strip, and I will be happy to lace your corset."

"I—I—" She swallowed the lump in her throat and pushed him away from her. "No!" She coughed. "No. A coat will be fine." Her face was burning as she stood from her chair and went to her wardrobe, fetching one of her long, thin coats, despite the summer air. Pulled tightly over her, he was right. No one would know she was half-dressed underneath.

He chuckled. "For shame. Although I do admit I would prefer to remove your clothes than help place them on you."

She put her head against the door of her wardrobe, the wood cool against her forehead. She prayed for patience from anyone who would listen. "Where will we walk, Count?"

"Wherever you wish. It is the company I seek, not the destination."

"I think you're lying to me." She turned to look at him and found him watching her with that softer expression once more. "I think the destination is all you seek tonight."

He grinned. It was both predatory and amused. "How quickly you learn, Miss Parker. Very well. I eagerly await the moment you no longer hide from me. But in my advanced years, I have come to appreciate the journey as much as I do the arrival." His eyes flicked over her body, and she fought the urge to tighten her coat around her. "Although...that may not be true in this case."

She turned her head away to hide her face and her inevitable blush. Her face went warm on cue. There she was again, hiding from him. She sighed and straightened her back, trying to find resilience. "Let us get on with it, then."

Vlad was smiling, but there was no mocking look on his granite features. "I will see you outside. I wish to ensure that your new intrepid *houseguests* do not lay in wait for me."

"I—"

Vlad vanished, and she watched a dark shadow slip across the wall and the floor, as if it were cast there by some unseen light. It slipped over the sill of her window, under the closed pane, and was gone.

"Must I put up with this now? Really? Bad enough he is unstoppable. Worse yet that he is of a constantly impermanent location." She didn't know who she was complaining to and decided it didn't matter. Glancing over at the table with her tarot cards, her eyes fell on the two in the final position. The Ten of Swords, or the Lovers. Which was it to be?

Which did she want it to be?

Shaking her head, she opened the door and decided that no matter which, leaving the vampire waiting on her stoop was likely unwise.

17

Vlad watched Maxine with deep curiosity as she emerged from the door of her home. Once more, he summoned, and she followed. He had donned a pair of sunglasses to help shield his eyes from the fading streaks of amber and gold that decorated the sky. It did not hurt him, but that was not to say he enjoyed the glow. It was far too bright for his tastes.

His children found the glowing orb far more deadly than he. Zadok would burn in time as if scalded by acid. Even Walter, ancient and purebred as he was, would suffer after prolonged exposure. Yet both men claimed they missed it terribly. Zadok would often wax poetic about missing the warmth of the daylight, although the Frenchman was never quiet and found himself expounding on topics more frequently than not.

Vlad did not care much about the sun or its absence when it was gone. But perhaps that was the nature of all men—to only desire that which they could not have. While that was certainly a flaw of his, he was faced now with the counterargument given flesh.

He could very much have this Maxine Parker. He

Heart of Dracula

suspected that in a matter of days, she would truly belong to him of her own volition. While he could take her—and he desired very much to do so—it would spoil the prize in the end.

But whether she gave to him her heart and mind this night, or in ten years, it did not change the fact that she was inarguably *his*. The brilliant child with the flashing dark eyes was even coming to understand it herself.

He held out his hand, and she eyed his pale skin and pointed sharp nails scrupulously. She did not trust him. She had no reason to, and if she did, he would call her a fool.

But it was for the precise reason that she was not an idiot that she put her hand in his and let him draw her gently down the stairs and to his side. They began to move down the sidewalk in thoughtful and delightfully companionable silence. No one glanced at them. They looked like any other couple. An odd one, perhaps a bit morbid as they were, dressed both in black and quite pale. He far more frightfully than she.

He would not rush her. Either to speak or otherwise. She was plenty quick enough for him.

"When do you plan to begin your war in earnest?"

He cast a glance down to her. It was how he spent every day of his life—looking down at others. Both literally and metaphorically. He smiled idly and looked back up to the fading rays of the sun. "When the other battle I wage is won."

"If you seek to convince me to surrender to your advances, Count, that is not the way to do it."

He laughed and, taking her hand, slipped it into his elbow so they walked together as the living did. And each time he placed his hand against her warm skin, he felt her pulse quicken. His nearness both terrified and excited her—

it was a quickly addicting drug. "I do not need any assistance in wooing you."

"Is that what this is, then? You are courting me?"

"I thought I had made that quite clear. Forgive me. Should I invite you to the theatre instead?"

"Perhaps."

"Consider it done."

"Please do not insult me by fooling me into thinking this is all not some sick game of yours. Do you find yourself a toy to play with in every city you destroy?"

He watched her, curious at her sudden ire. "You are trying to find any excuse you can muster to refuse me, aren't you, Miss Parker? If not the validity of your curiosity and desire toward me, if not my murderous ways, then you would paint me a malicious womanizer? You would shun me for that you think I am merely after the prize you keep between your legs?"

The muscle in her jaw twitched as she watched the street ahead of them, those amber-brown eyes of hers stormy and thoughtful. "You could have far better prizes than me, Count. I can't imagine someone with your experience finds it entertaining to dally with those who know not where to begin in such physical affairs."

"Enough. I will hear no more self-defamation from you. I am here with you this night, no one else. I ignore the threat of your houseguests to walk with you."

"Why?"

"You know why."

Her wince betrayed that yes, she did. That her clever mind had already worked out the secret he had refused to speak out loud. He needn't bother. She could hear it plain, each time he touched her.

She could see the whole of him. She could hold the

Heart of Dracula

facets of him and know him for what he was where all others might fail. That was what he wished for.

See me, empath. See my soul...and love me for what I really am.

Hope welled in his chest. A terrible, insidious thing.

"Why do you let me walk free? You could just as easily have me in chains and keep my mind in thrall to yours. I cannot fight you. You've proven that much quite clearly."

"And if perhaps you had known me a few thousand years ago, such would be the case." He could not help but let himself imagine her shackled to his bed, her body naked and prone, tears stinging her eyes as she begged for mercy, the pleas changing into desperate need for him as he entered her mind and eased her fears away. Her agony would turn to bliss as she opened herself, whimpering not in terror but instead for his touch. It was a delicious sight, and he felt his heart lurch once in his chest as his body found life at the thought of it. But he forced it away. "It would be a terrible waste."

"A waste of what?"

"You."

And there was the delicate blush on her pale features. It came to her so quickly, and he found it amusing to draw from her. It was fascinating to him how furtive and shy she was—a beautiful thing like her—and it made her all the more precious to him. That she was unaccustomed to the advances of a man was not what he found interesting. He had no care for whether a woman was untouched or more experienced.

Indeed, she was not wrong. A woman who was not ignorant of the pleasures of the flesh was preferable to him, if he were given an otherwise equal choice. Purity was a human conceit. Empty mortal lies layered upon women to shame them and keep them powerless and a commodity. He cared not for it.

It was that she did not see in herself her own value that he found both troubling and served as an inspiration for how much he delighted in teasing her. He understood why the living avoided her. He could smell the feeling of the unnatural in the air about her, her connection to the aether that mortals found so unappealing. She was a reminder to them, whether they could sense it or not, that their lives were not quite as they saw them.

He had watched her at the gala thrown by that insipid little man Zadok had pretended to be and subsequently had taken for his own amusement. Vlad had stood in the shadows and observed her as she waited for the cruel Vampire King to arrive for nearly an hour.

The living avoided her. Men would glance over to her thoughtfully, then seem to shudder and look away. Like a lonely cemetery angel, standing guard over the corpses and souls of the deceased, she was both beautiful and loathsome to them.

She saw too much in those dark eyes. They looked into the soul. It was too much for the living to endure.

But not for him.

"Why did you dance with me at the gala, Maxine?"

"Hm?" She was startled at his sudden question—they had been walking for silence for some time—and she glanced up at him curiously before she turned away once more in thought. "I thought it would be rude to refuse a man's request to dance."

"I do not think you are one to care much for being rude. You were there to bait and potentially attack me. You had a very dangerous game playing out around you. Yet you took the chance to dance with a stranger. Why?"

Heart of Dracula

She paused. He witnessed the moment she came to her conclusion and found it sorely lacking. She took a defiant expression instead. "You know why," she accused him.

"What makes you say that?"

"The only questions you ask me are the ones you already know the answer to, Count Dracula."

He chuckled. She was correct. "Then why do you suppose I ask them at all?"

She hesitated, and when the answer came to her, she flinched. Watching her untangle his strings was an addicting game. He had moved a piece upon the board that she had not expected and found herself cornered. She would have to sacrifice a pawn to move her queen to safety. "You ask them to see if I am brave enough to answer you."

"Correct." He slipped his hand over the back of hers where it rested at his elbow. "Why did you dance with the man who approached you? Did you find the face I wore more appealing than my own?"

"No."

"Then why take his hand?"

"I felt…something else about him. Something deeper. Something I now recognize as you. Or you were hypnotizing me."

"I was doing no such thing. You can sense when I am in your mind. You would have known me for what I was in that moment."

"Why did you pretend at all?" She shook her head. "Why hide yourself? You know my home, and you need no invitation to come inside. You could have taken me or introduced yourself in any other manner. Why like that?"

"You know the answer."

"Yes." A playful grin crossed her features. Oh, how he treasured that look upon her face. He adored her fear. It was intoxicating, but he looked forward eagerly to the day it was replaced with that—her fire—instead. "I suppose I am seeing if you are brave enough to answer me."

"Touché, madam." He bowed his head once. "I drew you out into the open because I wished to better know my opponent. I wanted to see if you could recognize the situation in which you had been placed and how you would play your hand. Also, by doing so, I better ensured that you were not simply some whimpering, terrified thing lying at my feet, begging for your freedom. I admit I tire of attempting to converse with catatonic individuals."

She laughed. That was not the response he was expecting. "Then perhaps you should stop frightening them so."

"Precisely why I approached you in the manner I did." He hummed. "And now I am glad for it."

"You mean to say you enjoy speaking with me, Vlad? That this is not merely the means to the ends you seek?"

"I seek many ends." He grinned. She slapped him in the chest. He blinked at the sudden show of violence from her, then roared in laughter. "Oh, Maxine. I do enjoy you very much. And not simply because I enjoy playing with my food." He cast her a wicked grin and was delighted to see the pink rise in her cheeks once more. He paused, and added, finding the inspiration to be honest with her, "I danced with you wearing a false face because I wished to see how you would speak with me if you were not aware of what I was. How we might have been, should the circumstances be different. If this were to be another world, and I a living man."

"It is not your vampirism that troubles me, Vlad." They had come to a small park in the road, a gathering of a few benches beneath several trees. She turned to look at him, stopping their progress. She reached out to touch his elbow, and he obediently turned to face her.

It was so rare that others chose to touch him.

"Oh?" He challenged her assertion that it was not his inhumanity that was the source of her unease. "I have trouble believing that."

She shook her head, insisting. "It is what you seek to do that troubles me. That you are what you are is...frightening. I feel as though I am in a cage with a hungry tiger each time you look at me. But I do not blame the cat for thinking me its food. I do not fault you for your nature."

"Then what troubles you? Why do you hide from me?" He lifted a hand to her cheek and let his fingers brush against the warmth he saw there. He knew his touch was tepid. To her credit, and his deep pleasure, she had not once flinched away from it. "Shall we speak of our dream, now?"

He felt her soul there, close to his, an inexplicable and uncanny sensation. It was truly unique. He was eager to discover how it might join them when they were paired in other ways. He idly wondered who would be inside whom.

Her face went crimson nearly in an instant, and she drew back from him. He let her go, and he watched as she paced around the bench, a hand against her cheek where he had touched her. "I...I am sorry that happened."

"I enjoyed it."

"I am not apologizing to you." She glared at him, and he chuckled at the indignity in her eyes. "I am as I said—sorry that it happened at all."

"Why? Did you not find pleasure in it?" He let his voice drop into the sultry purr he knew was so wonderfully effective on her. "Reality will be much more enjoyable, I assure you."

She growled in frustration and turned her back to him, putting her head in both her hands. "Stop teasing me."

"Never."

She laughed, a weak, defeated sounding thing. She sighed and looked up at the sky, now pale purple as the stars began to emerge. "And when you have me, Vlad—"

"When." He pointed out to her the choice of words.

She hesitated and nodded. He grinned to himself, glad she did not see the expression upon the tiger who waited for her in his cage.

"When," she repeated. "What then?"

The emptiness in her tone—the forlorn quality to her question shattered his sense of victory and pride. He stepped to her side, and slipped a hand onto her shoulder, but did not turn her to face him. "What are you asking me, Maxine?"

Dark amber-brown eyes met his and sliced into his soul like a knife. "Will you forget me like all the rest?"

Who was this little mortal child, who could dig her hand so deep into his chest and tear out his heart without even knowing the damage she had done? He could not hide his grimace of pain as he turned away from her. The cards she had read for him, detailing that he had chosen to be numb to world to avoid feeling anything at all, had been terrifyingly accurate. He was both the helpless pauper and the terrible king in the same breath. She had seen that his egotism was not a lie to cover his helplessness—she understood that both could be very true at once.

She could see straight to the core of him, and she had no qualms about tearing him to pieces in the process.

It was only fair, he supposed.

Undone and exposed by a child, he hung his head. "Maxine, I—"

A gunshot rang out.

He felt pain in his shoulder.

She screamed.

―――

Bam.

The sound of a rifle echoed loudly in the courtyard. Vlad twitched backward as if something had punched him in the shoulder. His hand went to it, and it was instantly stained red. He grimaced in rage, not in pain, fangs distended and long.

She screamed.

Vlad hissed and vanished into an explosion of bats.

"Maxine!" Eddie raced up the street toward her, a long rifle in his hands. The barrel was smoking. He slung it onto his back. He reached out and took her forearm and pulled her a few steps down the road. "Maxine, we need to go—"

"Eddie?"

"I can't take him on alone." He huffed as he was now running down the street with her, pulling her down the street. "I can't—"

"No. You very well cannot."

That was the voice that brought so many people so much fear. It was dark, it was expansive. And it was furious. He stood in the center of the road, blocking their path. All pretense of humanity was gone from him. His face was a mask of anger, and his eyes...were pure red, from lid to lid. The wound on his shoulder was already gone.

Eddie pulled up to a screeching halt and pulled two revolvers from holsters at his hips. He pointed them at the vampire. "Back down, you toothy cunt, or I'll fire."

"And you think you can stop me?" Vlad sneered. He

wore the expression of something that thought of the boy as nothing more than an ant. And he was likely right. "You? Where all others have failed? Tell me, boy, have you even struck puberty yet?"

"Fuck you, you—"

"Enough!" She stepped around Eddie, stunning him. She took hold of both barrels of his guns and pointed them straight down at the ground. "Eddie. Please. This is how you die, if you do this."

"Maybe I can stop him," the boy insisted. "I can." His words were strong. But what she felt from him was only terror.

"No...you can't," she murmured and placed a gloved hand on his cheek. "And you know you can't. It's all right."

"Maxine," Vlad's voice echoed easily in the empty street without trying, "come to me."

She glanced over her shoulder. "I leave with you, and he lives. Neither you nor any of your creatures touches him."

Vlad bared his teeth once more like a feral animal. "He seeks to kill me, empath. You would have me foster mercy for one who seeks *my* death."

"He seeks to stop you from murdering a city! You are not some helpless innocent lamb. Do not pretend you are somehow wronged by him."

"Mind your words."

"And you mind yours, vampire." It was her turn to be angry. "You spare his life until the dawn comes tomorrow, or I take his gun and bury a bullet in my brain. Then where will you be without your new shiny toy? Left to return to your siege of the city, I suppose."

Vlad flinched. His anger faltered. She wounded him. She could feel his hurt from where she stood some twenty feet away. She regretted it immediately, but it was too late to

Heart of Dracula

take it back. "Maxine…" When he blinked, his eyes were no longer pure red from lid to lid. His voice was no longer angry, but…mournful. He held out his hand to her. "Come to me."

It was no longer a command. It was a plea. *Do not harm yourself,* it whispered. *Let me protect you.*

Did he honestly care? Did she honestly matter?

She turned to Eddie, who was watching the whole thing as if someone was putting on some sort of farcical play in the middle of the street. "Ma'am, don't ask me to do this. I can't leave you."

"You can, and you will. Your word, Vlad Tepes Dracula," she called over her shoulder to the vampire. "I will have your word."

"He will not be harmed. By neither me, nor any of my creatures. I am not to be blamed if he is struck by a carriage in the street, am I?" And there was the Vampire King she recognized. Cynical. Jaded. His wound in his heart had already healed like the one in his shoulder.

Or it had on the outside, at any rate.

"Go, Eddie. Please." She put her gloved hand on the boy's cheek once more and stroked it. He would be a handsome man. If he lived that long. "With me, he is distracted. He will not wage his war until I am dead, or his. I will hold on as long as I can. I will buy you all time. Now please…go. Save yourself a pointless death."

His Adam's apple bobbed, and he nodded, clearly sick to his stomach at the thought, but unable to argue. He glared over her shoulder at the vampire. "Fuck you."

"Children these days."

Maxine rolled her eyes at Vlad's snide comment. Eddie backed away several steps, then a few more, then turned and ran. When she was alone and the boy was gone, she turned to face Vlad. He still stood where he had been before.

"I was foolish and lowered my guard." His expression softened, but barely. "You seem to inspire that in others." He held out his hand. "Come with me. You will live as a guest in my home. Every need shall be cared for. You shall not be kept in a cage."

"Do I have a choice, Count?"

He dropped his hand to his side. "No."

She nodded. She suspected as much. She may not have a choice whether to become the "guest" of the vampire, but she could choose whether she went sobbing and screaming or with her head held high.

She walked up to him and felt his gaze on her every step of her approach. As she drew near, he lifted his hand again. She sighed and slipped hers into his. With a firm pull, he yanked her into his chest and banded an arm around behind her back. His other hand caught her chin and tilted her head back to look up at him. "Do not mistake my kindness for weakness."

He was furious. She saw it now, seething in his red eyes. The night had not gone the way he had wished it to. He had lost this round of the game and was now trying to make it very clear that the board was still his.

"I never would." She let her hands curl into the fabric of his coat. "Do not mistake my surrender for submission."

A dangerous grin flashed across his chiseled features, and she watched in fascinated horror as his canines grew long, sliding from his jaw like the fangs of a snake. "We shall see about that…"

She did not fight him as he tilted her head away. She did not make a sound as his hand slipped from her chin into her hair, fisting it in his fingers, holding her still. He bent to her neck, and she only gasped as he slid his tongue up along the line of her throat, tender from the previous night.

It was only as his fangs broke into her skin that she made a sound at all. And it was not one of pain that he drew from her. It was a moan of pleasure, and she pressed up against him, searching for more.

She let her eyes drift shut.

18

Another vision. This time, she did not stand in a field of mud and gore. She was standing atop the steeply pitched roof of a tower of a castle. She squeaked in surprise as she saw how very close to the edge she was and flew back from the lip that would send her tumbling down hundreds of feet into the darkness below.

She impacted something firm.

It chuckled.

An arm snaked around her waist, holding her against his chest. She knew who it was without looking. She could feel him there around her. She recognized the evergreen forest before her. She had seen the mountain range before in her mind, images stolen from his memories.

"Vlad?"

"We are sleeping in my home. Your gift is insistent and difficult to avoid."

"Does it bother you?"

"Hardly."

He was wearing a long, black, crimson-lined cape. It whipped in the wind around her. It was tattered, ragged, and

Heart of Dracula

torn. Holes in the rich fabric revealed the stars and the crimson moon behind it. For all the world it looked like jagged, broken claws tearing angrily at the sky.

He was a monster.

"This is who I am. This is what I am."

She shivered. He had bitten her again, and everything had gone dark. He had put her under. She had no idea where she was, but she knew it was with him. "You can hear my thoughts now as well?"

"Yes. You are part of me now. I held it at bay yesterday as best I could to keep from alarming you. But here, in this place, I fear it's inescapable. Your blood beats within my heart."

Her hand went to her throat, but here in the dream, she had no marks to remind her of what he had done. Only the memories of how it had felt. She felt her face explode in heat as she blushed violently at how wantonly she had responded to the pleasure it had brought her. She knew if he had rolled up her skirts, she wouldn't have stopped him. She would have let him—

He could hear her thoughts. She shoved them back into a dark corner and screamed at them to be silent.

He chuckled again, his arm tightening slightly. "There is no shame in what you felt. Or in what you feel now."

"As you've said. You hope that is true. I do not think it's proven fact."

Something white breezed by her face. She turned to find the source, looking up at the man who towered behind her. He was another older self once more, with long white hair. His face was as stern, regal, and aristocratic as she remembered it, but the features were different. His clothing was older, perhaps five hundred years or thereabouts, and the garments of a man who was royalty. He was, after all, wasn't he?

But she knew those crimson eyes. She knew the feeling of his mind around her. His soul.

"I am very old, Maxine Parker. Never forget that." His words carried such weight that she could not find the words to reply at first.

She looked back out at the forest stretched out before them. "Where is this place?"

"Somewhere I once called home for a time. Carpathia."

The simple word—home—was enough to shatter the dream around them. Something wrenched her back out of his memories and into hers.

Home.

A terrible word.

It was something she had never truly had.

No, no! Damn it! No! Not here...not now...not like this!

She knelt on the carpet, her dress around her feet. She was weeping into the blue brocade pattern. Her head was in her hands. Her mother had been shouting at her. She had felt the sting of her mother's hand against her cheek. That was what put her where she was now, squarely in the center of the floor, sobbing.

There was someone else in the room with her. He had been the cause of her mother's ire. He had been a soldier. Blood covered his gray uniform, put there by the bullet holes that had punctured his lungs and ended his life.

She could speak to souls. Living or the dead.

And after the great war that divided their country, there were many...many dead to be heard.

He did not speak in words but in grief. In sorrow. He was so very sorry for how he had lived, and now it was too late to change anything. He was just a boy of seventeen. Now he would never see the rest of his life.

She had been talking to him, trying to console him. Her mother had once more found her talking to the empty air. Terrified that she was losing her daughter to insanity—something Maxine herself had pondered—she had flown into a rage.

She knew she would bruise from the slap to her face.

A hand took hers. One that was cold to the touch. He pulled her up from her knees, and as she rose, she was no longer the frightened, heartbroken seven-year-old girl. She was herself once more. She didn't turn to look at the face of the man who had lifted her up from her memory. She felt his presence all the same.

A dark rumble came from behind her. "You fled this place."

"She tried to kill me, after my stepfather…after—"

At his stunned silence, she pulled her hand from his. She wanted to weave her fingers between his, to find comfort in his embrace, but she had to remember who—what—he was. And to remember his game. She was his prey.

She felt his curiosity. His burning need to see.

"Please. Don't make me." She put her hand over her eyes. "No one has ever…I've never told anyone."

"Maxine." His voice was soft, gentle, with more compassion than she could have expected from him. She looked up at him, meeting his gaze. She couldn't hold it. There was too much there. She turned away and walked around the now-frozen memory of the ghostly and bleeding soldier boy. She had finally succeeded in convincing him to let go of his lost future and all his regrets. He had faded from her view as something akin to a current pulled him onward.

Leaning against the window frame, she looked out at the Virginia countryside and the white columns that decorated the front of the manor. "She was a well-to-do woman. Social appearances meant more to her than anything else, especially since father died. More to her than even me, her only child. She was convinced I was going mad. Honestly, at the time, I wasn't so certain she was wrong. I talked to people who weren't there. I told people what they were feeling. I always knew when other people were lying. That might have been enough for her to withstand. She would only keep me out of the public eye long enough to marry me to some unsuspecting gentleman and I would no longer be her problem."

She picked at the paint of the sill with her fingernails. There was a small gap in the paint there that she remembered. It wasn't the first time she had stood here and done this. Although her company was quite remarkable this time. "But then...she remarried. He was a nice man. He never said anything wrong. Never did anything out of line. He was gentle. Sweet. But there was a darkness in him. A seething, terrible sickness that I could feel whenever he was near me. It crawled over me like insects. I couldn't stand him."

A hand settled on her shoulder. Cold, but not unwelcome. She shut her eyes and tried to force herself not to relive the memory of what followed. But it was hopeless.

Her bedroom. The dead of night. The moon was bright outside, casting shadows of the mullions across the floor. The windows were open, the lace curtains blowing in the breeze. They danced like figures at a ball.

A ball she wished to attend someday. She had been a child. She had dreamed of being a proper lady like her mother wanted. She dreamed of being a princess, and

Heart of Dracula

having some dashing prince sweep in like a fairy tale. But it was all simply that—a pointless dream.

She stood in the shadows of the room, watching her smaller self as she lay under the covers. A girl of twelve, maybe thirteen. She didn't really quite remember. It hadn't mattered at the time.

The door clicked open. A figure slipped into the room. A man. Nothing more than a shadow of a monster. He slipped to her bed and under the covers with her.

Then...she had felt his hands.

Her memory of herself screamed.

Muffled against a hand against her small mouth.

"This was the first time it happened," she whispered to the vampire standing at her back. "The first time I destroyed a soul. I had always been a sensitive creature. I could always tell others what they were feeling, or I knew when they were lying. But until this point, I wasn't a danger to others. It wasn't until he attacked me that I could no longer touch another."

The man screamed as well. He howled in ear-piercing agony. He fell from the bed, landing with a heavy *thump* on the ground, limp and lifeless. But neither was he dead.

The little girl screamed. And screamed. And then couldn't scream anymore. Servants came in carrying lamps. The light washed over the face of the man on the ground. His eyes wide, mouth open in a silent scream. His chest was heaving. He was alive.

But empty.

She turned from the dream and forced it away. She was back in her old parlor once more. Tears streamed down her cheeks, unchecked. She had cried over that night many times before, and she would do it many times again in her life.

Arms circled her, pulling her close to a broad chest. She leaned her head against him and let herself take the comfort that was being offered. When he broke the silence, she felt the rumble of his voice against her cheek almost more than she heard him. "What happened next?"

"He starved to death. My mother blamed me for it. She didn't know how I had done it, but she knew that somehow, I was at fault. I tried to tell her what he had planned to do to me. I felt his intention the moment he touched me. But she didn't believe me. She hit me, saying I was lying, disparaging her second dead husband. She told me that if it wasn't for me, neither he nor my father would be dead."

A hand stroked over her hair slowly, soothingly. "The cruelty of humanity knows no bounds."

"I'm sure you've seen far worse in your years than a mother ill-fit for the job."

"I have. But it makes the proof of it sting no less. What happened next?"

"Please, no more of this." She pushed away from him and walked across the room, returning to the window by which she had spent so many years reading, or dreaming, or doodling. But it seemed she could not escape him, not even here.

A hand on her shoulder turned her to face him. A chill finger curled under her chin and urged her to look up at him. Crimson eyes flicked between hers, searching for something. His scrutiny was hard to withstand. When she tried to pull away from him, he pressed her shoulder against the wall firmly to keep her there.

He would have her whole story from her. She sighed and found herself looking at his cravat and the ruby that sat pinned at the knot to avoid watching his eyes. She could not take the scrutiny she saw there. "One night, a year or so after my stepfather died, she snuck into my room with a blade. She meant to end my life."

Maxine touched a spot on her ribs, over where she had the smallest scar. "She had the blade a quarter inch into my flesh before I touched her. I was going to tear her soul to pieces like I did his. But I...I couldn't do it. I came close. She screamed at what she felt, fell into the corner, and would not stop crying. I do not know what she saw when I put my hand on her. Perhaps she saw the piece of my stepfather's soul that I still carried inside me and the mental poison he suffered. I was fourteen, maybe fifteen. I gathered all I could fit into a bag, and I left."

"A girl of fifteen, out in the world alone."

"Yes. But I do not begrudge it. I've met many others who have had it far worse. The first few months in the wild were...unpleasant." She cringed. "I joined with a caravan of circus folk and Roma. They did not judge me for what I could do. One of the Roma, a real psychic, could see that I was an empath and sought to teach me. They saw the chance to make money from me, and I saw the chance to have a tent over my head and food in my stomach."

He chuckled. She felt him stroke a hand through the long curls of her hair, combing it through his fingers. "Clever girl, joining them. They would certainly covet the chance to profit from someone with true skill and not simply well-spun lies."

His touch made her shiver as he settled his hand at the back of her neck, still tangled in her hair. He pulled her forward and away from the wall. She went rigid, but the embrace was too alluring, too comforting, as he brought her against his chest. He slung his other arm around her, holding her to him. "What sent you away from them?"

"I thought perhaps I could control my gift. I thought, as I

aged and grew in skill, I could stop myself from destroying those who touched me. There was a young boy. He was kind. He was sweet. He was a true son of the Roma."

She smirked slightly and shut her eyes. She felt the memory around her, but she felt him, most of all. "He was like me, a little bit *other*. Able to speak to animals in a way that was not natural. He kissed my cheek one day." Her hand drifted to touch the spot where that boy had only expressed the most innocent of young loves. "His name was Chal." Her voice choked, but she had to finish her story. "He never woke."

Silently, he pulled her to him, urging her back into his arms. She bowed her head as he pressed her cheek to his chest. She could not hear his heartbeat. He had none, after all. Well...not normally. Even still, there was a strange kind of consolation in his touch.

"For such reasons you distance yourself from the living."

"Yes. I do not like to be reminded of what I cannot have. I hear their thoughts, their feelings, their love for each other. I cannot share in it. Besides, most others do not find a general desire to be near me. I unsettle them by my very presence. You understand."

"I do."

Her childhood "home" melted away from around her, and instead she found herself in a parlor. The wallpaper was a rich crimson damask. A tall chair stood by a roaring fireplace, filling the room with much needed warmth. Darkness clung to the edges of the room, and she could almost envision eyes there looking back at her. He had taken them away from her melancholy past and into his present.

The hand on the back of her neck shifted, curling around her chin, tilting her head up to look at him. "You are meant to be mine, Maxine..." His thumb trailed along her

Heart of Dracula

lower lip, and she shivered. "Feel me, and you will know it to be true."

She placed a hand over where his heart should beat. The silk fabrics of his clothing were soft underneath her touch, but she could also feel the strength that lay beneath it. More than the undeniable power in his body, but what dwelled deep beyond that.

She knew to what he was referring. She had tried to ignore it up until this point—something about him that was pulling her close. She blamed it on his charisma, his undeniably seductive charm. But there was a far more insidious current that drew her near him. When he twined with her, when she felt him there in the darkness of the ether, tangling around her like roots of a tree, it was not horror she felt. It was not disgust. She could feel his thousands of years. Time immemorial that stretched behind him. A future that spanned a million times longer lay before him. A road that stretched for eternity in both directions.

It was empty. Save for one figure upon it.

No matter the face he wore, no matter the name he chose, she could see him for what he was.

He was alone.

Skies of stars that she did not know. Trees, and desert sands, and white cliffs upon the ocean. Cities, and markets, and all of humanity filled him. Love, and loss, and grief, and tragedy. Joy, and agony.

He was all those things.

Sinner, saint, husband, murderer, tyrant, fiend, demon, and lover. A hundred thousand facets of a ruby, one for each of the souls who had touched him. Nearly maddening in its expanse.

And he was right. It felt like *home.*

God help her, *gods* help her, whoever might listen…she

looked into that emptiness and sought only to do her part to fill it.

Gods help her, she was falling in love.

Crimson eyes shone in the darkness like the ruby in her metaphor. "Where others may turn away from you, I find I am drawn to you like a moth to a flame," he murmured, echoing her own thoughts. "I shall have you, and I shall not let you go."

"And if I wish to be free?" It was an empty threat. She did not wish for such a thing, and he knew it.

The flash of a grin, of too-sharp teeth, were all she could see as the dream around her faded to nothing. With it came the rumble of his voice, dusky and dangerous. "You shall never be rid of me."

19

Maxine awoke in darkness. She felt an ache on her throat, and she lifted her hand to touch the sensitive spot she found there. It stung to the touch, but not terribly.

She did not feel as awful as she expected. She did not feel dizzy, or woozy, or strange. All the opposite. She felt oddly rested. It was the second time she had felt the kiss of a vampire, and she knew Vlad had been exercising restraint both times. He was trying to show her that he could be trusted. That his touch was not to be feared.

The jury was still out, in her opinion.

If only she could see where she was. This was not her own bed this time. Once Eddie had opened fire, her window of freedom—a ruse and a lie as it may have been—had slammed shut. While she knew where she was not, it did not help her know where she *was*.

Lifting her hand into the impenetrable darkness around her, it hit something six inches above her face. Something covered in silk fabric and upholstery. Odd. Reaching to her side, she felt a similar surface a foot to her right. And to her left.

She was in a box. An upholstered box.

I am in a coffin!

Panic struck her, perfect and instantaneous. It overrode everything else. She squeaked out a cry for help as both her hands struck the lid. It budged, if barely. There was hope! There was—

Hands caught her wrists. She screamed, loud in the tiny space. *Monsters! I have to escape—*

A dark laugh came from beneath her. She was not alone. The feeling under her had not entirely been the base of the coffin. It had been him…Vlad.

She was lying in a casket with the King of Vampires.

"Be still, my dear." His voice resonated through her. He folded her hands over her. It was also about then that she realized she was not wearing her coat. Or her dress. She felt a thick blanket over her, and beneath that the silk of her slip.

"You undressed me?" She took shelter in her indignancy.

"I could not abide by sleeping with such a tangled mess of fabric. I doubt it would feel any more comfortable for you." He was deeply amused. "Did you not sleep better last night than you did the prior two when I left you fully clothed?"

She sputtered angrily before snarling at him. "It might also have had something to do with you drinking my blood and—"

"I did not take enough to leave meaningful impact. You slept well because you had company, I think."

She sighed, frustrated. She hated how right he always seemed to be.

"If you have a chill, I can fetch you another blanket. I apologize I bring no warmth of my own to this affair."

"I find it rather alarming to be in a coffin with you, and

Heart of Dracula

now nearly naked as well. My issues with this arrangement do not include the fact that you are cold to the touch."

"Good." He shifted. She squeaked as he rolled onto his side, placing her against the upholstered base of the coffin. The tendrils of his hair brushed against her cheek. She felt his breath pour across her cheek. Her hand flew to his chest, and she felt a soft cotton shirt over an otherwise bare chest. Instantly, her face grew hot.

He quickly made it worse. One of his hands slid underneath the hem of her shift and splayed over her stomach. "I am very glad my touch does not trouble you."

She pulled in a startled gasp and grabbed his wrist, trying to pull him away. "It does!"

"Oh?"

"Not the temperature, perhaps, but its presence!"

He chuckled darkly and lowered his lips to her cheek, kissing her there, slow and sultry. "Truthfully?" His hand slid to her side then traveled northward underneath the silk. Threatening to travel farther. "Our dream the other night would have me believe otherwise."

She felt his desire. His amusement. His hunger for her. She felt them as if the emotions were her own. Skin to skin, soul to soul, there was no separating his mind from hers.

His desire drew hers from behind her fear, coaxing it forward like a frightened foal in the back of a barn. Urging her to trust him. Promising that there was no reason to be afraid.

She jolted, swatting at his chest. Suddenly, the air in the casket felt hot, thick, and too close. He paused in his upward drift of his touch, instead content to draw slow circles on her skin with his fingertips. The slight scratch of those long nails sent goosebumps flooding over her body.

He was too much. She was standing on the edge of a cliff, and he was urging her to jump. "Please, I can't—"

"You can." He feathered his kisses slowly lower, traveling to her throat, and she gasped as he kissed the spot where he had bitten her. When his tongue rolled over the wound, she whimpered and writhed beneath him. "You enjoy my embrace. Do not lie to me. I can see through you, even as you see through me. It is not only my desire I feel, is it?"

It felt so good when he had bitten her. Both times, the pleasure had been nothing like she had ever felt before. She had never been with a man, but she couldn't imagine it felt anything like that. She found herself wondering what it would be like to share herself with the vampire over her. Images of her dream flashed in her mind, of the feel of him between her legs, buried deep inside her.

Did he truly want her?

Or was this all a game to him?

A deep, angry growl rumbled in his chest. "Do not ask such foolish questions." His lips hovered over her ear. "You are too intelligent to be such an idiot."

She bristled but felt her face grow warmer at his words. She forgot he could hear her thoughts. He knew her doubt for what it was. "I—"

"You are afraid. I understand. But you have nothing to fear from me. I swear it. Do you want me, Maxine?"

She was too ashamed to answer. "It's not...it's not you that I am worried about."

"That is a small consolation. If not I, then what?"

"You see what happens when you kiss me or if I sleep in your embrace. Our minds become...muddled. If you saw too deep into me, if you...found me lacking, I do not know how I would survive. I—" She broke off. She didn't want to admit to him the truth. But she might as well have been hiding the

Heart of Dracula

moon for how much good it did her. He could see through her.

"You fear rejection. You fear I will abandon you like all others have done."

She remained silent, knowing that was well enough a confirmation for him. Still his fingers traced circles along her ribcage. The sensation was distracting. It made her feel something like electricity was crawling over her. It sparked something in her that was exciting and terrifying in the same breath.

"My darling Maxine..." he purred as he kissed her jawline, his breath growing warmer. "I will never spurn you. I do not give up an inch once taken. Once you are mine, I will never let you go."

She wanted this.

She wanted to run away.

She wanted desperately to remind herself that she was his prey. She was his prisoner. He had threatened to take all that she was. She fought hard to cling on to that thought, but it shattered and fell away like a shield made of thin ice.

So, she sought another defense. "I might hurt you. I might lose control."

"You might. You can harm me. I may not be as fragile as a mortal soul, but you could do me damage if you wished it. Do you?"

"What?"

"Do you wish me harm, my sweet? Do you wish to rend my soul to smithereens and send it to the void? Rid both me and this world of my curse?"

"I...I don't understand."

"You hold me in the palm of your hand, even as I hold you in mine. I am trusting you with my very being. Do you mean to end me? Remember our accord. No lies between us."

Any lie would be pointless now. He could hear her, feel her, sense all that she felt. And in return, she did him. And his words were the truth. She could destroy him.

And she found she despised the idea of even trying. "N... no." It was true.

"Even to spare this city?"

"Please, do not be so cruel to me."

He did not heed her plea. "Even to spare this world?" He leaned down and kissed her throat again, rolling his tongue along her. She let out a gasp and arched into him, pressing herself against his hand still roaming her side.

"Please—"

"Go on." He slid his hand farther north, over the swell of her bare breast. She gasped as he squeezed the flesh that he found. He was not shy in his embrace, and she found her back leaving the coffin to seek out more of him as he cupped and toyed with her. "Save this world from my curse."

She could only moan as he groped at her, his touch firm and insistent. His fingers found the hard peak and pinched it lightly. She bit back a howl, tossing her head away from him, squirming. He had thrown kerosene into the fire that had already been left smoldering. It roared to life, and she felt as though she could barely breathe.

Destroying him was the last thing she wanted. It was the last thing on her mind. She wanted him. She wanted to feel him. Gods be damned, she was beginning to yearn for his touch. "No. No—I can't—I—"

"Good girl..."

She whimpered at his sultry words. He did not let up from his attentions. His lips were at her throat again, kissing and lapping at the closed wound, sensual and seductive, that low purr rising again. She clung to him in desperation, her hands seeking the bare skin of his chest underneath his shirt. He felt like velvet over marble. Just the slightest softness over what rippled beneath.

She should tell him to stop. She should push him away. She could not find the words. He gave her ample opportunity. He had not bitten her. He had not placed her in his thrall. There was no one to blame for this but her.

She had never known such *need*. And she did not know what to do.

"What do you wish from me?" His breath against her throat was no longer cold but hot, pooling against her. "I could take you as a man, as a vampire, or as both…all this will come to pass in time. I can be gentle, or I can be cruel. Whatever you desire, it will be yours."

His hand released her breast, sliding back down her stomach, slipping underneath the drawstring of her undergarment. She gasped, her eyes flying wide as he unabashedly slid his hand between her legs and cupped her core.

"Wait—"

He chuckled darkly. She could feel his grin against her shoulder as he clearly took great pride at what he found. Her body had answered his call with a rabid fervor. "You lie to me still, my Lady of Souls."

"I'm not—"

"Shush." His fingers began to explore her, and her words cut off in a soft cry. She was helpless to stop him, namely because she found no desire to do anything of the sort. His sharp claws brought an edge of danger that only served to quicken her heartbeat.

"I can't…I can't do this. It's too much. Please—"

He let out a thoughtful hum as he rolled his tongue over

the puncture wounds in her throat. "Allow me to bring you pleasure, Maxine. Allow me to do this much, and I will go no farther this night."

When his thumb nudged over the sensitive bud at her core, she bit back a startled cry at what it did to her and at the sensations that ripped through her body. She felt as though she were made of molten lava, yet she felt as fragile as glass.

If he left her now, she was not certain what she might do. She was too scared to let it progress, but too desperate to let it end. *I am a goddamn bloody fool.*

She nodded.

He growled, a sound of hunger and desire, and she felt his fangs pierce her throat again, reopening the wound he had paid her. This time, there was no pain at all. She merely felt the pleasure rush over her.

As he drank, his hand deftly toyed with her body, careful not to prick her with his sharp nails. He was skilled. Too skilled. She whimpered and moaned beneath him, twisting weakly in his grasp.

When the purr began again, she was undone. She arched and writhed, her mind going pure white as ecstasy crashed over her in a wave. It was like nothing she had ever felt. No memory, no stolen dreams, could have ever compared to what washed over her. Her mind went reeling into bliss. She cried out.

"Vlad!"

She cried his name as her pleasure consumed her. Vlad shared in it like it was his own, and he nearly spent himself then, without ever being touched. He growled in frustration.

Heart of Dracula

This link of theirs—their shared minds and emotions—was as troublesome as it was amusing. While it was an intoxicating drug and a wonderful game, it challenged his control.

He nearly broke his promise. He wanted to split her wide, to bury himself in her volcanic heat, to feel that trembling and quivering body he held in his hands clench tight around him. He wanted to feel them joined in all ways at once—in body, in blood, and in soul. He wanted to take her like she had wished for in her dream.

Patience, you old bastard.

She was panting for air as he pulled his teeth from her throat and let his fingers cease their ministrations. She was twitching, her hands weakly tangled in his shirt. One of them had found its way to press against his chest, her palm over his beating heart.

It would still its tempo soon enough, but for now, he would relish in the warmth she shared. He had barely taken a mouthful of her. It had been enough.

It had certainly served its purpose.

She had asked for his bite. She had asked for his pleasure. She had wanted him. She was too afraid to do much more—yet—but he would lead her down that road by the hand. He knew now he would not have to drag her behind him.

He placed a kiss to her lips, knowing she would taste her own blood on him. To her, bitter and copper. To him, the bliss of life itself. But she did not turn away from him. She did not resist him. She kissed him back.

Beautiful girl. So innocent and yet so wicked in the same breath. I think I have become besotted with you.

If she heard him, he did not find that he cared. He was an open book to her—a library with all his tomes and pages thrown open for her to read. There was nothing he could hide from her. No sin of his that she could not see. He belonged to her. And she was kissing him back.

Perhaps that was what drew him to her now. Perhaps that was what brought him so much joy to watch her twist in his arms.

It was still midday. He could feel the position of the sun, and it was pulling on him to return to slumber. He nuzzled closer to her, tucking her head against his shoulder, and wrapped his arm over her. Her heart was still pounding a rapid rhythm in her chest, but it was slowly calming. He pulled the blanket up over them both. It was for her benefit, not his. "Sleep, darling Maxine." He kissed the top of her head. "This time, I shall do what I can to leave your dreams alone."

He felt her pull in a shaking breath and let it out slowly. He knew how she wished to fight him, to rail against him. To push him away and weep because she wore invisible chains about her neck. She was torn.

And he could also feel how he comforted her. How she took shelter in his arms. He had kept his word. He had brought her pleasure and nothing more. And in turn, she did not send him to the void.

He wondered if she yet realized the chains in her hand did not run to her own neck. They ran to his. He belonged to her, his beautiful empath, his Lady of Souls, who held his very eternity and cradled it so carefully to her breast.

She could ruin him.

Instead, she embraced him.

She tucked her head closer underneath his chin, and he found himself smiling at the guileless and innocent gesture. He pulled her closer and felt her curl her hand against his chest. The wicked girl enjoyed what he did to her, and somehow remained a sweet flower all the same. It made for a wonderful combination.

Something blossomed unexpectedly in his heart.

Something dangerous and deadly.

He fought the urge to swear aloud.

Gods below, may you rot in your graves.

He loved her.

But he would not say the words. He would not frighten her so. She would ignore that which she must know to be true. She was too afraid, too overwhelmed, to see it for what it was.

At least...not yet.

20

Vlad had promised to try to stay out of her dreams. To his credit, it had worked. Either because he had stayed true to his word, or because she was too tired to rifle through the mind she felt so near to hers as she slept.

Wrapped in his arms, held close to his very being, she had felt safe. Cared for. She hadn't felt alone. As she woke, she reached out for him without realizing what she had done. But her fingers touched a pillow, not a vampire. She was still lying in the casket, but she could feel the pillow beneath her head. A thick fur blanket was pulled up over her, warm and comforting.

There was a faint light in the room, and she looked up to see the lid of the casket was hinged open. It was one of the styles of coffins that was tapered at the toes and the head. It was as lavish as she would expect from him. She could see the bits of shining black lacquered wood where the silk and piping had been carefully tailored to end.

She sat up, holding the fur blanket to her chest. She was still in her silk slip and undergarments. The curtains were pulled back, and the sun was setting, casting the room in

Heart of Dracula

ruddy hues of orange and amber, mixing with the blues and purples of twilight.

And there he stood at the glass, watching.

He was a breathtaking silhouette against the light. She was in awe of him. Handsome, beautiful, and terrible. He sought to destroy her city. To kill thousands to "feed his wolves." And what wolves they were, a cornucopia of beasts and monsters.

He has done such terrible things.

"I have."

She cursed under her breath.

Her invective made him chuckle. "Not accustomed to being the one whose thoughts are privy to others, I take it? How hypocritical." He was teasing her, but the expression on his cut-granite features was still hard. Something was troubling him. "Did you sleep well?"

"I did." No point in denying it. "Why must you sleep in a coffin? Isn't it a bit too apropos?"

He smiled faintly. "Perhaps. Perhaps I enjoy it. It also suitably blocks the light. My eyes are incredibly sensitive, as you can imagine. Even the thickest curtains cannot keep it from disturbing me. Yet I find the dankness of a basement or a tomb utterly unappealing."

"I cannot argue that point. I think if I found us now in some vaulted mausoleum I would be rather upset."

"Noted."

Pulling her legs underneath her, she kept the fur blanket tucked up over herself. It was a sad attempt to maintain her modesty—especially after what had transpired between them—but she felt obliged, nonetheless. "I think I may need my clothes."

"They are on the chair there." He gestured toward a pile

of fabric. "I have sent Walter to fetch you the rest of your belongings while the hunters remain distracted."

"I can go myself."

"No. You will not leave my home without me at your side."

"Why?"

"The boy marksman saw you choose me over a bid for freedom. You will now be suspect in their minds. They will think I have corrupted you."

"Have you?"

"Have I?" He cast a wicked and playful smile over his shoulder.

She resisted the urge to roll her eyes. "I am now officially your prisoner, then."

He turned to her, and his expression hardened. "If that how you wish to view this, then very well. The hunters you welcomed into your home will now mean to take you away from me. This I cannot allow."

"You do not own me, Vlad Dracula. You will let me go. You will set me free."

"No."

"I will leave this place."

He grinned, this time an entirely unfriendly expression. "You shall not. Not unless I stand by your side as you do it."

"You cannot—" Before she could react, before she could even make a sound or finish her sentence, she was suddenly on her back in the coffin. His hand was twisted in her hair, pinning her. He was over her, straddling her thighs. She went to scream, but his other hand snapped over her mouth, silencing her.

"Oh, but I can." Crimson eyes glittered down at her, catching the fading light of the sun and making them seem

Heart of Dracula

somehow even more unnatural than they were before. "I am a monster, make no mistake. You pondered it yourself."

He lowered himself, sliding his hand from her mouth, and replacing it with his lips. His kiss was angry and possessive. It was reminding her of her place in all this. Her head reeled with the passion behind it. The hunger. The desire. And how she seemed to be more than willing to throw all she knew of his truth away if only he would kiss her a little longer. When he broke the embrace, she struggled to catch her breath. Her heart was pounding in her ears.

His face hovered close over hers, his cold breath washing over her cheek. "You can tear my soul from my chest. Do it. Do it, if you wish to be free of me. Or your words are only bluster. A bluff."

"I should."

He pulled his head back, straightening enough that he could peer down at her in curiosity. There was no surprise or anger on his face—merely fascination. "And will you?"

"I don't...I don't know how." This was how she died; she was certain. Right in this moment, she was going to be obliterated.

He placed his hand over her throat. He did not squeeze, he did not lean down, he did not dig his sharp nails into her flesh. He simply placed it there and waited. "And if you knew how, would you do it? Would you destroy my soul and end my eternal life?"

"I—"

"Do not lie to me."

She swallowed the lump in her throat. "I don't know."

He smiled cruelly. "Good."

She would not cower from her fate. She watched him and forced her pounding heart to calm. Forced her fear away. "Will you kill me now? Tear out my throat like you have so many others? Certainly, it's the wisest choice."

His smile faded. "I see now you will mean trouble. I suppose I should do as you recommend." He lifted his hand from her neck and curled his fingers into his palm. He let his knuckles trace over her cheek slowly. "But no. I shall not kill you. It seems we are mutually incapable of destroying the other to save ourselves. Nor shall I release you. You are mine, Maxine."

"You cannot truly mean to keep me here."

"If you wish to walk the streets, you shall. If you wish to picnic in the Common, you shall. If you wish to sail the seas, you shall. If you wish to reside in London, or in Serbia, or travel to Egypt, the path is yours. I lay the world at your feet. Whatever you desire, you shall have it. Money and means are no longer any barrier you will ever know. But you shall do all this with me at your side."

"And when you tire of me, as you have all the others I see in the sea of blood in your mind? All those you have killed and lain in waste? Will you forget my name as well?"

He laughed, cruel and dark, and he sank down over her again. She held her breath as he nuzzled his cheek against hers and kissed her earlobe. "Pray that I do. For if you remain as enticing as you are to me now for even but a day's length longer, I think I shall never grow bored of you. I fear then you will come to hate me even more."

When she felt tears escape her eyes and streak into her hair, he let out a low disappointed hum. He kissed the tears away, one side and then the other. "No. No tears, my darling. You are too strong for that." He straightened. "I can hear your thoughts. You are caught in turmoil. You fight me, even as you wish for me to hold you in my arms. Why do you resist the happiness I can bring you? Why do you insist on remaining alone in this world?"

His words left a gaping hole in her armor. Then it came to her. The answer to his question. She tried to keep it away, tried to hold it back. But it was like holding back the tide with a teacup. It was futile.

And he could hear her thoughts as she could sense his emotions.

He grinned fiendishly. "Oh, my darling child..." He tore the blanket from her, tossing it aside, and he was suddenly there in its place, his leg between hers, his dark peacoat draping over her.

He kissed her again, and this time insistence and desire was what spurred him on. But it was no less bruising. His fingers slipped to the back of her neck and lifted her into him, wanting more of her.

It isn't the death he's caused that scares me.
I'm not even afraid he'll kill me like all the rest.
I'm afraid in the end I won't matter. I'll be another cobblestone in the empty streets he walks alone.
I do not want to bring him more heartbreak.

He chased away her thoughts with his embrace. Pushed away those emotions and replaced them with his own. He would have her. He would keep her. He was all that mattered now. His fingers twisted in the drawstring of her underwear, and she knew what he planned.

Something tore through her like lightning.

Her hand flew to his and stopped him. He parted his lips from hers, and she felt his breath, warming as it was, against her cheek. "You are correct. These things should not be rushed. And in my coffin is not where you should be taken for the first time."

He climbed off her and back out of the casket and

tugged on his clothing to straighten it. "I wish to take you to the opera tonight. Will you join me?"

She looked down at her lap for a moment and thought it through. She had no real ability to say no. More terrible was that she wanted to say yes.

She nodded once, silently.

"I will have Walter bring you some proper clothes." He leaned his head down to kiss her forehead. "I will return in an hour. I have some business to attend in the meanwhile."

Before she could say a word, he was gone.

She jolted, startled. She would have to learn to adjust to his abrupt comings and goings. She shook her head. She was torn in two.

I fear him. I want him. He walks in darkness alone, but so do I.

He is a monster, bathed in blood. This means my death...

She shut her eyes.

But perhaps he is right. Perhaps this is meant to be.

AS HE HAD PROMISED, clothing was brought to her. The red-haired vampire was a bashful thing, for all his outward stoicism. Walter didn't even look at her as he placed the stack of fabric by the door and nearly fled the room. She donned her corset and her dress, even if the laces were not pulled as tightly as society would have insisted. She found no means by which to pin up her hair in the supplies she had been brought. She was certain her hairpins were omitted on purpose.

He did very much prefer her hair down, it seemed. She sighed. It was improper for this day and age, but she also decided he likely did not care.

Heart of Dracula

She did her best to braid her hair. Finally, once she was dressed, she went to leave the room and explore her new "home." Upon opening the door, she yelped and jumped as there was a man standing on the other side. He was leaning an arm up on the jamb, grinning at her.

A vampire, at any rate.

"Good evening."

Zadok.

She was growing to loathe him. She glared at him accordingly. "Please get out of my way."

"I was told to see to your every need. And as my Master commands"—he placed a hand against his chest, fingers splayed wide—"so I must obey." The wicked smile on his face displayed that he had a great many ideas on what might constitute her needs.

"I think I rather dislike you."

He gasped in mock hurt and clutched his heart with both hands. "Oh, how tragic. And here I had hoped to don some leather gloves and take you to bed. Even with a layer between us, I know I could show you great joy." He grinned. "What do you say?"

She blanched and shook her head. "You are rude."

"That I am. *C'est la vie*, my love. Come. You must be hungry." He stepped from the door and walked down the hallway. "I have prepared you a small meal before you attend the opera with our beloved Master."

"He is not my Master."

"Mmhm." He shot her a playful wink over his shoulder. "Of course not. Come, come, the hour grows late."

Letting out a beleaguered grunt, she followed him. She had little else to do, and she was indeed starving. She touched the mark on her throat. She had found a silk scarf to wear to hide it, but it was tender.

The building was beautiful, if dimly lit. *Vampires likely have little need for bright gas lamps,* she realized. It occurred to her how little she knew about them.

Despite his showboating, there was something about Zadok that intrigued her. One thing only. "For someone who is so utterly brash and irritating, you are quite lonely, aren't you?" She would enjoy cutting him to the quick. Men like him deserved to be lowered a peg or two.

He paused in his steps and turned to look back at her. "I never sleep alone."

"You may sleep with flesh against yours, but you still sleep alone."

"And how do you know this?"

"I can hear all your emotions, Monsieur Lafitte. Your sadness, your loneliness, your wish for a family. Perhaps if you did not drive everyone away with your callous behavior, you would have one already."

"Uncanny..." Zadok breathed. His eyes were flashing in excitement. "Truly uncanny. You are a marvel."

She didn't like how he was watching her, and she gestured for him to continue to lead her away. With a flourish of a bow, they continued their trek. "How old are you, Zadok?"

"The lady takes interest in me!" He gasped in playful dramatism. "I thought perhaps you could not see me."

"You will quickly make me regret asking you anything at all."

"Touché, my lovely. I was born in the year 1442, in the north of France. I died twenty-five years later to the fangs of my sire."

"And what became of him?"

"He grew tired of his state of being and sought to greet the dawn." Zadok glanced at her again. "We are not all

Heart of Dracula

suited for immortality. Our gift is not a blessing to all. With him died the family you clearly know I desire. I serve our Master to fill that gap you so plainly see." He brought her to what looked like the kitchens. A plate of fruit, of meats and cheeses, and several slices of bread sat on the counter next to what looked like juice. "Please, eat."

She was happy to change the subject. "Are you well-versed in nursing your victims back to health?"

"Hm?"

She gestured at the plate of food.

He chuckled. "Oh. Yes. I fear I am. I tend to enjoy the spark a living companion brings to me. Your kind experience love with such brevity that you do so like wildfire. Our kind grow cold as the years climb on. When I find someone—"

"Like the poor aristocrat you've likely murdered by now?"

"Like Arthur," he continued with a sly smile. She sat on the stool in front of the food and began to eat as he talked. "I tend to ensure I do not end them too soon. He lives."

"And will you end him?"

"I will turn him if he wishes it. I will not kill him. He is a playful, morbid thing. I enjoy him too much to kill him for the fun of it. Why do you care?"

"I suppose I care for the fate of everyone. It is the curse of being an empath. Along with my inability to be touched."

"Dracula has found the means to do so."

"He is rather unique in his own gifts."

"I have my own *unique* gifts that might allow me to play with you too, you know."

Suddenly, he was also standing at her back and to her side. There were three of him in the room. Startled, she went to stand, but he pressed her back down. The one across from her took her hand in his and raised it to his lips. He kissed her ungloved fingers slowly, one by one. There was no soul behind it. Only the sensation of it against her skin. The other one was nuzzling into her hair. It happened too fast for her to respond, and when she went to pull away, she found she couldn't. He had her in his snare once more. His hypnotism had taken hold of her.

"I take good care of my pets," he purred darkly into her ear. "Spurn our Master and join me in my bed instead. I can be anyone and everyone you desire. I may not touch you with my own body...but you shall never know the difference, I vow it."

"Zadok."

A second voice. A sterner, colder one. Walter. At the interruption, Zadok snarled, baring his fangs and hissing at the other creature. But the illusion shattered, and there was only one of him once more, standing across the room, leaning against the counter and sulking. No. He was pouting.

Zadok unloaded on the other man in French. *"Damn you to the pits, Walter Northway. You rotten-dicked piece of trash! I could have had her if you hadn't ruined it."*

"I thought you were all immortal," she responded to Zadok dryly in his own language. *"I doubt it has rotted as you say. I would slap you if I had my gloves."*

Zadok blinked at her, surprised. *"You speak French, my dove?"*

"I was raised to be a lady, and I traveled with the Roma for many years. I learned several languages. So, I recommend you mark your words. And no, you cannot have me."

He laughed in enjoyment. *"We shall see, my dove. We shall see."*

"I apologize for whatever just transpired." Walter moved

Heart of Dracula

to stand near her, looking down at her with an almost sympathetic air. Almost. She wondered if it brought him pain to show emotions.

"It is quite all right. I do not think he can be helped."

"No. That is quite true."

"Such wonderful manners." The Frenchman was still grinning like the proverbial cat who ate the canary. "I am jealous of the Master."

"You've made that quite clear." She lifted the glass of juice and sipped it. It was very much required. She hadn't realized how parched her throat was until that moment.

Walter was smiling, if faintly, as he sat at the counter next to her. His expression faded a second later. "Are you well, Miss Parker?"

"As can be expected. I am the prisoner of the King of Vampires. I do not know how I am supposed to react."

"You are attending the opera with him tonight."

It was a statement, not a question. "Would you have me reduced to hysterics instead?"

"No. I am merely making an observation."

"He has made it quite clear that there is nothing I can do to escape my predicament. If he wishes me dead, he can have it. If he wishes me to go insane, it is in his ability. If he wishes me to attend the opera, so be it." Her only chance of escape was to destroy his soul. But that thought brought her an insurmountable dismay. She did not wish the vampire dead, even for all his impositions upon her.

A hand settled on her shoulder. She looked up to the red eyes of Walter, so very similar to the man who made him. But his, despite the fact he was a fraction of Vlad's years, felt so much colder, so much harder than those of his sire.

"Do not fret."

She forgot how obvious her emotions were on her face. She never had much cause to hide them. "How shall I not?"

"It is clear you are attracted to him," Zadok interjected. "What is the matter with that?"

"I should not feel any such things." She sipped the juice and continued to eat the fruit and the meat. She knew she would likely need whatever she could get to survive the night. "This is wrong."

"By whose standards?" Zadok chuckled. "Certainly not ours."

She glared at him again. "Yours is a low bar."

"Oh, woe is me." He placed the back of his hand to his forehead and mimed fainting. "I have been dealt a terrible blow!"

She glanced to Walter, who clearly shared her beleaguered annoyance with the other vampire's antics. She wondered how the red-haired vampire had survived so long in his presence without going mad or killing Zadok.

"If I might provide some advice." Walter studiously ignored the childishness of his counterpart. "I think you would be better served to decide what is 'right' and 'wrong' upon your own opinions of him. Before you resort to anything dire, I recommend...thinking it through. He is a different kind of creature. What he has done—to take you—to him is no crime at all. Errant as that may be, it is simply who he is. He is from another time when such conquest was not a sin."

"He is a murderer."

Walter's lips twinged in the barest attempt at a smile. "Aren't we all?"

"I would hope not to that degree." She shot him a wry smile. "Although we have not talked for long."

Walter chuckled and bowed his head. "That is true. I

fear I came to fetch you for that the carriage has come. I am to take you to the Opera House."

She stood from the stool, rather glad to be done with Zadok. "Good night, vampire."

"And you, pretty dove." Zadok grinned and switched to French. She assumed that Walter did not speak it. *"If the Master is too much of a brute for you, say the word and you will be at my side."*

"He would disembowel you for the insult." She rolled her eyes. *"Do not tempt me to claim that I wish for such a thing for that reason alone. It will be a marked improvement for you to be without your intestines, I think."*

He laughed hard at her slight, and she knew her insult had only spurred him on.

Walter sighed, clearly frustrated and tired of the whole thing, as they stepped out of the house and to the black carriage that was waiting for them. The same eyeless thing sat in the driver's seat. She cringed and did her best not to look at him.

Silently, the vampire offered her a hand into the carriage. She sat on the bench and watched as Walter sat across from her and shut the door behind him. A crack of the whip, and the carriage lurched into motion.

"Dracula is your sire?" she asked after a long silence.

"Yes."

He was not a talkative thing. "Does he do that frequently? Make others directly?"

"No. Few can survive it. His curse is…strong."

"And therefore, so must you be."

"I suppose."

"Still, you suffer the likes of Zadok. And the impositions Dracula forces upon you."

"Such as what?"

"Escorting me about. It is clear there are many other places you would rather be."

"You are preferable company to the Frenchman." There was a ghost of a smile on his pale lips. It faded. "I do not dislike you, Miss Parker. I worry for what chaos you may portend."

"In that, we are agreed."

He took in a breath and exhaled it in a sigh. It was a show. He did not need to breathe. But old habits were likely hard to break. "Do you mean to harm him, my lady?"

She looked out the window as the city traveled past. "No. I do not think I do. I struggle with what that makes of me. But if I were given the chance to hurt him"—*and I have*—"I do not think I could bring myself to do it."

"Why?"

"I...wish to understand him. As much as anyone can."

"Then you are a gift, and I wish all this might resolve itself easily." Walter was watching her curiously, his red eyes catching the light of the city lamps as they passed. "I wish him nothing but happiness and peace. He is my Master, he is my maker, but he is also my dear friend. If you can bring him these things that he has never truly had...then I will do all I can to see it done."

What an oddly compassionate, frozen, disgruntled thing. She was not certain if his words were meant to comfort or threaten her. Was he swearing to protect her, or to ensure that she never escaped? *Most likely both.*

Maxine looked out at the street on the other side of the window. At the people passing along, smiling and laughing, enjoying each other's company. A happiness she had never known. One she had never had the chance to obtain. Until now.

A morbid, shattered version if it, perhaps. And in the

Heart of Dracula

arms of the King of Vampires. A tyrant and a monster. But a lonely, hurting thing, whose heart bled even as he drank from others to refill it. A cold and cruel exterior surrounding a wound that had been paid to him long ago.

After several more minutes in silence, the carriage rolled to a stop. Walter climbed out first and offered her his hand as she descended the stairs.

Once she was on the street, he looked down at her dourly. "Do not intentionally bring him pain, Miss Parker. That is all I ask."

"I do not know as if I have much choice in anything I do."

"Ah, but you do. Enjoy the opera, my lady." He climbed into the carriage and was gone.

A figure caught her attention, standing amongst the crowd, who parted around him and gave him a wide berth. They could sense what he was—a shark in a school of fish.

She let out a wavering breath.

She did not know for certain what would happen this night, but the glint in his crimson eyes told her what she might expect. The shark had singled her out, and tonight, she would feel his teeth once more.

Tonight, there would be no stopping him from having all that he wished to take.

21

Vlad bowed deeply, one arm folded in front of him. "My lady."

Maxine tried not to laugh. She shook her head. "I am not your lady, Vlad. I am your prisoner." It was as much of a reminder for her as it was for him. She seemed to need it constantly, especially in his presence. It was so easy to forget around him. So easy to be swept up in how he made her feel.

He straightened, and his expression was a stern one. "Is that how we are to begin our night?" It was clear he was disappointed. It almost made her regret her words.

But her life was not a game.

"I must seem so small to you. So brief." She watched the couples pass them. No one glanced at her. She didn't need to ask why. Dracula either had them all in his thrall or he was masking their presence. "I can understand why you would treat me like a toy."

"You are correct." His hand touched her hair, stroking over it, gathering the end of her braid in his hand before he began to

Heart of Dracula

unwind it. "You are more fleeting to me than a flash of a firefly in the night. Barely will I even have registered that you exist before you are gone. Even if you were to wish for my eternal kiss, you will fade to dust before I can do little more than blink. All things drop away from me and are gone. You observed it as such, did you not? All to me is as sand within my grasp."

When his hand combed through her hair, her eyes slipped shut. Something about his touch was hypnotic, even without the aid of his literal supernatural ability. When he began again, his voice was a dark rumble that came from close beside her. "I am surprised, though, that you would fault me for this."

"I do not fault you for what you are."

"Ah, but you do. You bemoan the symptoms but say that you sympathize with the cause. Yes, I delight in my games. Their brief diversions are the only pleasures I have left in this world." A touch of a finger tilted her head up to look at him. The feeling of him came over her like the surge of the tide. It was not nearly as alarming now as it had been before she realized she could swim. Bit by bit, embrace by embrace, the sensation of his soul against hers was becoming less disturbing. It was becoming—she could not find the right word for it. Comforting. Familiar.

Enjoyable.

His expression was still aristocratic and exacting, but something had grown softer in his crimson eyes. "Do not resent me for the games I play. That I toy with you is not meant to demean you. You are not, nor shall you ever be, little in my eyes."

She wasn't sure what to say. He robbed her of her words once more. He stepped closer to her, and she could smell roses upon him. He slipped his hand to cradle her cheek, and she found herself leaning into his touch, searching for more of it. Of him.

"If you wish to go, say the word."

She smiled faintly. "You will not let me leave without you at my side."

"No."

She sighed. "Therein lies my complaint."

"What is it you wish that I cannot grant you? What do you desire that you cannot have?" When she couldn't answer, he smiled knowingly. "You bristle at the notion of being restricted, even though your chains know no boundaries. I will not force you to be my lover. I will not demand you lick my shoes. I will not ask you for a single thing you will not give me willingly. There is nothing in this world I will not grant you, should you ask for it."

"Except spare my city and the lives of the hunters."

He shut his eyes and sighed heavily. "Do you not see what an opportunity we share?"

"I do. It is because I recognize what you are to me that I stand here. Attending this opera as you requested, at your side. That I come to spend a night with you...and I do it willingly. Walter did not need to drag me here."

"Yet you continue to request I spare this city."

"You said there was nothing I wished for that you would not give me. I was merely pointing out that you were false in your words." She poked him in the chest once, feeling quite brave.

He smiled, taking no offence at her gesture. Indeed, quite the opposite, it seemed. "On the topic of things that we have recently said..." He pulled her close to him.

"Oh, no."

"You say you recognize what I am to you. Please, do tell. I am so deeply curious."

Heart of Dracula

"I misspoke, same as you."

"No lies." His voice was a low rumble as he playfully scolded her.

"It is personal, then." She tried to push away from him, but his hand snaked around her, holding her close. She would worry what the crowd might think, but the audience was blind to her and the vampire.

"Even better. Speak."

When she didn't, he paid her an arch of a dark eyebrow. She felt her face grow warm as she looked away from him. "You have me at a distinct disadvantage, vampire."

"How so?"

"My condition has made me particularly vulnerable to your...methods of securing my attention."

He laughed, a mirthful, genuine sound. She decided she greatly enjoyed the way it resonated in her. "So bashful in your words. 'Securing your attention.' What you mean to say is that your inability to be touched by others makes you easy for me to seduce." His fingers turned her back to look at him with a press against her cheek.

Damn him and that exacting, arresting crimson gaze. "Yes. Very well. That is what I mean to say."

"You discount my skill in such regards, then? I am insulted."

"That is not what I meant."

"You are also rather adeptly avoiding my question. I asked you what I have become to you. Am I only an idle romp, then? A roll in the proverbial hay? How knavish." He was scolding her playfully again. "You have an itch that you have never been able to scratch, and I am just the means of sating your need?"

"I—No—"

"Then, what? Correct my assumptions, lest I think you

are simply here with me for what I can pay you between the sheets."

"Stop teasing me." Her face felt as though it was on fire. She managed to look down and away from his smile.

"Never. You are lovely when you blush, even more so when you find yourself cornered. You are beautiful when you are flustered." He leaned down, and she felt the press of his lips as he placed a kiss to her hair. "Do you enjoy my company, Miss Parker?"

No lies. She let out a long, defeated sigh. "Yes."

"Do you enjoy speaking with me?"

"Yes."

"Do you enjoy when I touch you?" His hand slipped to the base of her neck, and she shivered at the sensation of his fingers lacing into her hair. The points of his nails scraped against her skin, and she broke out once more in goosebumps.

"Yes," she whispered. "You know I do."

"Then go. You are free. Your chains are no longer mine. Walk from me now, take the closest horse and carriage, and head for the horizon. I will not follow you. Your chains are broken."

She looked up at him, shocked. He slid his other hand to gently cup her cheek, his thumb resting in the hollow of her chin below her lower lip. She had no words. She was too stunned.

"Or...you may choose to stay. To attend the opera with me. To spend the evening in my embrace. But know that this is your one opportunity to leave me. I am a covetous creature. I do not surrender the things I desire. And I desire you *very* much, Miss Parker. As much as I enjoy this game you claim we play of prisoner and warden, it brings you undue strife, and I will not have you conflicted over your actions in

Heart of Dracula

my arms. Go. Be free of me. Return to your hunter friends and seek to end my goals here in this fledgling city, or flee. The choice is yours. I will not stop you. I release you."

He took a single step back, his touch slipping away. The sensation of his soul there against hers, of crimson velvet and black satin, of teeth, and wings, and gore, and passion, faded.

But it did not vanish.

He would always be there with her now.

As a far deeper, far more wicked poison than any hypnotism or imprisonment he could levy against her.

Damn you for showing me what I have been missing.

"There are worse things to condemn me for, believe me." Vlad smirked with a hint of sharp and too-long canines.

She swore. Yes, right. He could hear her thoughts. Her blood was in his body. No one on the street registered her obscenity—as loud as it was—as they passed. She would go unnoticed by them, no matter what she did.

She took in a breath, held it, and slowly let it out. She shut her eyes and placed her fingers to her temple. This creature before her was going to give her a headache. *I am a fool. An utter and complete idiot.* She could almost hear the Roma witch who had taken her in yelling at her to turn tail and run. That another day of life was worth more than his embrace.

But was it?

A life alone?

She had become inured to the cold, standing out in the lonely winter night of her life. But now that someone had beaconed her inside to stand by his fire...she looked back out into that frozen darkness and did not know if she could survive it.

She knew she did not wish to try.

"Come to me, Maxine." His voice was that low rumble that carried without effort, both pleasant and foreboding in the same moment. She looked up to see him holding out his hand to her, palm up. Asking in his own way for her to join him. "The curtain rises soon."

This is my choice. If I take his hand, I can no longer pretend that I stand against him or the horrors he wishes to commit.

"You may always seek to better my nature, Miss Parker. Walter would certainly love the assistance. The poor bastard has been alone in playing my conscience for a very long time." He smiled tenderly. "I will never fault you for it, if you do not loathe me for when I do not comply." And still, he held his hand to her, waiting.

Damn me to the pits where I belong.

She placed her hand in his.

She accepted him, and this, and what they were to become.

He pulled her toward him slowly, giving her every chance to resist. To change her mind. But she did not. He banded an arm around her back and, with the crook of a finger, tilted her head up to meet him.

"Miss Parker...I think you may have stolen my heart."

He did not wait for an answer. Instead, he kissed her, and she sank against him and into his embrace. He filled her mind even as his tongue danced against hers. The passion that burned in him threatened to consume her. And like a torch to a drum of oil, he lit her aflame in response. Her hands were tangled in his lapel, and she pulled him closer.

His hand slipped down to grasp her rear, squeezing it tightly. She shoved against him, but he didn't relent. He kneaded her flesh in his grasp, unconcerned by her struggles. She slammed a fist into his chest.

He growled low in his throat, a needy sound, and it

Heart of Dracula

seemed to take every ounce of his self-control to finally separate from her. "I will never tire of your kiss. You wish to fight me, and yet you cannot help yourself. You are like stolen fruit from a garden. Sinful and sweet."

Maxine slapped him.

Not a single person near them even flinched at the sound. The impact rocked his head to the side, although she was certain it was entirely from surprise and not because she had done him any amount of pain or damage.

She, on the other hand, felt as though she had struck a rock. Her fingers stung. She waved her hand and winced. "Ow."

He laughed. She expected it to be cruel. But instead, he sounded truly mirthful. When he looked down at her, warmth creased his eyes, and she found him smiling at her with a genuine affection that made something in her heart hitch. The sight of his granite features grown tender was a beautiful thing.

"You really are quite perfect, you know." With the tips of his sharp claws, he tucked a strand of his dark hair that had escaped the silk tie when she struck him behind his ear. "Come. The show is to begin, and we have not fetched our drinks or taken our seats."

"I…"

"You have every reason and right to strike me, Maxine Parker. It troubles me none. Do it as much as you see fit. I will never be angry at you for it. Indeed, I may enjoy it." He tilted his head to the side slightly as he watched her, as if the change in angle might provide him new insight. "Loathe me, love me, fight me, obey me—I will take it all with joy. But you have made your choice, and the moment has passed. You cannot escape me now."

She was stunned. He was overwhelming—there it was

again, that word. He took her hand and led her inside the Opera House, and she followed him in a daze. His hypnosis was not to blame. She found herself lost in her wheeling thoughts as he led her to their private box. Before she could do much else, she was seated in a chair next to him, a glass of wine in her hand, looking out at the rows of people beneath them.

"Are you quite all right?" A knuckle stroked her cheek.

She nodded once. "You are a rising tide, Vlad Tepes Dracula."

"Truer words have never been said." When she glanced to him, he was smiling. "You haven't even asked me what we are seeing this evening."

"To be fair, it is the least of my concerns."

He chuckled and pulled a pamphlet from his pocket. He passed it to her. The program for the night proudly exclaimed that tonight they would be watching a production of *Faust*.

She shot him an incredulous look.

He laughed. "Too on point for you?"

She had to join in his laughter, and she handed the program back to him. "Tell me. Are you Mephistopheles or our misguided alchemist?"

"If there is one thing I have learned, my darling Marguerite, it is that one man can very well be both." He let out a thoughtful hum and sipped his wine. "If Gounod or Marlowe had any sense at all, they would have written it to reveal such a thing instead."

"I argue that they have. The theatrics are there for simply that—melodrama. The devil in this play is only taken literally by those who do not see the story for what it is meant to be—a parable for human weakness."

"Have you seen it before?"

Heart of Dracula

"Yes."

"Are you a fan of the stage?"

She smiled. "Very much so. I attend whenever I am able. Especially when they tend toward the more fantastical. I was glad to have had the opportunity to visit the Grand Guignol in Paris. I loved to watch their special effects. Especially the blood. I convinced one man to let me down beneath the stage to see how it was done. Wonderful contraptions."

He grinned. "You are a morbid little thing."

"With all the human suffering I can remember that far outweighs my own years, I think I would rather have to take on a morbid outlook to keep my own sanity."

He was still smiling broadly, a warmth in those red eyes of his. "And I am all the happier for it. So many with your manner of gifts wind up in an early grave."

"Have you met many like me?"

"Like you? No. Those who scratch the surface of what you are? Most definitely. I have met soothsayers and fortune tellers, those who see that which is unseen, and more. I have known warlocks and witches, wolves who have become men, and vice versa. I have seen it all." He picked up a lock of her hair and twirled it through his fingers. "But none quite like you."

"Now you flatter me, vampire."

"Is it working?"

She laughed and swatted at his knee. His hand caught hers and twined their fingers together, resting against his thigh. She looked away from him shyly.

"Do you regret your choice?"

"No. But I fear what I have done."

"Be nervous, but not afraid. All I ask is that you do not

hide behind your troubled thoughts as false reasons to refuse me."

"I promise I will not hide behind my doubts and misgivings. I will be honest with you about what I feel. I do not think I could hide it from you if I wished. But for all my talents, I worry that you can."

"What do you mean?"

"You are strong enough to lie to me, if you wished to. I am left to simply ask you, like anyone else would—please do not lie to me. Play games with my life if you must, but not like that. Do not claim I hold your heart in an attempt to secure my own. That is too cruel for me to allow."

"I still do not understand."

"I know a great deal of how the living wrong each other. I know how they betray, they hurt, they steal, and how they kill. I know how men and women might spin tales. To say that they might love another, that they are their sun and moon and stars in the sky, but to have it all be but a falsehood. All of it as means to an end. Once the goal is achieved, the game is over. Do not tell me I have stolen your heart only to be a lie, I—"

His hand was on her cheek. He was towering over her, his hand resting on the armrest of her chair. He had moved so quickly she hadn't seen it. He was suddenly there, caging her in, his clothing still settling with the inertia of his movement. His sudden presence stopped the words in her throat. "You think I do not mean my words? Even if I could hide such things from you, why would I bother?"

"I do not know."

"Without an ulterior motive, what could inspire me to act as you fear I will?"

"How do I not know you are simply exploiting my weakness?"

Heart of Dracula

He turned his head away to laugh, a low, dark, mischievous sound. Turning back to her, there were a great many things burning away in his expression.

"I—"

"No." A finger landed on her lips, shushing her. "It is not I that you do not trust. It is yourself, isn't it? You honestly think yourself undesirable." He tutted her. "Perhaps to foolish mortal men you may be. I am no mortal man." He grinned. "If I thought you amenable, I would have you on my lap, here and now, and I would make love to you until the curtain fell upon the stage."

"M—"

"Shush. My games are not those of mortals. I do not lie about that which I want. Tonight, you shall share my bed. Tonight, I shall show you the pleasure which I am capable of paying you. And you, Maxine Parker, will have come into my spider's web of your own accord. I will take you to the heights of bliss that you have been so grievously denied until now. You will lie down before me, and I will show you that you hold my heart in your hands, even as you do my soul."

And as quickly as he was there, he was gone. She felt too hot—her heart was pounding. He was sitting back in his chair, smiling a wry, over-pleased smile. He sipped his wine. The lights began to dim. "Enjoy the show, Maxine."

22

Save for his rather lascivious speech prior to the opening overture, the vampire behaved himself. He barely touched her more than to simply hold her hand, and they discussed trivial things, far away from the morbid arrangement in which she found herself. Of the performance quality, of the acting, of the set production. He was well-versed in every aspect of the stage and seemed to be a wealth of knowledge on all subjects. There was nothing she could speak of in which he was not well-educated. *"I am so very old,"* he had said to her before. And the weight of those years was clear. She could feel it when her fingers were twined with his.

The heavy burden on his shoulders. It would have crushed a lesser soul and sent them reeling into madness. *He is here to destroy my city. Is that not a kind of madness? He desires to live or to die, not to be trapped between the two as he is now.*

A thought came over her—a small realization. More of a question, really. *Does he play these games with hunters in hopes they might discover a way to end him?* She looked over to the vampire and found him idly smiling. Merely a small, knowing twist of those lips. He could hear her thoughts, after all. And she could hear his soul.

There was nothing more substantial than wax paper that separated them in truth.

The idea of how close they would be before the dawn made her stomach lurch in fear and excitement. There was terror, yes, a deep instinctual need not to leap from the cliff into the ocean. But there was also an anticipation that pushed her forward.

During intermission, she sought his hand, lacing her fingers between his. Crimson eyes watched her with curiosity and surprise as she lifted his hand to her face and kissed his fingers. One at a time, exploring him. He did not move and let her do as she pleased.

Touching him was addictive, she realized with no small amount of dismay. She bent her cheek to rest it against the back of his hand, wondering if she could warm him by touch. If she could give him shelter from the storm.

"Yes. You can." His voice was low and thick with emotion. Her silent yet well-heard question had carried more meaning to him than she intended. "Does the cold truly not bother you?"

"No. Although I do not have much to compare it to." She smiled faintly. "Does it trouble you? To be so frigid?"

"Rarely. Only in the moments when the warmth leaves me."

She placed a kiss against him again and lowered his hand to her lap, keeping it grasped within both of hers. He squeezed, reassuring and thankful. "Your compassion will be your undoing."

"I am an empath. All I am is compassion." She chuckled. "Sometimes I wonder if I am real at all."

"What do you mean?"

"I am filled with memories that are not my own. If I shut my eyes and ponder, I can feel heavy, mud-slicked boots on my feet. I can feel the crunch of bone and hear the screams of the dying that *I* have maimed. I feel their ichor on my hands. I taste their blood. I feel the weight of the sword in my hand. I remember the battlefield that I was shown when I touched that brooch of yours. That memory is now mine, added to all the rest. That is why everyone believes me to be far older than I am at first glance."

She let her fingers run over the wood armrest of the chair in their box seat. It was an elegant piece. She caught the grooves in her fingertips, glad she wore her gloves. She was certain the chairs had seen several instances of exactly what Vlad had teasingly threatened her with earlier. How many couples had stolen passionate embraces in the darkness of the theater when they thought no one could see?

"All we are, in the end, is a product of our context." She continued to circle her fingers along the wood grooves thoughtfully. "A series of events that surround us and define us. You are what you are because of the life you have lived. Some of it was your doing, much of it was not. But it is what created you all the same."

"You mean to say that we do not have a soul."

"Oh, no, that is not what I am saying at all. But when we begin, we are a seedling. A tree, or a flower, or a great immortal redwood like yourself. Our soul defines our potential. But our context—bad winters, dry summers, a perfect spring—define the branches we might sprout. The bark we might grow to protect us. Whether we bear fruit, or if we become grizzled and empty."

"My empath is a poet."

She chuckled. "I am no such thing."

"You are. You speak in metaphor."

Heart of Dracula

"I think in imagery. In photographs of another time. I describe only how I process the world."

"Sounds exhausting. No wonder you always look overwrought."

"Stop teasing me." She still couldn't help but smile.

"Never. Please, continue, Sophocles."

"I would like to think I am far more attractive than he was."

"You are. And far less irritating after a glass of wine."

She looked up at him curiously. He spoke as though he had met the man. Then she realized...he very well could have. He was ancient. Older than she could fathom. He merely smiled at her tenderly and watched her through half-lidded, crimson eyes that caught the lamplight and flashed occasionally, reminding her that he was a wolf who had taken it upon himself to walk at her side and not devour her whole.

"Please. Continue." He squeezed her hand again.

"If we are all merely a product of what we have experienced, then...most of what I know has not been my own. I wonder sometimes if I am only an empty vessel. A collection of other people's memories and context. I seclude myself from others not only because I cannot touch them, not only because they can sense that I am distinctly *other*, but because within the noise, I lose myself." She looked down at the crowd that was beginning to take their seats again. "I do not feel real. Sometimes I feel as though I am only a dream."

"When this world burns to dust, and the sun swallows it whole, I will have seen all of humanity come and go before me. I can control the nature of the world around me. I am expert in what is *real*, my darling. If you are a dream, then it is one from which I do not ever wish to be woken."

Her face bloomed with warmth, and she looked down at her lap, at his hand still twined with hers, and smiled. "Now you are the poet."

"Perhaps."

The overture began to play, heralding the beginning of the second act, and she fell silent as the lights lowered and the curtain lifted. In the darkness, she released his hand briefly to pull off her gloves and lay the black silk on the arm of the chair. In the first instance of such a thing ever being the case, she preferred to feel him against her skin. To feel him closer to her. His touch no longer scared her. His soul against hers was no longer jarring. It was welcoming.

She leaned her head to rest it against his arm. Soft fabric over a frame that could crush steel. A beast that was so very powerful, but still remained affable, and...benign would go too far.

"You inspire such genial things in me."

The show recommenced, and she found herself smiling throughout the second act. She dared say, it felt *nice.* He had asked to show her his kindness, and she found herself enjoying it greatly. It was as though they were any hopeful lovers enjoying a lavish evening on the town.

The curtain fell, and she found herself both a little sad for it and once more eagerly anticipating with both fear and delight what was to inevitably follow. At the end of the production, they headed to the street with the rest of the crowd.

There was no carriage waiting for them outside.

"Come. It is a beautiful night. Let us go for a stroll."

"You are not planning to turn us into bats and whisk us off once more, are you?"

He struggled not to smile, but his lips twitched. "No."

"Liar."

Heart of Dracula

That was enough to break his resolve, and he smiled fully. "You will become adjusted to the disorientation, I promise."

"I do not think I believe you." Regardless of her mistrust, she tucked her hand into his elbow as they walked down the street. He was a knavish thing. For all the appearance of a King and aristocrat that he wore, he was a rogue deep down.

She found her heart no longer torn in two. Her mind flicked to the point in time maybe only an hour away when he would have what he wished—what they both wished. When her silly dream became reality. The image of him over her, his heavy, broad frame against and inside hers, made heat pool dangerously in her body.

"Mind your thoughts Miss Parker, or I will not be able to wait, and our first real foray will be over that bench right there." He pointed a sharp-nailed finger into the distance.

She swore loudly and colorfully in Romanian. "Damn you. Reading my thoughts is cheating!"

"Turnabout is fair play." He laughed again at her side. "You rummage about inside my emotions and my memories. It is only fair I might pry into a few of yours. Don't you think?"

"You find the most inconvenient moments to do so."

"No, only the most embarrassing to comment upon."

She growled.

He chuckled and squeezed her hand. "That was rude of me. But you are quite charming when you are perturbed."

"Mmhm."

He grinned. "You could make a sailor blush with your vehemence. You learned such things from the Roma?"

"The only words I managed to retain from them were swears."

"Then I think you know roughly two-thirds of their

language and could be considered fluent." He made a face. "Lovely people. Creative in their invectives."

"You lived there for a time, you said?"

"Yes. Several hundred years ago now. I have traveled about since then. Italy, Germany, most recently London. I tired of the old world, though. I wished to experience youth. So, I came here."

"This country is hardly new, and you have picked the oldest city within it."

He shot her an incredulous look, one eyebrow raised.

She realized her foolishness, and she chuckled. "Two hundred years is not new to those of us who live sixty if we are lucky."

"If I have my way, you will live to see a thousand and more."

She looked up at him curiously. "Do you mean to turn me?"

"Only if you wish it. I will not force it upon you. That is a sin against nature not even I would wish to commit." Vlad frowned. "But I do not like the idea of losing you so soon."

She glanced away to watch a few others across the street, walking arm in arm as they were, enjoying the evening air after the opera. So similar, and so disparate, from her situation. The couple were young lovers. She and Vlad were... something very different from that.

"I could not possibly mean enough to you, that you would wish me to be at your side for—" She squeaked in surprise and bit back a scream as he picked her up around the waist with both hands and planted her feet on the edge of a stone railing that marked the front edge of someone's property, a good twelve inches up from the brick sidewalk.

"Stop. Enough of this. I will have no more of it. It ends

now." He was pointing at her face, lecturing her like she was a child.

She was twelve inches off the bricks, and for the first time she could stand eye-to-eye with him. Mostly. He still managed to be an inch taller. She laughed.

"I am tired of your—what? What is funny?" He narrowed his eyes, frustrated at her laughter.

"By God, you're tall." She kept laughing. "You poor bastard."

"You have only realized this now?" He raised an eyebrow.

"Oh, not in the slightest. I have but now measured the specifics. No wonder you defy fashion and do not wear a top hat. You would be a monolith." She rested her hands on his shoulders over the fabric of his dark peacoat. "You must spend your days with a sore neck."

His stern expression flickered into amusement. "I am accustomed to it. I do find this arrangement more convenient; I will admit." His hands rested on her waist. "You are so very small."

"I am of perfectly average frame. You are the anomalous one."

"Then everyone is simply too short."

"Is that why you turned Walter? Do you only pick out the spindly creatures so that you do not get a crick in your neck from glowering down at everyone?"

"I do not glower."

"Oh, yes, you do. I am quite convinced you invented the expression." She slipped closer to him, sliding an arm along his shoulder until it draped casually behind his neck. His dark hair was held back in a simple red silk ribbon, and she toyed idly with the end of the fabric. She pulled the glove of her other hand off between her teeth, drawing a low growl out of his throat at the action. Something darkened in his expression.

She slipped her fingers along his neck, feeling the muscles and the tendons there. The strength in him. The power that burned beneath her hand, though it was chill. He had no heartbeat.

Yet.

She wondered how quickly she could change that.

He growled again, louder than the first, and his hands at her waist tightened. "Do not tease me, Maxine. You will regret it later. I have every intention on being quite delicate with you this night. Do not tempt my control."

"I find it fascinating that you of all people can find the strength to handle anything fragile."

"I do not think you are, but I will treat your first night with the respect it deserves. I do intend on testing your resilience soon enough."

She trailed her touch up to his cheek and let herself explore his features. Let herself truly examine him, now that she had made her choice. His eyes slipped shut at her embrace, and he seemed to lose himself in the experience, same as she.

She ran her thumb along the line of his lower lip, and before she could second-guess her impulse, she tipped her head forward and kissed him. She wanted to feel him. Taste him. She could no longer hide what she desired. She could no longer resist what she wanted and hide behind a mountain of *should nots* and *maybes*.

And in the wake of his fire, her doubts melted away. She felt his surprise at her kiss and felt as it faded. He wrapped an arm around her to pull her flush against him. His other hand cradled the back of her neck as he took her curious, exploring embrace and deepened it.

Heart of Dracula

"Be mine, Maxine." She heard his thoughts echo inside her mind. It was not a request. It was a command. It was a *need* that burned in him. There were no lies within him. Nothing to betray any plot or any scheme to use and betray her. There was only a void, an emptiness, that he urgently demanded she fill. It called to her. It drew her close. It was what had sung to her like a siren the moment they had met. *"Be mine. Come with me."*

She had never once been needed by anyone in her life. Her heart soared. Even if this was only temporary. Even if her life was short, or his need was fleeting, it did not matter. *Yes, vampire. I shall.*

His grasp on her tightened as he heard her silent reply. His tongue flicked against her lips, asking for entry, and she granted it. He took her greedily, claiming her as his own. And she sank into him, wishing for nothing but more.

If this was to be how she died—at his hands, in his arms—then she could think of no better way. If she died his prey, she would do so with a smile. It was only when her head began to spin that she urged him away with a press of her hand.

He broke the kiss with a primal, irritated, and impatient snarl.

"One of us needs to breathe," she reminded him.

"Overrated." He grunted and leaned in to kiss her again. She was still reeling from the last one, and she urged him once more to give her a moment. Unhappily, he obliged. "Tell me that you love me, Miss Parker."

"What?" She blinked, astonished.

"I wish to hear you say the words. Tell me that you can see into my very core, straight through to the whole of me, and that you love what you have found. That you love this foolish cretin, this gargoyle, this monster, this *cannonball* of a soul you hold in in your hands."

She could not help but laugh quietly at his reuse of her bad metaphor. She put her palm to his cheek, and he leaned into her touch. His skin was not as cold as it was before. His heart had begun to beat. "That is what you wish from me. You wish for someone to see you for what you really are—all of you, not merely a facet—and declare you worthy of love."

"Maxine." His voice was little more than a whisper. Something shone in his eyes. For a moment, she worried he might shed tears. "Please…"

She intended to answer him with a kiss. To press herself to him, to whisper that he should take her away to some dark place where they could become what they needed in the other. She would whisper to him in his embrace *yes*. How she could, even in this moment, hear his answering call.

Odd as they may be.

Tragic as they might become.

God forgive her.

She loved him.

But she never had the chance to tell him.

The ground rushed up to meet her. Grass and dirt stung her hands. It was a second later that she heard the rumble of gunfire in the distance.

"Vampire!"

She recognized Alfonzo's voice, coated in anger.

The hunters had come.

23

VLAD PUSHED Maxine to the ground. The marksman was a careful shot, but he could not risk it. He felt the bullet tear through his shoulder. A second burst through his neck before he let his body take the shape of bats and fill the air.

The wounds burned, revealing the presence of magic in the lead that punctured him.

Wrath. That was the word for what he felt. He would destroy these humans. Tear them to pieces. For taking from him that which he had desired for so long—*so very long*—at the very second he was to receive it.

Knives, flying through the air, propelled by a psychic force, skewered several of the large black bats that filled the air. Bullets took out several more. He did not care. He had only one goal—kill them. Kill them all.

Somewhere beneath his anger, he knew he was at a serious disadvantage. Like the warlord he was, he surveyed the battlefield and found his own position sorely lacking. He ticked off a list as to why he found himself in an unfavorable position. The hunters smelled of magic, and the Helsing man was skilled. Vlad was already wounded. He had been caught off guard. Maxine forced him to lower his defenses, and he had been utterly distracted by her.

Cursing himself for his foolishness, he swarmed high up into the sky. The young blonde huntress was helping Maxine—*his Maxine*—to her feet.

And therein was the reason he would not retreat, despite it being very much in his interest to do so. He was immortal, he was eternal, but he was not unstoppable. The tactician in him screamed at him to take to higher ground. To seek another way around the front lines that was presented to him in the form of three very capable fighters who wished to see him defeated.

But he could not.

They had something he needed.

Redemption—as much as he would ever have—in the form of a beautiful young woman.

You belong to me!

The barbarian in him overcame the tactician. Rage overcame reason. Beast overcame man. He would not let them take what was his.

Diving low, he struck.

———

"Maxine, are you all right?" A hand took her by the upper arm and helped her up to her feet. She turned to see Bella standing there, watching her with concern etched on her face.

Why was the girl worried for her? It took her half a beat to remember that, to them, Vlad was the enemy. Rightfully so, they believed her to be his prisoner. They did not know she had chosen to take his hand.

Heart of Dracula

To them, he was a monster trying to destroy the world. To them, he was a demon who had stolen her away.

It was far more complicated than that. But not from their point of view.

"I—I'm fine, thank you," she finally managed to answer. She was still stunned and reeling from what had happened. One moment she had been about to kiss the King of Vampires, to tell him that she loved him, and another moment she had been face-down in the grass, with the boom of rifle fire echoing through the street.

"You belong to me!"

The words echoed inside her head, impossibly loud and not her own. She winced and placed her hand to her temple. She did not realize Vlad could holler inside her mind. It was disconcerting at best. But they were linked together in ways she did not yet fully understand. Her blood was inside his veins, and more than once she had touched her soul to his and rummaged about inside his memories. Such things were bound to leave ties.

The sound of screeching bats grew louder as the black cloud of flapping wings dove low, meaning to attack them. Bella lifted her hands, and daggers swarmed around the two of them like a shield.

Maxine gasped and drew closer to her, eyes wide. She had never seen anything like it. She had seen Bella demonstrate her power in a far more limited sense, but a swirling wall of knives was another matter entirely.

The bats were forced to abandon their attack. Still, the echo of gunfire continued. One after another. With each *boom,* a bat dropped from the sky, landing on the bricks or the cobblestone with a wet thump, blood pooling around their small forms.

Then there was Alfonzo. Standing in the center of the

street, a long blade at his side. It was glowing. Honest-to-God *glowing*. The steel shone a brilliant white, casting shadows around him and glinting off the pools of crimson on the stones.

"Face me, monster!" Alfonzo shouted up at the swarming bats.

The bats coalesced into the vampire. He stood, a towering and terrifying sight. With another *boom* of a rifle, something hit some strange kind of wall that sparked and glowed with crimson lightning near him. He had magic of his own. *Of course, he does.*

You are the one ill-suited for this kind of thing. They are warriors. They have done this dance before. Maxine wanted to shrink away into the shadows, to hide from what was about to come. But the swirling wall of daggers posed her as much harm as it might the vampire. She was forced to stay by Bella.

Who, bless her heart, was holding Maxine's hand tightly in hers as if she were in need of consolation. As if to promise that all was now well, and she was no longer in danger.

They were "saving her," after all.

Vlad's expression was both a hard and stoic mask and one of pure unadulterated *hatred*. But he was bleeding from the chest. Several bullet wounds shone as wet spots against black clothing. He was already wounded.

Three against one. He may be a demigod, but she did not like those odds.

It was in that sudden, jarring moment that she realized she wanted him to win. The hunters had never been anything but kind to her—friendly with her—in a way she was not often shown. She did not wish them harm. She wanted neither party to come to blows. "Stop this. All of you."

Heart of Dracula

No one heeded her words. No one even glanced at her.

"You die here and now, monster." Alfonzo lifted his sword and held it aloft with both hands, readying for a fight.

"We shall see." Vlad sneered. "Many of yours have come and gone, Helsing. Many of yours lie dead in the ground from my hands."

"And many of mine have sent you to the grave."

"To what ends? I always return."

"And we will always be here to stop you."

Vlad laughed. A cold, cruel sound. Empty of the mirth and the amusement she had heard before. This was who he was to others—*this* was the creature they fought. A tyrant, a fiend, and a demon. "No. You will not. I will outlive your ilk. I will outlive all. I will be the last to stand upon this wretched Earth when humans have lain it all to waste. When your plague has destroyed all the creatures of this place, and you have consumed it all in your fathomless greed, *I* shall stand alone in the ashes. So come, hunter, and try your will against mine. You will fall."

"We shall see!" Alfonzo ran at Vlad, sword raised.

The daggers around her shifted and changed direction like minnows in a pond. Bella jumped forward, taking her weapons with her, and joined the fray.

Eddie appeared, shouldering his long rifle, and pulled two revolvers from holsters at his sides. He opened fire.

Three against one.

Vlad was left to defend himself against a sword, against daggers, and against bullets.

And he was going to lose.

Shadows spread out from the vampire, and he fought with magic the likes of which she had never even imagined. He was faster than the hunters. Alfonzo was bleeding from slashes that had been paid to him by Vlad's sharp claws or lashing swipes of glowing red *something* that seemed to come from nowhere at all. It was not quite fire. It was not quite glass. It was not quite lightning. It was power itself, cutting through the air and clashing against steel and sending the hunters staggering back. And the moment that the arcs of crimson appeared in the air it was gone again.

I am not suited for this new world in which I find myself.

Despite his strength, the vampire was forced to play defense against the three who did not let up from their assault.

It was in one ill-timed step that Alfonzo took his opening and drove his sword deep through Vlad's midsection. He hissed in pain, and his lips pulled back from long, vicious fangs as he snarled down at Alfonzo. His hand gripped the blade in his stomach.

Alfonzo yanked the blade back, tearing open the vampire and sending blood pouring down around his feet. Vlad fell to one knee.

"Now, you die, vampire." Alfonzo raised his sword, clearly meaning to lop off his enemy's head.

"No!"

She had not realized she had shouted. She had not realized she had moved until she was standing between Vlad and Alfonzo. But there she found herself, rather inexplicably, her hand on the vampire's shoulder behind her, the other held up in front of her, as if that alone could stop Alfonzo's swing.

The vampire hunter paused, looking at her wild-eyed from shock. "Maxine, what are you doing?"

"Stop this. Stop all of this!"

"He must die. We have to stop him. He means to destroy this city and all who live here. Including you!" Alfonzo shouted back. "Get out of my way."

Heart of Dracula

She hesitated. "No."

The hunter looked crestfallen. "You are corrupted by him. You have fallen to him."

"I...I have not." She tried to sound resolute in her words, but they were as uncertain as she was. "I cannot allow this."

"We may only have this one chance, Maxine. Please. Get out of my way. He has poisoned your mind. Let me end him, and I will save you. His plague will end. Can't you see what he's done to you?"

"Maxine...go." Vlad's hand settled on hers. It was warm. His heart was beating. Bloodlust had spurred it on. But it was wet with blood. "You put yourself in danger. They will not understand. They will hurt you."

"We are not the monsters here, vampire," Alfonzo spat.

"Leave me, Maxine," Vlad urged her, ignoring the hunter. "I will not see you harmed."

She turned to face him, exposing her back to Alfonzo. It didn't matter. She couldn't stop him if he tried to hurt her, anyway. What could she do, a foolish empath? Her power could do nothing in a fight. She placed her hand against his cheek. *Go, vampire. I will not watch you die. Retreat.*

"*I cannot leave you.*" His words echoed silently in her head.

Nor shall you. This is not a parting. It is a pause. Go.

"Get out of my way, Maxine," Alfonzo warned. "I will not ask again. He must die. Say goodbye, and back away."

Go, vampire. I cannot watch you die. I will not survive the grief. She paused and let herself say the words silently that she wished she could say aloud.

I think I love you.

His expression shifted. No longer the cold mask of hate, but one so full of emotion that it cracked her heart in half. He gazed up at her in hope, in adoration, in awe. As if she

295

was some kind of angel come to Heaven to bless a wretch who had lived in darkness for so very long.

It lasted for only a split second.

Eddie raised his gun and pointed it at the back of Vlad's head. He would hit her too if he fired. They paused only for her sake. They did not want to hurt her. She was grateful for that. It gave her the moment she needed.

And the vampire vanished. He disappeared into his shadow, and she watched as it slipped along the floor and up the wall of a building and was gone.

"Damn you!" Alfonzo grabbed her shoulder and yanked her around violently. "Damn you, Maxine! What have you done?"

She shrank back from him. "I couldn't let you—"

"We may not have another chance. We could have stopped him and saved everyone." Alfonzo stormed up to her. "He's corrupted you. You're his thrall now, aren't you?"

"No, I'm not, I—"

She never got the chance to finish. Alfonzo balled up his fist, his leather glove creaking. With no other warning, the fist met her temple.

―――――

His Master was in a rage.

Walter was standing by the wall, his hands folded in front of him, head bowed. He made himself as much of an unappealing target for the elder vampire's wrath as he could.

And, oh, how he was wrathful.

Dracula had entered the home and immediately destroyed two pieces of furniture and ripped Zadok's arm clean off for having the audacity to ask what was the matter.

Heart of Dracula

Now, his King was sitting in a chair, his own fingers dug deep into the festering, burning wound in his chest, searching for the bullets that must have caused it. There was a deep gash in his stomach, but that had already mostly healed. It was the bullets that remained that were troublesome.

Blessed silver, no doubt. Two had been put straight into his heart. Several more elsewhere, judging by the blood, although those had exited out the back and the wounds had already healed.

It would have killed any lesser creature. As it was, Zadok was likely to be more the worse for wear come the morning than Dracula.

Vlad wormed his fingers into the holes in his chest up to his knuckle. His lips were drawn back from his teeth as he snarled and hissed in pain. He wrenched something free, and between his fingers was held a silver bullet. Walter watched as the flesh that touched it blistered and burned. The elder vampire tossed the bullet into the fire with a loud snarl and went to find the second offensive item.

"They took her," he growled through clenched teeth.

"I am sorry."

Vlad howled, a sound that was more inhuman than not, as he wrenched the second bullet from his chest and hurled the bloody thing into the flames. He stood from his chair, took two steps, and his knees gave out from under him.

Walter was there in an instant, supporting his weight and guiding him back to his chair. "Master, you are in no condition to—"

"I will not let them touch her!" Vlad hissed loudly in pain and collapsed into the chair, his hand pressed against the holes in his chest.

"You know not where they have taken her."

"I can sense her. I will find her."

"If they wished her dead, they would have shot her already. For now, she is likely safe."

"Safe?" he snarled. "Do not dare speak to me of what you—" He broke off in pain again, grunted, and tilted his head back to the chair, his eyes squeezing tight.

Walter sighed. "Take some hours to rest and heal before you go to fetch her. As you are now, you cannot succeed."

"These wounds will not kill me."

"Yet they nearly succeeded."

"I was distracted."

"These are not normal mortals, Master. You know this. We will win, and we will take her back, but you must be whole for us to do it. Anything less puts her at risk. While they may not kill her now, they may do so if you wage an assault."

That was what finally triggered reason in the enraged mind of the elder vampire. He sighed heavily, begrudgingly, and sank farther back against the tall chair. "Very well... Warn the others. Tomorrow, we find her. Tomorrow, we will wage our war."

Walter bowed at the waist, and in a swirl of mist, was gone.

Tomorrow, it truly begins.

24

"Maxine."

A voice called to her in her dreams. Somewhere far away. He was always so close, so near, and now he could hear her like wolves howling in the wood. Or perhaps he was calling for her because she was lost amongst them.

"Maxine!"

He was too far away to reach her without her help. He could not come to her on his own. She could hide from him if she wished. She could stay in the darkness of the woods that he could not see and ignore his calls. But more than his voice called to her. She felt his worry. She felt his desperation. She stretched out her hand to him. Reached for his presence and touched it with her own.

With the barest spark of contact, she was suddenly in his arms. She felt the fabric of his coat around her, smelling of roses. He held her tight. "Where are you?"

"I don't know." She looked up at him and saw his brow creased in concern. He tilted her head to one side, and suddenly his alabaster features flashed to a look of pure hatred. There must be a bruise on her temple. A low, terrible growl came from deep in his chest. Quietly, she tried to explain. "I think Alfonzo punched me."

"I will *rend the flesh from their bones.*" He was seething, and his hand was now hovering in the air near her, his sharp nails curled in like a claw. He clearly wished to hurt something and did not trust himself to touch her in his rage. His eyes, always crimson, were now consumed by it from lid to lid and seemed to nearly glow with their own light. His teeth were sharper, dangerous, animalistic. His humanity weakened as his anger grew. "How dare they—"

Struggling to control himself, he bit it back and squared his shoulders. He shut his eyes, schooled himself, and when he reopened them, they were his normal deep red once more. Taking in a deep breath, he let it out slowly through his nose. "Forgive me. I do not wish you to see me this way."

Shockingly, his anger didn't frighten her. It was terrifying, yes, but it was also fascinating. There was something beautiful about his wrath. Perhaps if it were pointed at her, she would think differently.

She placed her head against his chest and pulled herself close to him in an embrace. He hesitated, tense, before slipping his arms back around her to hold her. "What you wear on the outside is no less alarming than what humanity would hide within their hearts."

She felt his lips press against the top of her head. "I will find you. I will bring you home to me. I must take some time to mend the damage they paid me. But once I am well, I will destroy them."

"No. Please. Do not kill them. They mean well—they are trying to help me and save this city. They fear I have been corrupted by you. They do not understand."

"Poor, compassionate Maxine." He sighed and tilted her head up to face him. "There is nothing you may say to them

Heart of Dracula

—no words you might conjure, no poetry you might speak—that will ever convince them you are of your own sound mind. Not even you, my little Sophocles, could pen the verse that might inspire them to peaceably release you."

"Then what will we do?"

"I will bargain with them. I will tell them I will leave this city. I will take you and leave here with Walter and all the rest. Boston will be spared my wrath and my poison. We will go somewhere they can never find us. Perhaps the forests of the north, where the stretch of my illness will cause little damage."

"And what of your monsters? The wolves you seek to feed?"

"They will whimper and whine about being denied their city of prey. Instead, they will harass the local wildlife and terrorize the native tribes. They will survive." He furrowed his brow and, taking her hand, slipped her palm against his shirt and vest over his heart. "There is a great and terrible power that begs to be free within me, Maxine. I am a plague upon this land, make no mistake. I can contain it, and I will continue to do so if I must."

"Does it hurt you to keep it all…locked away?" She struggled to really understand what he was talking about.

"Yes. Immensely. But it is a burden I have become accustomed to. From time to time, I take a city as I sought to do here. I stretch my wings, allow those nightmares that dwell within me to be free. I allow some hunter or another to stop me. I rest for a time, then it begins again."

"But you would break this cycle now? For what reason?"

He smiled faintly. Warmth shone in his crimson eyes. "For you. Our time will be short enough." He traced his fingers over her cheek. "I will shoulder the strain if it means I can savor the time we will have."

She turned her head and nuzzled into his touch. It still felt so strange to have someone touch her. Strange...but wonderful. Yes, she could happily spend the rest of her life like this.

"Tell me...were you lying to me? Did you break our accord?"

She looked up to him curiously. "What do you mean?" He did not answer her, but his expression said it all. The hope in his eyes. The need. The aching loneliness she felt pouring from him. She tried to turn her head to look away shyly, but his hand on her cheek prevented it.

She had promised not to lie to him. She had also promised not to hide from him. Pulling in a small breath, she slowly let it out. "I love you, Vlad Tepes Dracula. All of you. Not a facet, but the whole."

He smiled dreamily, but there was sadness that stained the edges of his expression. A weariness. "For the fact that you believe what you say, I shall always treasure you and them. But you cannot yet mean them."

"I don't understand."

"You have not yet seen the worst of me. You will eat the steak, but you have not yet witnessed the murder of the cow. And if I were to give you the knife, would you be able to slit its throat, my compassionate, sympathetic, darling Maxine?"

"I..."

"You would not. You understand my horrors in theory. I wonder...will you approve them in practice?"

"What do you mean?"

"If the hunters do not return you to me, I will do what I must to have you back." He traced his hand over her hair gently, smoothing over her waves. "You are mine, Maxine. It is as simple as that. And I will not let you go. I love you, Maxine."

Heart of Dracula

She looked up at him in surprise. She didn't know what to say. She had felt something buried deep in his heart, but she refused to name it and crush her own childish hopes.

"Sinner, lover, tyrant, saint. I have been it all. I have more capacity, by benefit of all my years, for all the things that might make a man such a thing. Jealousy, anger, hatred, and yes...even love. While my heart may be cold in my chest, while I may be dead, I still feel."

"Yes. I know. Believe me, I know." She placed her hand against his cheek, stroking her thumb over his tepid skin. "It is that which I see inside you that I love. Not the things you may do with it."

He leaned down and kissed her, slowly, tenderly. When he parted from her, he leaned his forehead against the top of her head. She felt the dream begin to fade. "Tomorrow, we shall see if you mean your words. For tomorrow, if the hunters do not listen to reason...I will destroy this city of yours and all who dwell within it. And we shall see if your sentiment holds true."

She reached for him, but something held her back. Something heavy and strange was around her wrists.

She heard the sound of metal sliding on metal.

Maxine awoke in chains.

She was lying on a dirt floor. A pillow was under her head, and there was a blanket underneath her. She was still in her dress from the opera. When she looked down at her hands, she found them chained together with a foot of thick, iron links. Shackles were locked tightly around her wrists. A long, winding length of chain ran from one of her wrists and off across the dirt floor. It wound around a column, and a simple lock held two links together.

She knew this place.

It was her own basement, after all.

She sat up, confused and disoriented for a moment. And oh, how her head hurt! She placed her fingers to her temple and found she was still not wearing her gloves. She had taken them off before—oh. Now she remembered. Alfonzo and the hunters.

She sighed.

"Morning. Er. Afternoon, rather."

She looked up, surprised, and only then did she notice Eddie sitting by the wall in one of the chairs she had tucked away in the basement long ago. He was leaning against the stacked stone wall, the wood furniture up on its hind legs. On the table next to him was one of his revolvers intact, and the other disassembled. He was picking up a piece of the dismantled gun, piece by piece, and polishing it off with a cloth.

She shuffled to sit more comfortably against the wall. She was shackled in her own basement. She assumed she was going nowhere anytime soon. "I'm surprised I'm not dead."

"We don't want to hurt you, Maxine. We don't want any of this. Alfonzo thinks if we kill the vampire, you'll be freed of whatever spell he's put you under. He's done this before. Kept human...pets. Has he hypnotized you?"

"Once. Briefly. Perhaps twice. That's not what this is."

"Then it's something worse." Eddie put down one piece of his revolver and picked up another, cleaning it with the cloth. "We'll fix it. I promise. You're chained up for your own good. So you don't run off."

They fell silent for many minutes. They hated Dracula. Yet the vampire seemed to not know them save by reputation. There must be a reason they would not listen to her. "What happened to you, Eddie?"

"Hum?"

Heart of Dracula

"Nobody picks your life for fun and profit, I assume."

Eddie laughed, grinning. "No, ma'am."

She wanted to remind him not to call her that, but decided she was better giving up trying. "My father died from injuries he incurred in the Civil War before I was born. I never knew him. My stepfather tried to...he tried to hurt me. And when I tried to push him away, I tore his soul out of his body and destroyed it. That is why I cannot touch anyone or be touched. My mother—rightfully, perhaps—believed me to be a demon. She attempted to kill me. I ran. I joined up with the Roma and traveled with a circus for many years. And here I am."

Eddie watched her, wide-eyed. "I...um. Shit."

She shrugged. "We all have reasons for being who we are. For making the decisions that led us to where we are now. I am merely trying to explain mine."

"I saw him touch you."

"He is...not as fragile as a mortal soul. I have, over the years and quite by accident, destroyed eleven souls. I have sent them to the void. Not to Heaven, or Hell, or whatever might exist—but to nowhere at all. With him, it is not the case."

"But it's not only that, is it? You sympathize with him."

"I sympathize with everyone, Eddie."

"Even us? Alfonzo hit you. We've chained you up in your own home."

"Even you. Especially you. You are trying to save this city and everyone in it. To your own words, you've done this to protect me. I disagree, but I cannot fault you for doing what you feel is right."

Eddie nodded slowly. He moved on to cleaning the next part of his weapon. "My family died. All of them. My ma, pa, my little sister. She was eight. All of them. I...found them. Found what was left of them."

"From a vampire?"

"I wish." He paused for a long time. She could sense his grief from across the room. He was picturing that moment in his head as he talked, judging by his far-away look and the visceral tightness she could feel in the air around him. "The monster turned my sister. Turned an eight-year-old girl into one of *them*. She came home. Killed my parents. I... had been riding the property, checking on the fences. When I came back, it was too late. I saw her kneeling in our parents' blood, licking it up from the floor, crying because it had gone cold. She was a rabid animal. Like a dog, chewing off its own leg in madness."

"What did you do?"

"I do what you do with any rabid animal. I got my rifle. I put her down."

Maxine shut her eyes and lowered her head. "I am so sorry, Eddie."

"Thank you. It's long over. It's because of him that it happened. He's the source of the poison. I'm not the only tragic story. I'm not the only victim."

"I know."

"But you feel for him. I...watched you at the opera through my scope. You took his hand. You let him kiss you. You touch him. It isn't merely physical, either. I see how you look at him. You weren't his prisoner."

She felt the shame creep over her slowly. "No. I was not."

"He's a mass murderer. He's responsible for *millions* of deaths over the course of humanity. Think about that."

"I know."

"You know, but you don't understand." He put down the

last piece of his gun and began putting it back together. "You haven't seen it. I hope you never do."

"I fear that choice will not be up to me."

They fell back into silence. She lay back down on the blanket, shutting her eyes, trying to get her head to stop hurting as badly as it was. Alfonzo had hit her hard.

She wasn't certain how much time had passed before she heard a resounding *boom* from her courtyard outside like an explosion before a voice carried easily through the windows in the foundation by the back of the house. A voice that she would never forget.

"Hunters."

Dracula.

25

It was astonishing how quickly Maxine forgot how terrifying Vlad could be. That one word alone sent a tremor up her spine. That deep, resonant voice that was loud without shouting. Heard without insisting. It reflected the effortless power of the creature himself. Eddie looked as though he shared a similar reaction.

She looked out at the sun streaming through the window and furrowed her brow. He had come for her...in broad daylight.

It was clear Eddie had the same thought. "What the fuck?" He stood from the chair and quickly loaded his guns and tucked one into his holster. He kept the other down at his side.

The basement door was pushed open with a creak. "Eddie. Up here. Now. Bring Maxine," Alfonzo barked down the stairs.

Eddie picked up the end of the chain that attached to her shackles and undid the lock that fastened it to the column. He slipped the key and the lock in his pocket. Looking at her mournfully, he jerked his head in the direc-

Heart of Dracula

tion of the stairs. "C'mon. Let's go."

It was not like she had any say in the matter. And so, she stood and followed Eddie, picking up the weight of the chain to carry it as they climbed the stairs. He kept glancing back at her regretfully.

"I'm sorry about this," he muttered. "It's not fair. It's for your own good."

She nodded once, not knowing what to say. Bella and Alfonzo were standing by the large glass doors that led out to the courtyard in the back of her house. There, standing in the middle of the yard, looking freakishly out of place, was the Vampire King himself. The sun was shining. Her gardens looked peaceful and perfect. Save for the black inkblot that stood in the center of it, long hair loose and hanging around his gray and pallid features.

He did not belong amongst the life of the garden. He belonged amongst dead things.

Alfonzo turned to look at her and Eddie as they approached. She let the chain she had gathered up in her hands fall to the wood floor with a loud clatter, glaring back at the older hunter.

He didn't miss the point she was making. He sighed. "I'm sorry. I really am. But you are unwell. He's twisted your mind. You can't see it, I know, but you'll understand when he is defeated. When you're free."

I am not sure if I will ever be free of him, even if you are victorious. She opted not to say the words. She opted not to say anything at all. Her silence was unnerving him, and she wished to shun him for what he had done. Including for having struck her. Her head still ached.

She did not bother to ask for an apology for the blow. He was a soldier and lived on those terms. She looked back out to the vampire. She realized there was a white line in the grass, and he was standing at the other side of it. Curiosity broke her silence. "What is that?"

"A ward. He cannot cross it," Bella explained. "The house is protected from him."

Magic. More magic. She shook her head. She would have to accept the idea that monsters and magic existed and cared nothing for the fact that she needed time to become adjusted to it all.

"I lead. Bella, stay by my side. Eddie, keep Maxine with you and take up the rear. If she moves or runs toward him, shoot her," Alfonzo ordered.

"But, Al—" Eddie tried to argue but stopped as the older hunter glared at him. "Yes, sir." Eddie sighed and pulled back the hammer on his revolver. He looked to Maxine sheepishly. "Please don't run. Please don't."

She felt her jaw tick as she clenched it. She met Alfonzo's steely gaze for a moment and saw—and felt—that he meant every word. "You believe I am better dead than to live in the thrall you think he has placed over me."

It was a statement, not a question. Alfonzo shifted his grip on his sword, his leather glove creaking. "It would be a mercy. You do not know the things he does to those he keeps. You would be eating insects and tearing out your hair before long."

She highly doubted that. But she knew a zealot when she saw one, and there would be no arguing with him. She could only hope that he would take Dracula up on his trade. Looking back to Eddie, she did her best to smile gently. "I will not run, Eddie. I will not make you live with the regret. Nor do I have any particular desire to die."

"Thank you, ma'am. I greatly appreciate that."

Alfonzo pushed open the glass door and stepped outside. Bella followed at his side. Eddie gestured for her to walk in front of him, and with a shake of her head, she did.

Vlad's crimson eyes flicked to her as she stepped out onto the brick patio. Upon seeing her in chains, he grimaced. His features twisted in anger as he bared his teeth in a vicious snarl. She could feel his rage pour over her even from that distance, nearly palpable in the air.

He looked as though he had already healed from the violence the previous night. But the sun was out in full, and she knew from his own words that it weakened him, even though it did not seem to harm him.

"Give her to me," he demanded. *"Now."*

"No." Alfonzo moved to stand on the other side of the white line, within arm's reach of Vlad. Whatever barrier it posed was invisible, but clearly strong enough to withstand the vampire. Alfonzo had enough faith in it to think the creature could not simply reach forward and rip out his throat. "She stays our prisoner until you are defeated."

Vlad laughed, a cruel and quiet sound. "We shall see. Your hubris will be your downfall, Helsing. As it was your cousin in London. He was a fool. I see it runs in the family blood."

It was Alfonzo's turn to snarl and grimace in anger, although his was far less bestial than his foe's expression had been. "Do not speak of him or the lives you took."

The vampire shrugged idly. "They are of no consequence."

No consequence. To hear him speak of mortal lives with such dismissiveness was a painful reminder of with whom she had aligned herself. She wondered over his words in her dream—if she was truly naïve to think she could accept his callous nature and his monstrous hunger for death.

The vampire's voice was a low rumble. "I have come to

offer you a bargain, Helsing. A trade. The lives of this city, for her."

Alfonzo took half a step back to look over to her where she stood, a silent witness to the scene in front of her. She gripped the chain that ran between her wrists, needing something to hold. The cool steel links were somehow reassuring. Luckily, the links had not witnessed anything of any real importance. Her gloves were missing.

"Explain," the older hunter demanded as he looked back to the vampire.

"I will take my children and leave this place. We will go where we will trouble none. Give her to me, and spare this city and the lives of those within it. Refuse me…and their blood will be on your hands, hunter."

"You're lying." Alfonzo turned back to Dracula, his shoulders raised. "And do not *dare* try to pass the blame for your actions on to me! You are the monster here, not I. This cruelty is yours, not mine."

"Men are capable of far more evil than I have ever been. I am but a reflection of what cruelty you pay each other. You have taken a woman who has shown you nothing but hospitality and compassion and chained her in her own home."

"To save her from *you.*"

"I do not think she wishes to be saved."

"You twist her mind to your own ends. She cannot make these decisions for herself."

"She hardly looks hysterical to me." Vlad sneered. "Men. Always wishing to make decisions for the women around them. Tell me, did you enjoy hitting her? Did you enjoy putting the 'weaker sex' in its place when you struck a defenseless woman?" His expression grew dark and furious once more. "Speak to me once more of cruelty."

Heart of Dracula

Alfonzo growled and paced away from the vampire, fuming.

"Boss?" Eddie asked quietly from behind her. "Boss, shouldn't we consider what he's offering? I mean, an entire city—the whole city—for—"

"Shut up, Eddie." Alfonzo glared angrily at the young boy, who flinched visibly at the man's harsh tone. "No. No deal."

"What?" Maxine couldn't help but finally speak up in her shock. "My life is forfeit. It has been since the moment you arrived at my door with that brooch. I am one person. There are eighty thousand who live within this city, maybe more. And now he threatens the entire seaboard. Let me go. Take his offer."

"He is lying! He cannot be trusted. If I give you to him, he will still wage his war upon the human race."

"He is not lying."

"I cannot trust you, either. I am sorry, Maxine. But your words, and your loyalty, now side with him. You are corrupted by him."

"He is a man of his word," Maxine argued. "I—"

"He is no man!" Alfonzo pointed at the vampire who loomed at the other side of the barrier that kept him from simply sweeping in and likely killing all three of him. "And that you cannot see him for what he is proves my point. No. No deal."

"Boss..." Eddie interjected quietly. "Even if he's lying, shouldn't we take that risk? Isn't it better to roll the dice? Besides, I don't like keeping her prisoner. It feels wrong."

"Listen to the boy." Vlad smirked. "He seems to be the only intelligent one among you. Although, to be fair, the young woman has yet to speak." He glanced to Bella. "What say you?"

"I—ah—" Bella stammered, not having expected to be put on the spot. She glanced between Eddie and Alfonzo, then to Maxine, then to Vlad, seemingly searching for some way out of the spotlight. "I think—I think it is a risk we may wish to take—"

"No." Alfonzo slammed his sword into the dirt, point down. It cleaved easily through the grass and stood on its own as he stormed up to Bella and pointed angrily in the young woman's face. She shrank back from his anger. "You will not take his side on this. The vampire cannot be trusted. He will destroy this city. And even if he doesn't—" Alfonzo broke off abruptly.

"And even if he doesn't, what?" Maxine asked, walking toward the older hunter, the chain scraping on the bricks beside her. She reached the end of her tether a few feet from Alfonzo, but it would suffice. It was then, in that proximity, that she realized what was really going on. Her gift let her tap in to what he was feeling, and the undercurrent beneath his zealous anger was the answer to why he was not accepting the offer. "Oh. Oh, you poor, demented thing."

Alfonzo growled and stormed away. "Stay out of my mind, empath."

"It is not your mind into which I pry. It's your heart. It is not righteousness you seek. It's *revenge.*"

"He has taken everything from my family!" Alfonzo roared as he wheeled around to face her. "One after another, generation after generation, he has slaughtered us all. This is my chance—my real chance—to stop him."

"He cannot be stopped. Even if you defeat him now, you know he will return. It's just a matter of time. You would end so many lives for the chance to hurt him?" She shook her head. "That's madness."

"You do not know what he has done." Alfonzo stormed

Heart of Dracula

up to her then and grabbed her roughly by the upper arms, shaking her once. She heard the vampire growl at the show of violence, but there was nothing he could do. Alfonzo glared down at her. "You do not know what he is capable of. He impaled my cousin on a pike and left him propped in the front yard of his home. Abraham was a father of two children. He was *alive* when the wood met his flesh. He was left to slide down the length of it as it pushed its way through his organs. He was still breathing when the authorities found him. And he was not alone. All the rest who sought to stand against him met the same fate."

Alfonzo's expression turned knowing and cruel, looking down at her with a prideful kind of arrogance. "And do you know why they stood against him? Why they took up arms to defeat the vampire? Not because he wished to destroy London. Oh, no. Because of a woman. He hunted her. Seduced her. Fed from her."

"Enough." Vlad was seething, but there was nothing he could do.

"When Mina was too far gone, too corrupted, and flinched away at the sight of daylight for that he was feeding her his own poisonous blood, she begged for freedom. Abraham granted her that mercy. And the vampire, in his selfish rage, murdered them all."

Maxine yanked out of his grasp and took a few steps away from the hunter. She glanced over to Vlad, whose expression was an unreadable mask of stone. She felt from him only *death*. Death that he was—death that he would pay others. "Did you love her?"

He was silent.

"Vlad," she pressed. "Please."

He hesitated before answering reluctantly. "No. She was a bauble, nothing more."

She cringed and looked away. She knew he was ancient —he had told her in his own words that he had loved before. And how many "baubles" did a man like him take to amuse himself? She suspected as much, but to hear him say it was another matter entirely.

"Maxine...remember our accord."

Yes. A promise never to lie to each other. He was telling her that he loved her without saying as much in front of the hunters. She shook her head, wishing it all to go away. Wishing she could crawl into her bed and sleep.

Vlad sighed heavily. "Hunter. Accept my offer. Give her to me, and I will leave this place in peace. I ask one final time."

"No." Alfonzo yanked his sword from the turf and took a battle stance across the line from the vampire. "Fight us here and now instead."

The Vampire King laughed, cold and empty. Devoid of any humor, humanity, or kindness. "How I would love to grant you what you wish. But no. I will make sure you learn the cost of your revenge. I will ensure you will see what you have wrought in your foolishness."

"Coward. Fight me. Or is the sun weakening you too much and you know you will lose?"

"Hm?" Vlad smirked. "What sun?"

"Wh—" Alfonzo began to speak but did not get a chance to finish.

Vlad lifted his hand above his head. He reached toward the sun, sharp nails looking like talons that extended from long fingers. He closed his hand into a fist.

And all at once...it was dark.

The sun *was gone.*

Blotted out from the sky as if it had been swallowed into a hole. She looked up in awe, blinking at the sudden dark-

Heart of Dracula

ness. Her eyes struggled to adjust to the change. There were no clouds hiding the sun. But that was not to say there was no glowing disk hanging in the sky. There was.

But it was the moon. Huge, and full, and the color of blood. Stars glimmered about the terrible usurper on the throne.

The city fell deathly silent. No birds chirped. No wind rustled the trees. All the sounds of the city merely stopped. It was as though life itself held its breath.

Then...came the howling. Like a wolf in the distance, answered by another, and another. But the sounds were not like a canine, but something *else,* something *other*. Creatures of the darkness who had come to answer their Master's call.

Worse than the howling was what followed.

The screams.

Faint and far away, numerous and chilling. His army had already begun to feed. Maxine shivered and shrank back toward the house.

"What have you done?" Alfonzo asked through his shock, his eyes wide in horror. "How have you...how have you done this?"

Vlad laughed and smiled piteously at the hunter, as if he were a parent whose child had learned of gravity and scraped his knee. "You know so very little, Helsing, of what I truly am. Of what I am capable. I could rule this world if I wished it. You would be surprised to know how little in this world I desire. You will be horrified to see the lengths to which I will go to secure that which I do. Now, you will learn who I *truly* am." He looked to Maxine with those words. She knew they were meant for her. Vlad took a step away from the barrier and stretched his arms out at his sides. "You will now see the full reach of my curse. Come and stop me...if you think you can."

And with that, his form exploded into a swarm of bats and soared up into the dark sky above, little more than movement against the unnatural night's canopy.

She heard screams in the distance. They hung in the air like the morbid calls of birds, replacing their counterparts like the moon had stolen the sun. He had threatened to destroy the city...and now she learned Vlad Tepes Dracula was not a creature who bluffed.

Resting her back against the brick of her home, she looked up into the darkness. "Oh, Vlad...What have you done?"

Fin.

"Curse of Dracula"
Immortal Soul: Part Two
Arrives August 1st, 2020
Order it here!

ALSO BY KATHRYN ANN KINGSLEY

Immortal Soul:

Heart of Dracula

Curse of Dracula

The Impossible Julian Strande:

Illusions of Grandeur

Ghosts & Liars

The Cardinal Winds:

Steel Rose

Burning Hope

The Masks of Under:

King of Flames

King of Shadows

Queen of Dreams

King of Blood

King of None

Queen of All

Halfway Between:

Shadow of Angels

Blood of Angels

Fall of Angels

To stay up to date with all my upcoming releases and extras, join my Facebook Reader Group, or consider joining my monthly newsletter.

www.kathrynkingsley.com

ABOUT THE AUTHOR

Kat has always been a storyteller.

With ten years in script-writing for performances on both the stage and for tourism, she has always been writing in one form or another. When she isn't penning down fiction, she works as Creative Director for a company that designs and builds large-scale interactive adventure games. There, she is the lead concept designer, handling everything from game and set design, to audio and lighting, to illustration and script writing.

Also on her list of skills are artistic direction, scenic painting and props, special effects, and electronics. A graduate of Boston University with a BFA in Theatre Design, she has a passion for unique, creative, and unconventional experiences.

Printed in Great Britain
by Amazon